FROM
SAVAGERY

ALEJANDRA BANCA

FROM SAVAGERY

—STORIES—

Translated from the Spanish by Katie Brown

RESTLESS BOOKS

NEW YORK · AMHERST

First published in Spain by Lecturas de arraigo as *Desde la salvajada*.

Restless Books and the R colophon are registered trademarks of Restless Books, Inc.

First Restless Books paperback edition August 2024

Paperback ISBN: 9781632063588
Library of Congress Control Number: 2024937755

This book is supported in part by an award from the National Endowment for the Arts.

Cover design by Keenan
Jacket illustration © 2024 Pene Parker
Designed and typeset by Tetragon, London

Printed in the United States

1 3 5 7 9 10 8 6 4 2

RESTLESS BOOKS
NEW YORK • AMHERST
www.restlessbooks.org

Will this story become my own coagulation one day? Who can tell? If there is any truth in it—and clearly the story is true even though invented—let everyone see it reflected in himself for we are all one and the same person.

CLARICE LISPECTOR,
THE HOUR OF THE STAR

Translated from the Portuguese
by Giovanni Pontiero

An immigrant heart is a bird in the hand.
I have mouths to feed.
I have to eat.
I have to be eaten.

MARÍA FERNANDA AMPUERO,
HUMAN SACRIFICES

Translated from the Spanish
by Frances Riddle

CONTENTS

FROM
SAVAGERY

BARNA

TIBIDABO

MUERTE!

SARRIA

SANT G

PEDRALBES

N

PLACA DE SANTS

L'HOSPITALET
DE LLOBREGAT

SF

SANT

 AQUÍ CON LOS PANAS*

SAGRADA FAMILIA

 MI CASA ES TU CASA

 BAÑOS

 MACBA

* We are friends here

CARRER DE LA MURTRA
SANTA COLOMA DE GRAMENET
BADALONA
EL CARMEL
SANT ADRIA DE BESOS
MUERTE!
CARRER DE MOUNT
PARK GUELL
SANT MARTI
GRACIA
DIAGONAL
SAG FAMILIA
ASI
EL POBLE NOU
DIAGONAL
LACA D'OSCA
PLACA DE SALVADOR SEGUI
TS
EL POBLE SEC
MONTJUIC

DIRT POOR

How much? Three thousand dollars just for the plot? Angélica swallows and takes a deep breath. What about cremation? she asks. Depends. The most basic one's around five hundred, answers the voice at the end of the line. She couldn't afford either. *Where am I gonna find that much?*

Angélica taught at a high school in Maracaibo; she moved from Caracas because they offered her way more hours, but it didn't help. She couldn't even afford to eat. Her mother always said that when she died, she wanted to be buried, it was something she repeated all the time. Bury me, let the worms eat me. Keep me far away from those flames. Angélica couldn't even afford the flames. Going into debt was an option, but the amount seemed enormous.

Well, cremation then, she whispers, unconvinced, what do I have to do? Oh, I'm sorry, we're not offering the cremation service at the moment, there's no gas at the funeral home, the woman replied, apathetic, I forgot to mention it. So, when will there be gas then? A laugh, more like a sigh. Couldn't say, it's been like this for weeks. They keep saying they're going to supply us, but then there's no gas anywhere.

God, now what do I do? She's dirt poor. She can't even afford to die. It's hard to believe you have to go into debt to be eaten by worms. The Charon of this river only takes dollars and doesn't even guarantee you'll make it to the other shore.

To ration gas, the funeral home only offered cremation services on certain days and to a reduced number of people; only the lucky reached the flames. There was a waiting list for cremation. Normally, they kept the bodies in cellars until the gas arrived or the family, tired of waiting, and wanting to settle the matter and bring peace to the departed, chose to pony up and pay for a burial. In an ideal situation, if they had been prepared well, corpses could remain indefinitely, for as long as the family paid the fee to keep them there. But when electricity was being rationed, nothing could stay in the cellars: they were a conflict zone. There were cases—that is, bodies—of people whose families did not have the resources to keep them, cremate them, or forget about them; so, the funeral home looked for the fastest way to get rid of them. The stench of the poor is worse than the stench of the dead.

Look, Angélica, don't you worry, said Juan Pablo, her neighbor. My folks had a plot in the Cementerio del Edén, let me look into what we need an' I'll lend it to you, don't worry, he comforted her.

Angélica, distraught, like a lost soul, didn't understand how you could lend someone a plot in a cemetery. How would she give it back later, would she dig up her mom and then where would she put her? Juan Pablo made his inquiries. She still needed money.

You gotta buy two sacks of cement an' thirty cinder blocks, Juan Pablo advised. Why? she asked. Oh, honey, why d'ya think? To cover the coffin an' seal that shit over. You know people smash that shit up looking for scratch or whatever.

Angélica tried. She went to the hardware store. When she returned, her face was dirty with tears and snot, poorly wiped away on the sleeve of her T-shirt. No, Juan Pablo, I can't afford that either. Pablo grimaced, Fuck, Angélica, if I could, I swear I'd lend a hand, he said, but he couldn't help her, he was also just getting by, scraping two cents together.

She had no other choice. Calling her family was a joke, unthinkable. Five years ago, when her grandpa died, they all ended up fighting because no one had any money. The old man wasted away for months in a care home where he burned out faster than a match. When he died, nobody wanted to chip in because no one had savings for unexpected expenses. An aunt—by marriage, not even a blood relation—offered her own plot in the Cementerio del Este, but the corpse had to be transported from San Felipe to Caracas and that plus preparing the body cost an absurd amount. If they'd tried to put together the money between them all, they could have managed it, but they didn't make the effort. Angélica didn't go and see him in his final years. The old man didn't recognize anyone, and she preferred to hold on to other memories of him, she didn't want that image of a skeleton with no memory stuck in her head. They buried him in a pauper's grave, in a plywood coffin with a couple of tiny nails in each corner. Angélica hadn't realized just how badly they were doing until her grandpa died. This fiasco revealed the truth: they were all just clinging on. She had never thought about this before, just as she never thought that her mother would die so young, that she would end up completely alone in this hostile world, nor about what would happen and what the process would be before and after burying her, before covering her with earth. Did anyone ever think about such things?

At least she'll rest in peace. But how, if she can't even lay her body to rest? Angélica was lost, she didn't have anyone except her mom. Now what do I do, Juan Pablo? I don't have the cash for any of this, she said. Juan Pablo guided her. The only option was a mass grave. And the only cemetery that didn't charge too much was the Sagrado Corazón de Jesús. Even she, as naive as she was, knew that people rob graves there. They smash open the ossuaries, use torches or cigarette lighters to see if the deceased have any jewelry or anything of value. They take the skull or a femur, any bone still intact and in a good state. Nothing goes to waste.

Angélica's mom's body was still in the hospital. The nurse told her to make arrangements quickly, bodies were piling up in the morgue, and the refrigeration wasn't working. The blackouts damaged the whole refrigeration system, you understand? the nurse asked, raising his eyebrows. Angélica nodded, though she did not understand.

She was living through the whole process on autopilot, not realizing she was in shock. Unless someone spoke to her directly, she withdrew into her mind, remembering the voice of the man who called her: You have to come to the hospital, it's about your mother, señora Rosa. And, well, there she was, like they told her on the phone. Even though they explained what had happened several times, she didn't understand, the information wouldn't go in, her neurons weren't firing. She nodded, answered without knowing who was speaking for her, *but it's me. It's me?* She wasn't prepared for what awaited her in the coming hours and days.

Well, there's no way around it. Her head ached and her mouth was dry. When was the last time she had anything to eat or drink? She couldn't remember. Juan Pablo told her that she didn't need to go to the hospital again, he had a friend who worked there and could stand in for her. But she refused, insisted on going. The morgue was in the basement. Juan Pablo didn't accompany her on that crossing, I'll wait for you up here, it's best you go alone, he decided. She walked toward the side wing, at the end of the corridor she could see the stairs descending to the basement, hell itself. Even from above ground and from some distance, the stench was overwhelming. The place looked apocalyptic: unusable and abandoned objects, rusty and damaged stretchers, everything piled up and ruined.

On the stairs, she began to retch. She wasn't wearing a mask because there weren't any. Roger, Pablo's friend who worked there, went down with her. He wasn't even wearing gloves. Once inside the morgue, she wanted everything to be over as soon as possible. She found eight metal tables arranged haphazardly, loaded with bulks, each under sheets of different colors, *who brings the sheets?* The stench made her cry, stung her eyes as if she were chopping onions. The mortuary cabinets, those holes where bodies are supposed to be: infested, splattered, and encrusted. The floor stained with fetid blood. Roger stopped by one of the tables, much cleaner and tidier than the others. Angélica was shocked to see her mother like that: colorless, expressionless, without so much as a sheet to cover her naked body, her mouth slightly open as if she wanted to whisper something to her. She wasn't her mother anymore. *Yes, yes. It's her*. They left immediately and she was startled by the heat outside. There was no refrigeration, that's true, but down below, among the stench and the flies, she felt a chill.

People insulted the morgue staff because, so they said, they handled the dead as if they were animals. In that moment, they forgot the general plight. In their heads, the crisis had nothing to do with the way corpses were treated or the price of coffins. Surviving was difficult enough without having to think about what would happen to the bodies afterward. Even so, they were always surrounded by death: flesh and bodies. Four or five corpses would rot in the hospital morgue each week. Those left there forgotten, unclaimed, no longer even looked human by the time the flames finally destroyed them. A body had burst in one of the mortuary cabinets and nobody wanted to clean it up—with what?

I can't even. They get bent out of shape about every fuckin' thing, but, like, there's fuck all here. How am I supposed to clean this? Huh? There's no electricity, there's no masks, there's no gloves, there's no boots, no bleach, no disinfectant, there's nothing and no one to clean the cabinets. There's fuck all, only bodies, Roger complained, more outraged than anyone, his nails filthy and his eyes tired. There's people with AIDS and other shit, you can get sick too an' die like a total asshole an' leave all that crap for your family to deal with, he added.

Roger was depressed. He tried to comfort her because he knew señora Rosa, but his words weren't having the desired effect. He no longer knows how to comfort people, rather he needs comforting himself. He felt ashamed about her seeing the state of the morgue. Angélica didn't say anything, she knew it wasn't his fault or his responsibility. In the midafternoon, an aunt-by-marriage, the only one in the family who bothered to show up, arrived all in black and with a small suitcase, to stay with Angélica for as long as necessary. She was always her favorite aunt, even though they hadn't seen each other for years and just exchanged the occasional short message on Facebook. She held her tight. No need to speak. Taking advantage of the company, Juan Pablo and Roger went to find her something to eat.

You just can't stop thinkin' about what you see down there. You come outta that shithole rotten as a cavity. D'you know what that's like? Well, don't go back there, man, find yourself another gig, Pablo replied. Oh, bullshit, you kiddin' me? You say it like it's the easiest thing in the world, Roger grumbled. Well, it's an option. Jeez you're touchy today, seriously. I'm just sayin' it's up to you, Pablo added. I'm doin' better now. I was on the pediatric ward before an', cuz, that shit is fuckin' nasty. Every little one of 'em is contaminated an' new arrivals just end up gettin' sicker. There's too many little kids rottin' or waitin' to be cremated. Roger, Jesus Christ, Pablo exclaimed, bro, you gotta get yourself another job. You're gonna drive yourself crazy, man, you hear me.

They went to Pablo's. A large house where he lived with his parents, his sister, his brother-in-law, and his three nephews. They each ate a big, fat patacón. Juan Pablo kept one for Angélica, he didn't know when she'd last eaten.

What're you gonna do, then? Pablo's mom asked. There's no gas to cremate her an' no money to bury her. It's gotta be the mass grave, over in the Sagrado Corazón, he said. Sweet Jesus, that's awful! Pablo's mother crossed herself. And that place is horrible, the bodies are scattered about all over. You're going with her, aren't you? You can't let her go there alone.

The cemetery's funeral home didn't want to transport the body because the payment still hadn't gone through. The aunt helped out and was the one who transferred the money. *God knows when it will go through.* They had the remittance receipt, that should have been enough; but given the circumstances, they wanted the money in hand. Pablo intercepted, fed up. For fuck's sake, can't you see the receipt? You got eyes, don't you? It's already done, you cretin! It's done! he shouted. Everyone was getting worked up and irritable.

In the end, they agreed to transport the body, but only because they knew Roger. In passing, Angélica saw that they had wrapped her mother in a sheet that her aunt had brought. She had also brought the clothes in which they would later dress the body. Angélica hadn't even thought of that. *A sheet? Which clothes, which shoes? What for?* The gray skin, the naked body, the twisted mouth were engraved in her brain. They stored her in the hearse with other bodies in the same condition.

Angélica didn't want a wake. She had never liked the experience of going to see the dead, and anyway, who would come see her mom, four nobodies? The family hadn't batted an eyelid. Besides, there was no money for a wake or to prepare the body to last longer. Formaldehyde is a valuable commodity, reserved for those who can empty their pockets. Regular people are given a modest, not to say poor, embalming, washing, and makeup service. So, you have to rush the whole process. In the crisis, once again, there is no time for death because death is all-consuming.

They arrived at the cemetery and got straight to work. Angélica had never been to the Sagrado Corazón de Jesús. She'd heard the stories, but that's all. Her aunt was angry, as soon as they entered the cemetery the air was rank. *With what?* Cemeteries shouldn't smell bad. Quite the opposite, the air should be filled with the scent of flowers and freshly cut grass. The coffin she could afford was simple, like cardboard. Instead of nails in the corners, it had staples. There was nothing decorative inside, not even cushions for the deceased to rest on and comfortably support her limbs; just a flat space lined with a thin material.

Two men did the work. It wasn't just her mother's open mouth that she would never forget, or her feet hanging off the table. She would never be able to rip from her memory the succession of grotesque images that remained with her all the way from the cemetery entrance to the mass grave. As she walked, she felt her aunt's arms squeeze her shoulders tighter and tighter. Many of the mausoleums, almost all of them, had strange, visible holes. From some, she could see objects sticking out at ridiculous angles and some kind of powder or putty. It stank, the odor was everywhere.

To the left, in the distance, the enormous head of a pig, wrapped in black ribbons, hung from a tall mausoleum. That area on the left, which they avoided at all costs, was strewn with chicken carcasses, some intact, others rotting; feathers and guts, candles, concoctions in bottles, and splatters everywhere. When they reached the grave, the scene did not improve; a huge hole in the earth with many other barely covered coffins, piled one on top of the other. The stench was painful. Juan Pablo handed her the flowers, and she was surprised to take them. *Did I buy these? When?* Her hands were shaking. She likes carnations, she said, her voice sounded thick, she was holding back tears. Yes, dear, whispered her aunt. The only good thing about the Sagrado Corazón de Jesús is that at the entrance you can get the cheapest flowers in the whole area. It was a bouquet of black and white carnations.

But they mustn't open her, Angélica blurted out, overcome with emotion. They can't open her, tell them, Tía, she doesn't have anything. She doesn't have anything valuable, please, she doesn't have anything, she's naked. She's naked, she repeated. The shock spoke for her, her body trembled, her head swung in a neurotic denial. She doesn't have anything, they can't open her, she's naked.

Don't open her. Don't open her!

Once she started, she couldn't stop babbling the litany over and over. There was no priest to pray for the soul of the departed and give her a holy burial. There was only Angélica reciting her own version of the holy rosary and funeral oration, except she received no response from anyone but herself, repeating herself endlessly. There was no liturgy save for her voice rising in pitch as the seconds passed. In response to the pain that trembled through Angélica's body, her aunt gripped her shoulders more tightly and resolutely led her away. Nobody said anything. She led her toward the exit past the same area they had avoided earlier. The pig's head wrapped in black ribbon. The feathers. The blood splattered on the tombs. Chicken carcasses and candles. Bones left exposed. Remains of guts. The same stench.

They left the cemetery and kept walking, leaving everything behind them. Her aunt kept a firm grip on her arm. Angélica could breathe better, little by little she stopped sobbing, but the litany continued: Don't open her. She doesn't have anything. She's naked. Don't open her.

She didn't know how, but a door closed and suddenly she was in the back of a car, one of those old and rusty taxis that seemed like boats with wheels. They crossed Avenida Cinco de Julio under a blazing sun that was insensitive to death. Her eyes caught the gleam of Lake Maracaibo, beyond the Vereda, and Angélica moved in her seat, anxious to get out.

She opened the door while the taxi was still moving, terrifying her aunt. Angélica, what are you doing! she shouted as the driver hit the brakes hard. They got out of the car and stood there, silent and undisturbed, for at least another hour. With infinite patience, the movement of the water calmed her. The important thing was not to look away from the water, from the lake that seemed like a sea: vast, soothing.

Her hands hurt and her knuckles were white from gripping the carnations so tight. Her sanity depended on it. She approached the concrete barrier and threw the carnations into the water. Angélica, sweetheart, Angélica, her aunt called to her, shaking her gently. Angélica, let's go, the sun's going down, she grabbed her hand, as if she were a little girl. Come on, Angélica, it's time to go, she commanded. And while she watched the far-off carnations, scattered on the water, she remembered the man's voice on the phone: Am I speaking to Angélica Rodríguez . . . ? You have to come to the hospital . . . It's about your mother, Señora Rosa. An unbearable beeping in her head. *Does anyone hear that? Can't you hear anything?* They took her into the ER, the velvety voice explained, you have to come, please. Denial. *What's happening?* I can't go, is she okay? Put me through to her doctor, what room is she in? Where is she? her voice hysterical. Ma'am, they found her trembling on the floor, said the other voice, tired. He didn't want to give more details over the phone, but Angélica could not accept his words. She had a stroke, he explained. Angélica didn't know what to do or how to react. *What is that?* She went to Juan Pablo's, mute, petrified. Pablo returned the call, the voice was already exhausted, at least now he was talking to someone who was with it, conscious. They found her convulsing on the floor, she had a stroke. When they got her to the hospital, it was already too late. Her pupils were fixed, she was brain-dead. The body is in the morgue, I'm very sorry, but someone has to come . . . and the unanswered interruptions: Pablo, did my mom die? *How can they not hear the beeping? Where is it coming from, is it an antenna?*

Angélica, let's go sweetheart, it's night already, her aunt said roughly. She stretched out her hand, Angélica clung to it. Yes, Tía, she muttered, in a trance. The beeping again. *What makes a sound like that?* She looked to one side, thinking that the sound came from there; she felt that, at any moment, she would wake up and see her mom ironing in the living room. But the memories came, the man's voice, Pablo's expression and his head in his hands, the bones sticking out of the coffins, the smell, the pig in the black ribbon, the chicken carcasses. She blinked with these images on her retina, on her eyelids. She didn't want to think. She didn't want to admit that she had left her mother there: in the lions' jaws, abandoned to neglect.

BUM-BA-DA-DÁH-DA
DA-DA-DÁH-DA

The cramp brings her to a dead stop. Feet flat on the asphalt, hands tightly gripping the handlebars. Her womb contracts again and María Eugenia bites her lip. She doesn't have ibuprofen or anything for the pain. Her meds are stored away in a cosmetics bag hidden in her suitcase; she only uses them for real emergencies because medicines are expensive here. Menstrual pain doesn't come under an emergency, but, fuck, it hurts. She looks up: the street brings her back to reality.

Come on, María Eugenia, let's go. She settles onto the bike again and starts pedaling. The pain in her legs is nothing compared to what she feels in her hips. Her body shudders with the aftershocks of an earthquake and her belly is the epicenter.

Only a few more streets before she can deliver the order. She knows the last street will be the most difficult because it's uphill. *Freaking Carmel streets. Concentrate on pedaling to forget the pain.* Sometimes she imagines she's in a game and she needs to go faster to win more points; other times she thinks she's competing in the Tour de France. She tries to spur herself on thinking about the physical side: she's thinner, her legs are stronger, she has more stamina. Then there are moments when she lives with intense paranoia and fears for her life. She could get knocked down, she could have a bad fall and injure herself, she could even die.

Some days, she feels so miserable between pedaling and more pedaling that she only thinks about death. She heard someone say that if a Spaniard knocks you down, you're within your rights to report it and you could be offered citizenship, but she's not sure, it could be one of those rumors that run wild. She's also not entirely convinced she wants to stay in Spain forever, *hopefully not*.

Her calves start to burn, and she pushes harder. *Let's go, dammit, almost there*. The straps of her backpack chafe her armpits, she has to find out how to secure it to her bike, like Cheo does.

She slams the brakes.

She touches the ground with her toes and gets off the bike. Something moves, something oozes out, she can feel it. *Shit, fucking cup*. She pulls her panties out of her crack, pretends that nothing has happened, maybe it is nothing.

She's hot, she can feel the damp between her breasts. Luckily, it's winter, it's only twelve degrees and, luckier still, the place is on the first floor and she doesn't have to go up any stairs. She puts the backpack down, carefully takes out the

McDonald's bag and presses the buzzer. A guy opens. Hey!
I've got your order, María Eugenia greets him, holding the
bag out toward him. He looks at her, surprised. *Yeah, I know.*
I'm not Álex, but I've got your order just the same. Thanks, he says
and takes the bag.

She hopes he doesn't give her a bad rating because the
account's ranking would go down and the schedule wouldn't
open on time for her, she'd end up without enough hours. She
knows that she looks nothing like the person who, in theory,
should be making the delivery, but that's the game. Álex is
a friend who lets her use his account as long as she pays his
freelancer fee. It's not bad, bearing in mind that many people
who rent out their accounts don't just demand payment of the
fee, but also take a cut of the rider's earnings. Enjoy, she says
finally, as the guy nods and closes the door.

María Eugenia turns the bike around, straps her backpack
on again. She hasn't mounted her bike yet when the phone
shrieks *bum-ba-da-dáh-da da-da-dáh-da*. The sound of money,
of hunger. She checks where she has to go: a sushi restaurant.

An aftershock of the primordial earthquake rocks her
again. Anyone seeing her in that moment would know that
something was wrong. She waits a few seconds for the pain to
subside, like a wave rolling out, and then stands up. Getting
on her bike, she notices a strange dampness in her underwear.
She's still not used to the menstrual cup and has to adjust it
several times before, like magic, everything seems to fit perfectly inside her and it doesn't leak. It's been five hours since

she put it in and until now she hadn't felt anything. Maybe she can use the restroom in the sushi restaurant. She always goes to the McDonald's one as a last resort, when she can't hold it in any longer. With her period, it's more chaotic and she usually tries to go at home, or to work nearby so she can escape in case of a leak.

The sushi restaurant is a twelve-minute bike ride away. Google Maps shows more, but she's going to try to shorten the journey by taking different alleyways. She doesn't know what Google Maps was smoking when it designed its routes, but sometimes she only needed to go in a straight line to get to her destination. The app works against her. Better to memorize the names of the streets and bike paths.

The good thing about Carmel: going downhill. She cools down quickly in the breeze. Sometimes she gets scared and hits the brakes, but she usually enjoys it. She's on the flat once more and pedals calmly. She feels something ooze out again but can't check it, it's overflowing. Now she knows it's definitely blood; she feels the warmth filling her vulva. She knows when she's staining her clothes, though she can't explain how.

Fuck! At least my leggings are black, and my coat covers my ass. She tries squeezing her vaginal muscles as if she could hold it in that way. When she reaches the sushi restaurant, there are two riders waiting, both sitting on the low wall by the entrance with their thermal bags on the ground. María Eugenia leaves her bike and greets them, knocks on the restaurant's door. Hi, hello, I've got this order, she shows her phone to the Asian woman who approaches. Okay, a few minutes, the woman responds. María Eugenia can see them already putting some trays into a bag, presumably for the riders waiting outside. Hi, I'm sorry, would it be possible to use the bathroom, please? It sounds like she's begging. The woman looks at her and shakes her head, sorry, love, it's not allowed. Okay, thank you.

She leaves the restaurant and stands by her bike, waiting. Right then, they hand two bags to one of the riders, an Indian or Pakistani, she can't tell. The other rider is rolling himself a cigarette. She sees it and it makes her want a smoke too, but then she'd be thirsty, and her water bottle isn't that big. Plus, it's months since she last smoked, and it seems like this time she has finally quit for real. She feels like she can breathe better and that she's fitter, not to mention her ability to smell things that she used to miss.

She moves away to the corner of the restaurant and, trying not to be seen, puts her hand underneath her buttocks and pats the area. *I knew it.* It's damp. She looks at her fingers, they're lightly stained red. She smells them even though there is no need: yep, blood.

Shitballs! Okay, last one then I'm going home. This sucks, I smell like ass. She grabs her water bottle and cleans her fingers. She doesn't have any more black panties, she'll have to do laundry, and from now until it dries, she won't have any option but to wear colored leggings, the ones she doesn't like because they irritate her inner thighs. She wants to sit on the low wall at the entrance to the restaurant, but the tiles are white, she would leave a mark. She shifts her body weight from one foot to the other. While she waits, she replies to some messages. Hola mami, I love you too. Yes, all good, working right now. Heart emoji, sunflower emoji. Yeah, it's near Sants, I'll send you the address later, thumbs up. Hahaha LMAO that killed me, crying-with-laughter face. Sara, can you turn on the hot water? I'm coming home to shower coz I've leaked. Injection emoji.

Sara is one of her housemates, there are three of them: María Eugenia, Sara, and Yunalivi. Yuna is at work and Sara is the only one at home because she works remotely. Sara is also the only one who has papers, the contract for the rent is in her name. She sublets the other two rooms because paying for an apartment on her own would be a real pain. María Eugenia and Yuna pay three hundred euros each for their rooms, Sara puts in the rest. María Eugenia isn't too sure what Sara does, but she does know that she earns good money, that it's something to do with numbers and codes, and that she's always sitting at the computer typing.

Sure, Maru. Plugging it in now.

They decided to unplug the boiler when they weren't using it to save on electricity. Sara has a thing about wasting electricity or water. She also forces them into rigorous recycling and has slowly convinced them to use solid shampoo; now the three of them share the same bar. The menstrual cup, of course, was also Sara's idea. She had fabric panty liners and period undies that absorb blood, but María Eugenia didn't trust them. She was only giving the cup a trial and, look, it was already letting her down. Fuck, Maru, listen to me. Don't be afraid to really stick it up there, it's not going anywhere, she reassured her. It's got this stem for you to pull on. One thing though, you've gotta break the vacuum in there, otherwise you could hurt yourself.

The first time that Maru put the cup in, she panicked. Then she couldn't feel the stem and thought that she would have to go to the walk-in clinic for them to take the cup out, but it turned out that she just wasn't used to sticking her fingers very far up. Tampax have a cord to pull on and you can avoid the rest of it, with the cup she needed to explore a little. María Eugenia had put her fingers in and shoved; in that moment she thought that giving birth must be the worst and most painful thing in the world.

Babe, you've gotta relax when you put it in. If you're all tense, it's not gonna open properly. Look, what I do is fold it like this or like that, Sara explained folding the cup like a U, and bam, in it goes. Then I put these fingers in and gently touch the base to see if it's flat, if you feel a little lump or something, it's still folded. If it irritates you or hurts, you can put a little lube on it, but you don't really need it, that's for pussies. A gut punch doubles her over, squeezes her swollen belly. The waitress comes out again and gives a yellow bag to the other rider. The guy throws his cigarette to the ground and gets on an electric scooter. The woman comes back straight away and gives her a package; Maru stores it in her bag and looks at the delivery address, which is only revealed once you have the order. She has to go to Carrer de l'Arc de Sant Cristòfol, another fifteen minutes by bike.

She sits as comfortably as she can and without thinking too much about the stain spreading across her buttocks and inner thighs, she pedals. When she sees other riders, they greet each other, though she never feels truly comfortable because the vast majority of them are men. She has seen so few women that they all know each other.

It doesn't surprise her that female riders aren't very common. It's tough work, not just physically. She regularly encounters odious men who stare at her or find ways to make innuendos while she delivers their food. More than the customers, pedestrians or drivers are the worst of all. Alright love, enjoyin' yerself on yer bike? some idiot said to her once, licking his lips. He was with friends and all four of them laughed. The number of sexual comments she gets just for smiling while riding her bike is surprising: some people have such twisted minds. Enjoying her bike ride and showing it only provokes obscenities. Not to mention her fellow riders who mock her, exclaiming in a pack that she can't take more than five orders, at most, that she's not fit enough to make up to a hundred euros a day, like they do. She keeps silent and smiles, cursing them all under her breath. *Dickheads.*

Like in many other jobs, it's not easy for her to be taken seriously. They all think that she does it as a side hustle, that she's not biking all day. *Well, they're wrong.* Hey, mamita, you're so tasty, topped off with that repulsive lip-biting and eyes that penetrate her. *Just what I needed.* María Eugenia looks at the guy who is laughing and watching her from the sidewalk, grabbing his balls. She looks away, almost breathing fire. What she would really like to do is get off her bike, stick her fingers in her vagina and then wipe them across the face of that imbecile who is still shouting things at her. Force them into his mouth. *Take your mamita, that's tasty, huh? In your face, you toad.* The light changes and she moves on.

She is about to arrive when she feels that the reservoir of blood is now breaching its levee. She brakes in front of a narrow building with pretty little balconies, gets off the bike and notices the seat is stained. A darker patch than the black of the seat, shinier. She tries to stand up straight, but the pain in her belly doubles her over, she feels like a hunchback. She takes the order out of her backpack and approaches the entrance to the building. Before she can ring the bell, the door opens and a girl with curly hair appears. That's for me, thanks so much, the girl looks at her, surprised, of course, to see not Álex but a young woman looking pained. She smiles at her, and María Eugenia returns the smile with the corners of her eyes. She grabs the bag and offers her some coins that Maru accepts with profound gratitude. Sometimes angels do exist, in the form of people who give a tip, or so she likes to think. Oh, thank you so much, she says. The young woman closes the door and leaves her there with her pain and her stain. She puts the two euros in her koala, or riñonera as she should call it here, and gets back on her bike. She doesn't think she'll accept another order, she's hurting, she's done. Her head is starting to pound.

They'll probably lower her rating for not completing these peak hours, but she just can't; she needs to get changed, shower, throw herself into bed and cling to the covers. Now she will take an ibuprofen, because the pain is stronger than her money worries.

Only another fifteen minutes of movement before she can get home and give herself over to the task of relaxing, she no longer cares about the stain or if blood is still leaking. She managed to make forty-two euros in six hours. She can't do any more, she's not well today. Today she does believe the comments from her fellow riders: that she can't do it, that she's not fit or strong enough. *If only you all bled from your dicks and your balls hurt as much as my womb does, I'd love to see you then.* The image brings her comfort.

She thinks about her parents and her younger brother, still on the other side of the Atlantic, hoping everything goes well for her and that she's able to save at least enough money to bring him over. The thought depresses her, she tries to get it out of her mind by thinking about other things, but a bitter taste remains in her mouth. *Today it's period pain, tomorrow what will it be?* One of her worst fears is getting sick: with no documents, no money, no insurance, and responsible for three lives that depend on her. She bites her lips to keep from crying. *I'm hormonal, that's all. I'm fine.*

She finally reaches her street and as she opens the door to her building she feels the levee break, the great flood is coming. She goes up in the elevator to the fourth floor, opens the door to the apartment, and hears Sara typing at the computer. The hot water's ready for you, Maru, she shouts without looking away from the screen. María Eugenia places her bike on the stand they got to avoid marking the walls. She leaves her backpack in the corner and takes off her shoes. She only wears socks or slippers at home, Sara's orders, of course. Thanks, Sara, you're the best. So, has there been a murder in your panties? A massacre.

She closes the bathroom door and takes off her socks, then her T-shirt, and finally her leggings and underwear. *Shit.* She forgot to put on dark underwear. These are beige and the whole ass is now dyed burgundy, she'll have to wring them out by hand in very cold water to remove the stains. At least the blood hasn't fully dried. She puts them to soak in the sink. Twisting, she spots the scab of blood on her ass. She turns on the shower and waits a few seconds for the water to heat up. She sticks her fingers in and takes out the cup, blood spills over her hand and down her wrist; the cup is full and now there are clots on the shower tiles and running down her thighs. She puts her head under the hot water and relaxes.

The water flows, cleans the ceramic shower tiles, white again now, sweeps away clots, blood, and with them her frustration at only earning forty-two euros. *Don't think about that, Maru. Tomorrow you'll make more money.* She closes her eyes and massages her stomach, her hips.

Bum-ba-da-dáh-da da-da-dáh-da, bum-ba-da-dáh-da da-da-dáh-da.

Fuck! The goddam sound of money, of hunger. She'd forgotten to cancel the last hour. Where did she leave her phone? Sara, reject the order pleaaaase! she shouts, half out of the shower. The music insists. Sara! she shouts again, more forcefully, this time holding on to the shower curtain while trying to open the bathroom door. She miscalculates and slips. Falls flat on her ass, taking with her the shower curtain and the metal shelf where they keep the shampoo, conditioner, soaps, razors, and a thousand other things.

María Eugenia gives in; everything hits her all at once in an uncontrollable wave of emotions. She surrenders to the tears that are camouflaged in the water pounding her face.

The music stops and the bathroom door slowly opens.

Sara discovers the wrinkled mass of curtain on the floor, the bathmat soaking up water, and the corpse of poor María Eugenia sobbing under the flow. Are you okay? she whispers. Maru? she gets closer. No! I am not okay! María Eugenia covers her face with her hands. She weeps.

Sara can't help but chuckle, the scene is just too funny: María Eugenia sprawled in the shower like a jellyfish on the shore, surrounded by conditioners, the shower curtain a shroud, the poor thing sobbing with her hair over her face. They look at each other and both break into fits of giggles. They laugh nonstop until the *bum-ba-da-dáh-da da-da-dáh-da, bum-ba-da-dáh-da da-da-dáh-da* pulls them back to the present again.

FREELANCE WHORE

When I was still there, in my real home, I'd often go around to some friends from the estate to smoke. The oldest, who would've been approaching forty-five, was a chavista. He idolized Chávez, Che, and Fidel. Sometimes I got fired up debating with him, we started arguing and shouting at each other. After a few days, we calmed down and went back to talking as if nothing had happened. Deep down, I admired him because he really lived according to his beliefs. He didn't have many clothes or shoes, no luxuries, no TV, no latest generation smartphone. The house he lived in was left to him by his grandfather before he died, and it wasn't in good shape; he had a hammock in the middle of the living room, a radio, and a pile of books. He didn't have much food either, just some essentials, tea and coffee. He only thought about food when he was hungry. What little he had, he shared. He loved Alí Primera and had a photo with him in the middle of the living room, taken when he was only a teenager.

Without realizing it, Mateo was sliding into total poverty. All skin and bones too. Talking to him was like talking to sand on the beach that sifted away, running through your fingers straight to the bottom of the ocean, over and over. Trying to snap him out of it was like a proselytizing mission and after a while I gave up. We all gave up. I decided to accept him, just as he was, or to stop going to his house and spending time with him. I preferred the former. What did it matter? There were hundreds of other topics to discuss without getting bogged down in politics.

Mateo worked in Caracas, something to do with the radio. He had to go down into the city and back every day in his jeep. He didn't have a phone because they'd repeatedly stolen the brick he used to make calls. The last time he was robbed the thief pistol-whipped him, outraged at such an antique in black and white that could only receive messages in capital letters, and only offered as entertainment the game with the snake that grows and grows until it eats itself. He told me about his adventures and spoke of the dead along the highways in the early mornings; at least once a week they found a body. People used the highway to get rid of their filth. Noooo, yesterday when I went down real early, we got stuck in a tailback reaching almost to Mamera. There was a guy on the curb with bullets in his mug. Later, the PTJ turned up and found another one in the mountains, with a bullet hole here too, he pointed at his head. We were stuck there almost half an hour, all of us with our knees squashed together, uncomfortable, putting up with the heat. The only great thing about Mateo was that we could go to his house and smoke all we wanted, get wasted, blast music, play dominos, shout, dance, and he never said no to anything; he was very chill, probably because he didn't have any valuables that we could break and because he benefitted from everything we brought over without contributing a cent given that he provided the space. The racket wasn't a problem; the house was on a separate lot from the estate and he didn't have any neighbors. The bad thing was that there was no furniture and we had to sit on the floor, which got colder and colder, so we all wrapped up well when we went over there. We'd get together to jam for a while. Andrés would pick me up in a friend's car, I'd load the keyboard and the guitar, and we'd go to Mateo's to smoke and make music. Kids from the area turned up and we'd play all night. Sometimes some real gems emerged, ephemeral pieces that disappeared as soon as they were played, or if someone got confused with the rhythm, everything came down like a pack of cards. We were united by music and marijuana.

A year or so before I left, Mateo got himself a girlfriend. It was the first time we'd ever known him have a girlfriend and we knew it was serious because he moved her in with him, not giving a shit what anyone thought. Her name was Nataly, an exuberant and very friendly girl. She worked as

a masseuse. I've got my certificate an' everything, she confessed. Her hair was dyed dark red, a faded burgundy; her
breasts were obviously fake, giant for her stature, and she
was always made up: dark liner around those brown eyes and
lipstick the same color as her hair. Her high-pitched voice
was full of kindness. The first time we went out drinking
together, she graciously held my hair back from the toilet,
telling me: Let it out, let it all out, mami, don't worry, and I
thought this chama from Ruiz Pineda was a real sweetheart.
She was thirty-two, but her short stature made her look like
a small Minion with a boob job, she seemed younger than
she was and said that the key to avoiding premature aging
was to fuck a lot and cry very little. So, anyway, Nataly was
a masseuse and worked in a spa.

Spill, Nataly, I'd say, wheedling information out of her,
far from Mateo who, to our surprise, turned out to be jealous
and possessive. We all wanted Nataly to leave him; he became
more and more toxic and avoided us so that we couldn't spend
time with her. What's it like? I asked her.

Well, frustrating. Sometimes you get super annoying girls.
Annoying how? I insisted, in between giggles. Fuck, like,
annoying. Once I was doing a session on this girl an' every
time I'd start massaging her she'd, like, touch me up an' stroke
my arm an' I was like woah, chama, let me work, okay? I told
my boss I didn't wanna treat her no more, but that freakin'
woman didn't want no other masseuse, super annoying. I was
like this lesbian and her constant groping is such a pain in my

ass. I had another one who only came the days I was working an' when I started massaging her, she got goosebumps all over, got all nervous. Just great, an' it happened every time. Till one day she sent me a message, confessing her love. Look you're really beautiful, you know, we should go out. Let's party, you'll have a great time. Some beers, weed, pills, whatever you want, just go out with me. No, okay, no. Some of them are as bad as the pervy guys, no thanks.

In the end, Nataly left Mateo and came to Barcelona. It was inevitable that she'd leave him. Mateo's deprivation and lifestyle weren't for everyone. And if one thing was clear from talking to Nataly, it's that she aspired to much more than a hammock in the living room and composting. She wanted it all precisely because as a child she had nothing. What's more, she couldn't deal with Mateo's manipulation and toxicity; Nataly wasn't going to let anybody boss her around. Much less a loser like Mateo. If I wanted to be with a guy who orders me around an' yells at me every other minute, I'd stay with my stepdad. No, no, I'm getting far away from Mateo an' his mental shit.

One day, bright and early, just after Mateo went to work, Nataly put all her things in a bag and left without giving an explanation. She fell off Mateo's radar but not mine, and I found out she was saving up to go. She bought a ticket as soon as she could, not thinking too much about it, and threw herself into the adventure with only three hundred euros to her name. When she arrived, she worked in a beauty parlor for a while, but she wasn't making enough money and lived under the threat of her Chinese boss, afraid she wouldn't pay her because she didn't have papers. A visa marriage wasn't an option for her. No way, mami, that's too much money for nothing. I'll sort it myself, forget it.

She became a hooker and the money started to multiply. *Sex worker, Nanda.* Sex worker. Well, not multiply, but she did have much more money than before. She had been staying with a friend, in a small, one-bedroom apartment where every night she had to wrestle with the sofa to turn it into a bed. Now she could move out. First, she moved to an apartment in Sant Andreu; her roommates were French girls who went to the university, and she never felt comfortable there. They complained all the time about the noises Nataly made 24/7, attending to clients as a cam girl.

That's how she started out: a fake username, different wigs, and pretty lingerie. You don't have to get fully nude if you don't want to or you're not comfortable, they told her at the interview. You're free to do whatever you want in front of the camera, as long as people watch. After a few weeks, she was the girl with the most viewers, and some of them wanted more and more and more, hungry for flesh between their fingers, done with screens and pixels. They asked her to give up the camera and become an escort, which meant more money and more control of her time. She decided to go balls-to-the-wall, or rather, ovaries.

Through her work as an escort for that company, she met many clients who then made dates with her off-the-books, a bonus she didn't tell her bosses about. Those clients, in turn, introduced her to potential customers, so she always had steady work. She wanted to stop working for the company, but she wavered because, in the first place, she didn't understand the whole legal process or the paperwork to get set up with social security, and secondly, having the company as an intermediary seemed safer than looking for clients on her own. Going independent wouldn't just be more dangerous, but would also take up more time: taking photos, updating her profile, replying to messages, answering calls, booking dates, etc. She had to organize herself better not to feel overwhelmed with work. She also started selling used lingerie through a website and though it wasn't steady income, every now and then she made good money for no extra effort.

What she really wanted was to register as a freelancer, but she couldn't because she didn't have papers. Can hookers register as freelancers? Do they pay into social security and is income tax taken off them each month? *No idea*. The papers were the biggest stumbling block, but even if she were here legally, it's very unlikely that sex workers could register as freelancers. Nataly explained to me that being a sex worker wasn't illegal, but being a pimp or madam was. The problem's not if I can be a freelance whore, she explained, well, okay, kinda, the issue is that I'm a fucking illegal immigrant an', obviously, whoring ain't one of those high-class jobs that get you residency or a work permit, ya know? Even though, in theory, it should, coz if it ain't illegal, why can't you register as freelance?

On multiple occasions, she went to meetings with a union formed by a group of sex workers demanding labor rights. Her comrades made her feel part of something, but as she was still undocumented, there was no more they could do for her. Not for her, nor for any of the other foreign women who sucked the streets at night.

Nataly felt lucky to have regular clients, which allowed her to pay for her own apartment, while other girls lived crammed together like cockroaches and didn't even ask for labor rights or to pay taxes or plan for retirement; their needs were more basic: safety, food, clothes, toiletries. She decided to chill, to let it go for now, and help out those who didn't share her luck; she sometimes shared clients or brought them food, clothes, miniature bottles of alcohol, cigarettes, condoms, lubricant, whatever they needed. She didn't work the street because she had the clients the escort agency arranged and some other recommendations, creating a safer circle. On occasion, she accompanied girls she knew who worked alone pounding the pavement, just to be there in case anything happened. In the end, all those girls she met through the union and whom she now considered friends wanted the same thing: safety. That didn't mean more police patrols or raids; the police made them feel the opposite of safe. They wanted the police to stop hounding them as if they were dangerous parasites, forcing them to work in remote and dark areas where they were more likely to be hurt and abused.

Ever since she lost her virginity, she had always enjoyed sex, she had a voracious appetite and was uninhibited; she knew her body. Her break-up with Mateo was due to this, in part; his ideology was another key issue, but she confessed that, beyond his beliefs, his obsessive control, and his lifestyle, she had left him because the poor wretch couldn't please her like she wanted. Bitch, it's coz he don't eat an' he's always so weak, he don't give me what I want, you feel me? I need a strong man who don't give me no sob story 'bout how he needs more time after coming once, what the fuck is that? Oh sure, so he comes, then see you later alligator! And me? No, no, no. Any guy who wants to be with me gotta be ready for a marathon.

When she started as a cam girl from home, just undressing in front of the camera and masturbating several times a day, being monitored the whole time, she liked to think of her profession as a kind of hobby that brought her both profit and pleasure. Later, when she met in person the moneyed men who filled her pockets and bought her gifts, that image began to dissolve little by little; she didn't know how much was genuine pleasure or just faking it. Was there a difference, a dividing line? She was uninhibited and enjoyed herself with some, but others were pure torture.

She discovered that most clients weren't interested in her pleasure or her wellbeing. She was just a tool for them to achieve their own pleasure; sex was something they acquired, they paid for. Sometimes she didn't even feel like a person, she just pretended to be a robot, a machine dispensing pleasure to other people. To give pleasure, first she had to crush her own. And if she was good at anything, it was at faking: giving the impression that she was enjoying what she was doing to the full (sometimes she did actually enjoy it), pretending that she loved being with this or that client, that she found him attractive or he turned her on (many did), and even that she felt as satisfied as they did. She learned that many of the clients got off on the fantasy that she desired them too. What'd be the point of getting a hooker, if not? So she gives you dirty looks an' treats you bad? Uh-uh. Most of 'em wanna believe you think he's as fit as he thinks you are, that you really wanna fuck him, she said, blowing cigarette smoke out of her nose.

Nataly was a real character, she made an effort to be that way. She was very warm, very intimate with people, sometimes she'd come out with these crude expressions to break an awkward silence, a Natalism. She was very funny and always seemed so happy that her enthusiasm was contagious. She had a vibrant personality. But sometimes she got melancholy and philosophical, questioning life, why things happen, cursing the good fortune of others and yearning with all her heart for that other life she would never get back. Well, what's the big deal? I'm still a thousand times better off here. Bitch, I seem so stupid. Sure, I weren't no whore there, but I coulda been, I was this close to opening my legs for any rando an' you can forget about euros back there, no, back there they'd give me a packet of rice, a liter of oil, some shit like that, coz that's where we've ended up, that's for damned sure. Back to bartering. That or go to the border an' get killed an' left in a ditch, coz that's what they tell you is gonna happen if you start whoring: straight to the gutter. In those moments, she wasn't at all fun to be around: she was a wet cat, hissing and looking for shelter.

When she felt at ease, on very rare occasions, she showed her true essence. Calmer and more conciliatory, reserved to the point of becoming a complete mystery. A simple woman trying to survive whatever way she could, but just when you started to scratch the surface, her protective front and joie de vivre returned. She understood, she knew the impression she had on people. I think in part it was her role and she accepted it, but how tiring it must have been for her, and must be for many other women, living a double life, always having to pretend to be someone else.

Today she was particularly happy because she was going out with a guy in the evening. She turned down an invitation from some girlfriends to go partying, because she had a man who, so she said, was loaded. In every sense. He was German, Russian, or Italian, she shuffled the three nationalities, and, from his photos, she knew he was tall and handsome, blond and muscular. He had killer eyes and that was more than enough. I'm so into him, I ain't even gonna charge. She laughed at her own naughtiness. I asked him to send me pictures. Of course I did, babe, you know how it is.

That man hadn't been recommended by a friend or another regular client. She guessed the guy had found her details on the website. He didn't speak Spanish, could only stutter a few sentences. They communicated in a garbled English and messages poorly translated by Google, but she felt positive, smitten. *He's good enough to eat, delicious. So, what else matters?*

Before meeting up, they spent a few days chatting online and did a couple of video calls where they barely understood each other, but there were plenty of laughs. Nataly felt the same as she had as a teenager when she started to develop a crush on a boy in school.

Ar u from yermani? No, nyet, nyet. Ruskiy. Ya ruskiy. Soy de Rusia. Ah, mira tú, from Russia. Ameizin'. And there was Nataly thinking he was German. *Even better*. She didn't know anything about Russia, but then it's not like she knew much about Germany either. She imagined sexy country folk in the snow, *it must be damned cold*. That's a lie, she did know that they drank too much vodka, they ate some sort of gelatin with chunks of meat in it that seemed like the most disgusting thing in the world to her, and they wore furry hats that completely covered their heads; she thought they were super stylish, she had one, not from Russia, from the Chinese bazaar.

They agreed to meet at La Barceloneta, somewhere busy in case she got a bad vibe or wanted to retreat. It wasn't a job, he had asked her on a date. *Date*, he said, a word none of her clients had ever uttered. What's more, she never messaged or did video calls with clients to shoot the breeze, like they did, or to see what the other person was cooking.

It was eight thirty, still light, just about. Nataly left the metro looking for a tall man in a black T-shirt and, *fuck it*, there were several. She stood there to smoke a cigarette while she waited. A guy inched toward her; it was him. Just from seeing how he carried himself, the confidence with which he walked and the way he smiled, she knew it was him. They greeted each other as best they could, between an awkward kiss and nervous Spanglish. Alexander, he said touching his chest. Nataly imagined the scene from Tarzan, hitting his chest exactly like that, and felt a bonfire inside. For the first time in a long time, though she didn't know how or why, she got nervous and started playing with her hair. She who always grabbed the bull by the horns, who always spoke in a firm voice, who was used to giving orders or getting straight to it without much preamble, felt like moldable jello before this man. *Sasha*. That's what he said on the video call, she assumed it was a diminutive in Russian. Ar yu ok? Everything is fain? Yu look sou prity. Thanks for coming. I'm okay, yes. Thank you, gracias mi amor, for invaitin' me.

They walked around, trying to communicate through sounds, gestures, and the translator app. Sasha was pleasant, but he made very serious faces as if he were having sudden cramps, and that put her on her guard. Why was he making those faces out of nowhere? At other times, he stood staring into space for long periods, sharpening his gaze. More than once, she had to repeat his name to bring him back to the here and now. Hey, Sasha! Nataly thought maybe he was dopey or deranged, but that didn't make him less tempting, quite the opposite. She didn't know where they were going, but she followed him, trusting. Though they didn't have the best verbal communication, they seemed to understand each other, their eyes and their body language made them feel comfortable.

They walked a little farther and when Nataly realized where they were, they were almost at the port, passing Maremagnum. Sasha bought ice creams and they stood there a while, watching the boats. Nataly thought it was the most romantic moment of her life: seeing the blue sky slowly turn purple and pink, turning the boats into small dots that seemed to float in space, like stars. She licked her scoop of ice cream with abandon, wanting to show him how provocative she was, but he didn't make sexual gestures or play along, he was rather austere. He did say things to her, though, like yu ar sou biutiful, ai laik yur ais, never seen ais so dark before, ai like yur Spanish, yur accent, wiping the ice cream off the corner of his lips and licking his fingers, or laughing at gestures or faces that Nataly made unwittingly.

They kept walking, she didn't understand where they were headed, but wanted to get somewhere already. She was hot, her feet hurt, and her thighs were chafing. They walked beyond the industrial zone of the port. Everything was dark now and there wasn't a soul around; they had left behind the beach and the chiringuitos some time ago. The little voice in her head warned her, told her not to let her guard down, but how could she not let her guard down when this man who barely spoke her language felt so close, as if they knew each other from before: *Yo a ti te conozco de antes, he visto esos ojos andantes.*

Sasha looked at his phone and they stopped walking. He stood still, observing the emptiness. Nataly was about to ask what was happening when a black car appeared out of nowhere. The driver didn't even park, just drove close by them and threw out a bag. It was a large gym bag. Nataly couldn't believe what was happening, she was curious and nervous. *No fuckin' way. This is like a movie or some shit.* Sasha smiled at her, as if it were the most normal thing in the world; he was elated, his smile blinded her.

Tovar, tovar, he said, moving the bag, narkotiki. Great stuff, muy bueno. He joined his thumb and forefinger in a circle, muy bueno. Then he pointed to the mountain in front of them, Montjuïc. Walk, he said. He took out his phone and showed her a little dot in Poble Sec, on the other side of the mountain. House. He touched his chest again and Nataly despaired, longing to be at that little red dot on the map already. She imagined Sasha in bed and forgot everything else: her feet, her chafing thighs, the bag, the word narkotiki, everything. After so much time pleasing slimeballs and winos, with the exception of some clients who were real gems and treated her like a queen, she felt like this young, good-looking guy was the antidote to all her ills, the potion that would rekindle her spirit. *And what if he's not? What if I don't feel nothing after all? No pleasure, no joy, not even disgust or nothing?* She tried not to think about that. *Shh, enough already, just enjoy it. You ain't charging now, you're doing it coz you want to. Remember, sex ain't just work, people do it for fun too, for pleasure. Or have you forgotten how much you enjoyed getting laid before?*

It was complicated.

On the one hand, she genuinely liked her work, she enjoyed it; but sometimes she couldn't help feeling and seeing herself like a piece of meat. It depended on the client, of course. She couldn't deny that her personal relationships had been affected. Her characteristic confidence when she was with her regulars abandoned her entirely when faced with someone she liked for real. She seemed to have forgotten how to act without seeing herself as a product. She had mixed feelings. If I like what I do, why do I feel like this sometimes? I think it's normal, isn't it? As much as we might like our jobs, sometimes we feel sick of everything. There are moments when you just need a rest. That could be what's happening to you, Nata, you need a little break to get back to yourself, you know, we all need that space and time to look after ourselves and find ourselves again.

Work was consuming her: there was no way to create an official record of all those hours of her life she spent earning money to pay the rent and bills, to buy clothes or food. There was no way for her money, the cash they put between her tits or hid in the fold of her skirt, to be paid into social security, to allow her to register as a freelancer, or to pay her taxes like any other citizen who works and fulfills their obligations.

I work too, and more than most people. I break my back every night. Where's my pension for providing pleasure? Where's my food credits for making office workers forget their miserable lives for a second? My Employee of the Week plaque for putting up with the weepy fatso who hits me afterwards? I get nothing, babe. Sure, I make more than in any other gig, that's true, but I can't have days off. Vacations? What are they? No way, I gotta work my ass off. My profession is as necessary an' important as so many others. Why can't I register as a freelancer? If whorin' ain't illegal, why can't I have the same rights as other workers? It's so hypocritical . . . they're all ass-lickers.

Every day she tattooed on a smile, clenched her buttocks to give the best of herself and please clients. For everyone else, those who knew her profession, she was just depraved, an ignorant girl who hadn't had enough education, a victim of her own decisions. That's why, over time, she stopped saying what she did and preferred to lie: call-center operator, waitress, cleaning lady. She was sick of people seeing her as a victim or trying to save her. *Save me from what? They're ridiculous, the lot of 'em, I don't need no one to save me, don't you see? Let them go save the kids dying of hunger in Africa.* Nataly was the sex worker who wanted to register as a freelancer and vindicate her profession. *I got a master's in treating emotional traumas, a degree in curing dysfunctions an' inflating egos. A PhD in putting up with gobs of spit, insults, and mental garbage. I did my internship right here on the corner. I swallow the worst of the night so the mornings can be more productive. An' I can't pay in with that? I wanna pay my taxes, it's no problem, I can afford the freelancer fee an' then some. I'm an entrepreneur too, I made all this my business.* Little by little, she started to lose friends, because those who weren't sex workers like her saw her as a threat who would steal their boyfriends, or as dirty. The harshest criticisms came from women, those acquaintances who called themselves her friends and didn't understand why she did it, ripping her to shreds behind her back and telling her family she was a whore. *Nataly? Yeah, she's doing great. Working as a hooker over there. If she was gonna be a whore, she coulda stayed here. What a girl! She seemed so proper.* Her friendship group slimmed down until she could count her real friends on one hand with fingers to spare.

It's best not to think about that because it melts her face, her smile, her eyes. She looked at Sasha, he seemed to pick up all the unpredictable ramblings that jumped and danced in her mind. No kidding, there was a spark of compassion in his eyes, maybe because, just like her, he was a nobody, a person who becomes disposable for not having a good, respectable, socially acceptable job.

Sasha threw the bag over his shoulder. Nataly felt apprehensive at first. *Pff, I've seen too much weird shit in this life to freak out over a bag.* Okay, okay. Vamos a tu casa, mi amor. Wi go tu yur haus, yes. Let's go, pues, darling.

Walking again. *Dear God, how much longer?* They had to cross Montjuïc to reach Sasha's house. At least it wasn't a big mountain, more like a hill. Her feet would be destroyed when she got there, all because of those sandals. How was she to know that the Russian would make her walk across half of Barcelona? Because it was dark, she tripped on stones and branches, Sasha helped her. From up in the mountain, they saw the lights of the port and the same little boats in the distance, floating in space. Once again, the view intensified the feeling that she was in a movie, a romantic scene, where she wasn't herself, at least not today, not now. At first, she thought she only wanted a good screwing and then ciao, bye, spassiba. But then the whole adventure had become a very special date for her. *And the Russian is a ripped hunk showing me the last colors of the evening, better than any client's cash.*

At last, they got out onto the street and headed down toward Poble Sec. Sasha stopped outside a small, old building. Their impatience was palpable. Nataly wanted to stop, for a moment, being a woman-machine who only gave and obliged and yielded and obeyed, to become a receptacle for absolute pleasure and tenderness. She wanted to abandon herself to the sensation and let things be done to her.

As soon as they were inside, she pounced on him. Sasha returned her kiss and groped her, amused, but pushed her away firmly, raising both hands in an attempt to ask for time. Wait, espera. The apartment was small and unfurnished. *Like Mateo's, motherfucker.* A mattress, a table, a chair, a microwave, and a safe. Sasha put the bag on the mattress. Nataly went over. Sasha opened the bag and took a small knife out of his pocket. Pure white packages, lined up, filling the bag. Nataly brought her hands to her mouth, her eyes popped out, and she failed to stifle a cry of shock.

Sasha, qué vas a hacer con todo esto? What are yu duin? Ar yu creizy? She made circles with her index finger at the side of her head. Sasha smiled, moved his hands in front of his chest, excusing himself. Nyet, nyet. No loco. Work, trabajo. He cut open one of the packages, scooped up a little with the edge of the knife and sniffed it. Nataly let herself be wrapped up in the sound of a nose snorting something powerful and then the howl of appreciation when the coke is good. It was a universal language; she understood that it was world-class. Sasha offered her some. Nataly doubted for a few seconds. *What if . . . ? Or if . . . ?* She knew it was not always a good idea to accept everything clients offered, otherwise they think they have more rights, they feel powerful, invincible. And who was she to raise her voice, to shout out, to ask *please that's enough, stop, please, you're hurting me*. But Sasha wasn't a client, he'd made that clear from the start, they had been talking for days and there was something in him, she couldn't say what exactly, that made her trust him. She looked straight at him, boring into those blue eyes that were boring into hers in turn. They both seemed to be looking for the same thing in each other; at least that's how it felt to her.

Well, what the hell, I'm already in this mess. Nataly snorted the powder. *Uff.* An unpleasant tickle in her nose, a bitter taste in her throat. A glow in her brain. Giggles. In a second, she realized just how much coke the Russian had in a bag that someone had thrown out of a car, and she broke into laughter. How did they get from the ice cream and the sunset to this? Sasha started laughing too and they both threw themselves into the senselessness, the unreality of that moment, twisting, taking on a life of its own, outside of them.

Nataly was enjoying herself, she felt that, after so many bodies, so many rough tongues on her neck, she could be her genuine self without being judged, without worrying about not getting paid, without being hit or yelled at. She felt the idea of being a woman-machine evaporating, leaving her naked in the fibers of her senses, in her desires, and being just her, a woman.

Who are yu, Rusky? she asked, half closing her eyes and signaling him with an accusatory finger. Sasha. Just Sasha. Y tú? Who are yu? Soy yo. Just me, Nataly.

Nataly undressed in front of him, slowly. She was smoking a cigarette and didn't stop looking at him for a second. He had turned on the speaker and put on Buttechno to set the mood. I really like this music, she whispered. Nataly felt like they were alien sounds. There were several bottles of vodka on the table. Nataly drank straight from the bottle; so did he. She was naked within moments. Both their eyes lit up, shining. She leaned toward him; first, she took off his black T-shirt and felt his hard abs, then she pulled his pants down to his ankles. Sasha started to pull himself off in front of her, Nataly touched herself too. He grabbed her firmly, but radiating tenderness and desire. He licked her nipples, nibbled them gently while his fingers explored the cavity that opened up, wet and hungry. He kissed every part of her body, never looking away from her, and when they were both ready, unable to contain himself, he rammed her. They matched each other in their movements and their breathing, their eyes reflected in each other's pupils, their foreheads collided, their mouths overlapped. Nataly felt the awakening of the pleasure that for so long had been hidden, camouflaged.

At last, someone made her feel something, he wasn't just a sweaty man touching her body while she—in her mind, in her essence—was somewhere else, watching it happen from a distance. No. For the first time in months, she felt that her pleasure was just as important. And it was. Sasha wasn't going to admit defeat before bringing her to the threshold of ecstasy. *I ain't just a body, I ain't just meat. No. I'm a human being, I feel, I smell, I touch, I lick, I suck. I can take pleasure. I'm alive! I'm not a thing! I can say what I like an' what I don't, I can make demands an' I can come an' not feel bad or dirty or tainted.* They spent several hours that way, devoted to the rhythm and the climax, with brief breaks for cigarettes, vodka, and more coke.

Nataly reached the summit with the Russian. Or Sasha reached the summit with Nataly.

KARATE KICK

Eight a.m. and the heat was already fierce. Today it reached over thirty-seven degrees, easily. Cheo got up to piss, he had a morning boner. Pissing in that state was some feat. At least he only lived with other dudes, so they weren't too bothered about hygiene. Sometimes Cheo wished a woman lived there, to force them to be cleaner and neater. Just the fact of sharing a bathroom with a girl would impose certain basic rules of cohabitation: put the toilet lid down, wipe drops of urine off the seat and the floor, clean the hairs out of the sink after shaving, change the bath mat that's been there forever, remove solid lumps of toothpaste from the sink.

He put on the moka pot to make himself a strong coffee and get pedaling. He had loads of hours booked for today and wasn't sure when he was going to eat. There wasn't any food at home either, he'd have to stop by a Mercadona. *What a ball-ache.* He'd probably end up spending his tip, that is if anyone gave him one. *People are tighter than a duck's ass.*

If some kind soul did give him a tip, he could buy a cheap combo at KFC or a kebab. But first things first: shit, smoke while taking a shit, and get those legs moving.

Luckily, he had his own Glovo account now. He had been given his NIE for being in a common-law partnership with Andrés. It hadn't been complicated at all, at least not for him. They both handed in their cartas de soltería, indicating there was no impediment to their marriage, Andrés presented his work contract to demonstrate that he could "support" his partner while he waited for his papers to come through, and that was it. They didn't even need witnesses, unlike other acquaintances who not only needed witnesses but were subject to an exhaustive interrogation to see if they were really a couple. How many tattoos does your partner have? Any notable birthmarks or other areas? What is his favorite food and what color is his urine in the morning? Cheo and Andrés explained to the notary that they had lived together since Venezuela, but that gay marriage wasn't legal there, so now they wanted to become common-law partners. No one asked them anything more, or required any proof, nor did anybody come to check on how they lived, what they ate, or how they screwed. He thought about it and shat himself laughing, wallowing in his good luck, but with a knot in his stomach because he knew that they were the exception among thousands who really had to fight to be believed. Something like survivor's guilt.

He sent the best part of the money he made straight to his parents' bank accounts, back in Venezuela, and to his girlfriend, Andrea. He would have liked to send them the money in euros, but it was impossible; changing the money to bolivars at a bank was daylight robbery. Nor did he have a gringo bank account to use a money exchange app and cryptocurrency was not an option. He had no choice but to give euros to someone he knew over here, and that person would transfer bolivars to his family. *Spend them on whatever you need now, tomorrow they'll be worth fuck all.*

He was saving up to buy his girlfriend a plane ticket. He dreamed about their reunion: meeting her in the airport, maybe he'd even cry? Waking up and having her at his side, a vital boost that would push him to keep going in bleak moments, a companion in adventures and misadventures, in learning, in life. His plan was to put a ring on that finger. Deep down, Cheo was a hopeless romantic: flowers, chocolates, breakfast in bed, wine, and massages. His mind went from meeting Andrea at the airport to asking her to be his wife; the wedding and the celebration, which had to be lavish, within the limit of what they could afford, of course. Kids, family, a house.

If someone were to ask him what his dream was, beyond fooling around and saying something like *winning a green card or the lottery*, what he really yearned for was a family. He tried to return to that mental image when he felt he couldn't go on, when the desire to give up and throw in the towel seized him as soon as he opened his eyes.

Yes, he needed his Boo by his side to start making his dream a reality at last. What was the point of all this bullshit if not to offer her something better? Cheo had been with Andrea for almost six years, their relationship brought them together during late adolescence and they had been each other's rock ever since. Andrea's living conditions and experiences were not the best: when she was eight, her father was shot dead at an ATM. At ten, she became an orphan when her mother took her own life, unable to bear the loss. Her grandparents became her parents and from a young age she got used to scarcity, not in an emotional sense because her grandparents loved her and showed that love, but material deprivation. After high school, a public one because her grandparents couldn't afford much above medicines and food, she started to work and paid for her university studies herself. She was, as Cheo would often remind her, *a go-getter.*

He was having trouble shitting. Probably because he wasn't drinking enough water, he always forgot. His turds were like stones. This, added to a serious problem with hemorrhoids, made his ass like a bunch of grapes: lips hanging out, an orchid in the dark. Then he'd walk like a penguin, looking in the fridge for the magical cream to make the eruptions recede back into his body and bring the swelling down. No, you're nuts, you can't work like that, bro, you need to rest your ass.

At the walk-in clinic, they told him that he needed an operation, urgent surgery. He went twice; the first time, the only solution they offered him was draining the blood with a needle and reducing the swelling that way. *No, nope, no way, you crazy.* He left with the same pain in his ass. The second time, he felt so bad that he didn't care, and they punctured the swollen hemorrhoids with a needle. It was awful, but he felt immediate relief. You need to have surgery urgently, the doctor repeated. But how could he have surgery if social security didn't cover hemorrhoid operations and would send him to a private surgeon, which would cost a fortune? He needed to rest, but how could he survive without working? He works freelance, in other words, he can't just do nothing. If he doesn't work, he doesn't eat. Neither him nor his family.

No sick leave, no vacations, no bank holidays, nothing. *Get pedaling, you son of a bitch!*

First, he needed to save up for his ass surgery, survive the recovery period and get back to working flat out. But he also needed to save up to bring his girl over, send money to his parents, send them the medicines they asked for. It didn't add up, even with pedaling eighty-four hours a week. At least this way he made more money than anywhere else, for now.

Even with his papers, the jobs he found were . . . jobs. Receptionist in a hotel only doing night shifts. Cook. Waiter. Door-to-door insurance salesman. Door-to-door electricity salesman. Estate agent. Delivery driver for a restaurant. Vodafone call-center operator. *Dog shit.* The jobs he really wanted told him that he was "overqualified." A kick in the ass, straight to the hemorrhoids. *Move, you waster.* His only option was to take a ton of ibuprofen, smoke weed, listen to music, drink beer, and get pedaling. Who needs to go to the beach when they're a rider? He was getting tanned: the summer sun was making him darker, but only his arms, legs, neck, and face.

Marico, said Jordi, appropriating Cheo's words, before switching back to his usual Catalan, man, you have to put sun cream on. You'll fuck yourself up. No way, I'm a real man, he grumbled, playing it down, not like you, all gay with your sunscreen and skin damage and whatever. Time to go. Mate, you're so ignorant. Call me gay when you get skin cancer, Jordi spat, throwing him the sunscreen. Shake a leg, bro, Andrés shouted from the living room as a goodbye.

Helmet on and ready to crush it. First up was an order from a McDonald's where everything came out straight away. As soon as he got an order for closer to the city center, everything went haywire. He didn't know where he'd end up. He imagined himself like Mario Bros in different worlds and levels. Every order was a new adventure.

Biking everywhere, he had developed a certain affection for the city. He now knew it inside out and, little by little, he was forming associations with Caracas. Once, while we shared a joint after a few beers—here's where I show up—he became melancholy, nostalgic; he often thought about going back.

It's like, I spend so much time thinking about wanting to go back that, in my mind, I already have another reality, he told me. What do you mean? I asked. Shit, it's like I know it too well. Green paths and everything. Look, imagine Barcelona. The similarity with Caracas is brutal, it's the same layout. The closer you are to the mountain, the more prestigious. Where do you live at the moment? In Sants, I replied, that would be . . . ? Fuck, like Chacao. Further up's Les Corts, which would be like Altamira, and over toward Pedralbes we've got Los Palos Grandes, do you get it? Yeah, that's wild! Hospitalet would be Chacaíto. Totally. As you go farther down, things get more down-market here too. Where did you live in Caracas? Valle Abajo, around Los Chaguaramos, near the university. Oh yeah, near the stadium. Yep, where we used to go to watch Caracas FC and drink beers up at the top of the stands while you smoked your weed. That could be Marina here, I figure. Poble Nou? No, coz Poble Nou would be the cooler, classier part. I guess more toward Besós and Marseme, in fact there's even a street called Venezuela right there and that whole area is like Santa Mónica, Bello Monte, and Los Chaguaramos. And Las Mercedes is Eixample, which is right next to it. Well, that whole district, before Eixample, just next to it, San Martí. Coz Eixample is Eixample, it's its own thing. Sarrià obviously is La Lagunita, very douchey and full of luxury houses. Terrazas de Ávila was fucking cool, but it was near Petare, the Cota Mil, Santa María. Here the Ronda de Dalt is exactly like the Cota Mil, so that whole area covers Torre de Barró and Horta Guinardó, though I see that area more like Alto Prado. Anyway, remember that it doesn't match up exactly in terms of geography, well a little, but what's more important is comparing the neighborhoods themselves, what they're like. The people are similar too, aren't they? Too fucking right. People here do whatever they want, just like over there.

The grapes had retreated now, and he wasn't in much pain. It was midafternoon and he was sweating from pedaling so much under the sun. Thank god for public drinking fountains where he could rinse off and cool down. A high-paying order came in, he had to go buy something. He went straight to Gràcia, it was a sex shop. *Fuck me!* He went in and asked the salesman for a "butt plug." He showed him his phone because he wasn't sure he'd read it right. In fact, he didn't know what the hell it was, but he was real curious, not embarrassed at all. When the salesman brought out the package and he finally laid eyes on it, he was dumbstruck. *Shit, no.* He hoped that, if he was a homo, he wouldn't be one of those intense ones who didn't respect personal space or made him feel uncomfortable, because if Cheo was anything in this town, it was a man magnet. You're too damn sexy, wifey, Andrés would say to get a rise out of him.

He paid for the ass dilator, put it away before leaving the shop, and was off again, heading toward Raval. The object disturbed him. *Here I am suffering from hemorrhoids and there're people who go and stick this thing up their asshole, no way, bro.*

They were like pointy doorknobs, each one bigger than the last, a progression. *And how the fuck do they stick it in?* He felt his hemorrhoids tremble just thinking about it. *Well, as they say back in Caracas, everyone's free to use their asshole as a flowerpot.*

He arrived at the apartment block, a narrow building; he was used to them. It was a Raval thing to live in tight spaces, whenever he went to those buildings, things took a turn for the worse. He went in and had to carry his bike upstairs. Always the same story, everything repeats. Leaving it outside was not an option. If someone were to come downstairs at the same time, it would be impossible for either of them to pass, the space was that narrow.

He arrived panting. Wiping the sweat from his brow with his arm, he rang the doorbell. A short man answered, butt naked. *Fuck, not again, si us plau.* He was starting to think that every naked man in Barcelona had been assigned to him. And what if he were a girl? Would they at least have the decency to get dressed or would they not care? For the moment, he didn't know any women who'd had similar experiences, delivering packages to naked customers.

Cheo had never seen such a huge schlong. He wanted to look away, but he was stunned. The man smiled, aware of the reaction he caused. Cheo couldn't help widening his eyes and raising his eyebrows. The guy stroked his bald head several times, Cheo imagined he must be wasted because he stank of booze.

What's up, bro? Sign here, please, Cheo held out his phone for the man to sign. He signed and grabbed the bag. Wait, wait, he said.

Cheo picked up his bike again, ready to set off running. The guy disappeared into his apartment and then appeared out of nowhere with a smile. He gave him a ten-euro note. *Fuckin' A, in that case I'll deliver ass openers to everyone in Barcelona who wants a bigger hole.* He grabbed the note in disbelief; he wanted to hug the guy despite his nudity. The man, seeing the genuine gratitude on Cheo's face, couldn't help but laugh and they shared a friendly chuckle.

Thanks dude, enjoy it. *If anyone can enjoy having that doorknob deep inside them. No shit, just with a suppository I'm seeing stars.* He went down the stairs taking care not to kill himself and as soon as he stepped onto the street another order arrived. Toward Diagonal, far from apartment blocks and narrow streets. He skirted the cars, people were being dumbasses: using their phones all the time, looking at something on a tablet, distracted with talking or fighting, concentrating on anything other than driving.

The light turned green, and he pedaled. He had to make a left and was just doing that, in his bike lane, when out of nowhere a guy didn't just run the red light but went into the bike lane. Cheo braked suddenly and so did the car. Thwack! He smashed into its side, but nothing serious happened. Shock more than anything. Instead of helping him up or checking that everything was okay, the driver started to shout and insult him, as if it had been Cheo's fault. Soon he was back on his feet, and as he picked up his bike, Cheo hit his breaking point under the shower of insults.

Seriously, what's your problem, cocksucker? You ran the light and because of you I'm on the ground, you jerk. You're a wanker, mate. A wanker! Can't you see you're in the bike lane, jackass? Look, look how you've left my bike. Moron. You twat, go back to your own country. Come on, then. If you're so brave in your car, come on out. I'll show you, you South American cunt.

Cheo kicked the driver's door. The man had enough and got out. He was a burly fortysomething, with thinning, graying hair, pinkish skin, and bulging eyes. Barely out of the car, he launched himself on Cheo like a bull. Not knowing where his reflexes came from, but feeling like he was in *The Matrix*, Cheo swerved, turned, and slapped him. Bam! Take that, sucker. The man tried to kick him, but Cheo moved away in time. People were gathering around them, and neighbors were watching out their windows. It was the old fool who ran the red light. For god's sake, man, you're making a scene, an older gentleman said to the driver.

The man, in his blind rage, went to the car and opened the trunk. For a second, Cheo thought he was going to pull out a gun; he nearly shat himself. He visualized where his bike was so he could race away if possible. Some of the neighbors at their windows started shouting, waving their arms. When the driver closed the trunk, he had a pipe in his hands. I'm going to destroy you! Fuck you and fuck your whole family, you tosser. And on he went, insulting and threatening; he was going to kill him, he would get him deported. He waved the pipe around, hitting it against one of his hands and coming closer to Cheo, trying to trap him or maybe just frighten him. The crowd were shouting too, and a few were even filming the whole mess.

Someone tried to intervene and calm the situation, but he was threatened too, and nearly struck with the pipe when the maniac, exasperated to have no backing, tried to whack him. The roar of the crowd was growing, other bikers stopped, watching and looking where to go because the car was parked across the bike lane. It was a matter of minutes before the police would arrive.

Unable to control himself any longer, the man launched himself a second time on Cheo, who, while the crowd shouted advice at him, had a lucky escape. The maniac managed to hit him on the forearm, but in his rush to attack him, he tripped on the curb and stumbled. Cheo made the most of those seconds of distraction to center himself and when his assailant turned, he received a karate kick straight to the chest. Cheo had gathered momentum and without understanding how, because he didn't do any exercise other than biking, his elastic leg rose with all possible force. In the best Mr. Miyagi style. He felt the impact through the sole of his shoe, the hit almost knocked him over, but he managed to stay upright, expectant. Instead, it was the driver who fell on his ass, the pipe rolled on the ground, and someone rushed to grab it. The crowd celebrated the victory, the spectacle; they even cheered from the windows and jeered at the loser.

Amid the celebrations, Cheo, nervous and thinking that the police would arrive any moment, ran and got on his bike as best he could, and disappeared from the commotion. No one said anything to him because most of them didn't notice, distracted as they were with insulting the driver, taking photos, and filming the show; some men were holding him to the ground, and he was twisting about trying, unsuccessfully, to escape.

When he had some distance, Cheo realized that the handlebars were twisted and the front wheel was a little dented, that's why he was having such a hard time going in a straight line. *Motherfucker.* Now he had to spend money to fix the bike to be able to keep working and the worst thing was it was Saturday afternoon. *How do I work tomorrow? What about Monday's shift? Goddammit.*

He braked and took a moment to calm down and check himself over. Nothing seemed to hurt, but then he was wired, and the adrenaline was pumping. His forearm was swelling where he'd been hit, but he could move it normally so he didn't worry about it; nothing that a little Voltarol wouldn't cure. A knee was bleeding, but otherwise he was unscathed.

Even though he felt victorious, he was also in shock, looking around cautiously, alert. He didn't want any problems with the cops. For as much as the crowd had helped him, because it really was the driver's fault, the police made him so nervous that he imagined the worst, even though, in theory, he wasn't an illegal immigrant. *Better to vanish in a puff of smoke and act like I was never there.* The adrenaline rush pushed him up tough hills and he went full pelt, almost unaware of the effort, as if he were on an electric bike. The only thing that mattered was to keep pedaling. His heart was racing, the only thing that hurt was his chest.

Later, after smoking a joint and heading home, he realized that he had another injury to his arm. His shirt was stained with blood, but he hadn't noticed. How had he done that? He didn't remember. It was only when he saw it that he felt the pain. All that pain: his knee, his forearm, his other arm, his legs, his back. For all that time, his mind had blocked the feeling.

Andrés came out of his room and was surprised to see Cheo standing in the living room. What's up, bro, no orders? No, asshole. If I told you what happened. Just another day, a normal, ordinary day in the shitty life of a rider. Well, marico, you know how it goes . . . the dealer gets the worst hand.

LASME

Not long after I arrived in Barcelona, I started working in a bar. It didn't go well. I dropped the tray several times, I couldn't remember customers' orders or the table numbers, I didn't know how to enter orders into the tablet, I never managed to memorize how to make the cocktails, or where to find the ingredients. After going for three days straight with the best intentions of learning, they asked me—in a very friendly way, but without paying me for those days—not to come back.

After a few days of searching on JobToday, I found something in a store. They sent me an email asking me to learn a speech in English for greeting clients.

It was a boutique that sold cosmetics from the Dead Sea, beauty products: bath gels, exfoliants, creams, face masks. My job was to bring in customers, approaching them directly in the street, forcing them to enter via somewhat passive-aggressive means. Then I had to demonstrate the product to them: wash their hands, touch their arms so they could feel the effect of the exfoliant, smile at them, all while delivering the speech I had learned, without stopping for breath or breaking eye contact. What a sales strategy: pretty girls selling cosmetics. It didn't seem that complicated.

I showed up on my first trial day dressed in black, as the email indicated. At that time, I lived in a sketchy area of Barcelona. Well, sketchy according to the locals, I didn't think so. It was like a charming Chinatown. Though it was true that things could turn ugly now and again because it was right next to La Salut, a "dangerous" neighborhood on the edge of town. The nearest metro was El Fondo, on the red line. I sat reading until Urquinaona and then changed to the yellow line; a couple of stops and I was at Jaume I.

When I reached the address indicated by the little red dot, I saw it was a tiny store. A man not much taller than me was standing right in the doorway. His eyes were turquoise, incredible eyes. I can't remember his name, but he was from Jordan. Let's call him Abdul. He and his beautiful wife were the owners. I don't remember her name either, I know she was from Israel, maybe it was Débora. They introduced themselves as husband and wife.

There were three of us salesgirls: a young Black girl called Lasme, Camila, and me. We each had to stand outside the shop and try to bring in the biggest number of potential customers. We had to do at least five demonstrations and they were very strict with this, they were always counting or reminding us that we hadn't done enough demonstrations. I felt terrible pressure in my chest and the urge to launch myself at people: *Please, let us do a demonstration for you! Please, let me smear your hands with cream while I regurgitate this spiel that I don't even understand!*

On the second day, I realized that the three of us were very attractive in our own ways. Lasme was a total beauty: tall and slim, with glowing, flawless skin; she seemed older than she was. Camila wasn't as tall as Lasme, though taller than me; she carried herself like a model, had green eyes and a perfect smile. And then me, petite and slim. Abdul sometimes walked among us making inappropriate comments about our bodies, telling us to try being sexier with the customers. He was constantly comparing me and Camila to Lasme, who had already been working with them for six months and always dressed provocatively. She had a lively personality and a silver tongue, perfect for sales. I'd say that, for every five demonstrations, she got two or three sales; she was very good. Camila only came for the first three days, then we never saw her again.

In the days that followed, I was just with Lasme, trying to learn as much as possible. I followed her advice. I also saw a ton of touching between her and Abdul. Lasme played along, smiling; I didn't take it too seriously, though Abdul made me feel uncomfortable. It was my first public-facing job, and at times I even believed he was just being relaxed and friendly with us. He would pass close by us—if I'm honest, there wasn't much space in the store—and always found a way to graze Lasme's butt, which was at the same level as his stomach, he was that short compared to her. Sometimes they would disappear out the back, to the stockroom, leaving me alone out front. I thought they might be organizing things or replacing products, but once, when I tried to get in, I was met with a locked door and I didn't keep trying. It was all very awkward, bearing in mind that his wife was around. As soon as he came near me, I moved away, tense, and started doing odd jobs to avoid him: sweeping, organizing the shelves, talking to a tourist.

Lasme and I stayed late to lock up. Abdul and Débora left around seven, so we were in charge of cleaning, tidying, and leaving everything ready for the next day. Lasme kept the keys because she'd been there longest. We took the metro home together, because we lived near each other: we got off at Fondo, where she would catch a bus to Badalona and I would walk home.

On one of those metro journeys, Lasme told me that her family was from the Ivory Coast. They came to Spain when she was five. Her parents didn't speak any Spanish, only the basics, so she had to be their interpreter. She spoke perfect Catalan. She had a baby sister. Her father sold counterfeit goods on the street and her mother sewed and mended clothes. I don't know why the store paid her under the table, in cash, as if she didn't exist.

I never asked her much about this, maybe it was because she was underage, I don't know. But they could decide not to pay her and she wouldn't be able to file a complaint or do anything about it; I asked her if she wasn't afraid that one day they would decide not to pay her, a common practice among employers with workers in irregular situations. She wasn't worried in the slightest, she had been working for them for months and they never once let her down.

She suggested getting together one day and going to La Maquinista to try on clothes and watch boys skateboarding; sometimes the age gap between us was so obvious, especially when it came to our tastes in music. I gave her my headphones and played her some band from the nineties or noughties she didn't know, she called me old for listening to prehistoric music, and in turn she played me her favorite songs from bands I didn't have a clue about, mainly trap.

On my fourth day there, my level of discomfort rose precipitously. Abdul always wanted to offer us to the customers. He did it through tongue-in-cheek comments that were meant to be funny, but they were so repetitive I could read the truth behind his mask of laughter: for him, we were just another product in the store. If they were Arabs or Russians, even better; their eyes would light up in lust and he would move us to show us off better. I felt like a thing, an object. I sometimes tried to catch Débora's eye, the few times she was around, but she avoided any eye contact—any form of contact with us, in fact. It became very clear to me that she was another extension of the business, more merchandise for Abdul to use at his whim. Why didn't she say anything? Was she afraid of him?

Half-kidding, half-serious, Abdul would tell customers what time we would finish work and even told us to go out the back with whoever we fancied, no need to be embarrassed, always laughing, winking, trying to be amusing, playing down the issue with a wave of his hand.

I didn't want to go back, but if I finished the week, they would have to pay me for it.

On the sixth day, Débora went out back to do a demonstration for two Russians she brought in from the street. They were big and pale, brawny. Abdul turned the music up and carried on attracting customers, as if nothing were happening. The son of a bitch wanted to pimp us out.

After a while the Russians came out, spent at least three hundred euros on products and left. Then Débora came out. Her eyes were glassy and her face burning. *Shame? Rage?* I approached her, not knowing what to say. She dodged my gaze and my hands, went upstairs to the tiny room where we ate our lunch.

At the slightest distraction, Abdul would look daggers at me and indicate with a nod that I should return to my place—standing outside the store. He would grumpily tap the little pad hanging from our waists to keep track of how many demonstrations we had done. At seven, Débora came down and left without saying anything to anyone. Abdul didn't even notice, he kept humming, making wisecracks and complimenting tourists who walked past the store.

That night, when it was time for us to close up, three guys from the UAE approached us slowly. We had done a demonstration for them that afternoon and Abdul told them when we would finish work, they took it very seriously and there they were.

Lasme was crazy nervous; she'd already told me that she thought one of the guys was super cute and he had told her how beautiful she was while she demonstrated the exfoliant. They invited us for a drink, something chill, they said in English. I didn't want to go, I didn't feel comfortable going anywhere with three strangers and even less after seeing the side hustle going on in the stockroom. Lasme did want to go, only to be with the one she liked, a man who was easily twice her age. We stood with the shutters down, discussing our options in whispers.

No, no. Let's go home. If you want, we can go to La Maquinista and have some drinks, just us girls. Come on, babe, come with me, she insisted. It'll only be a few beers. I don't wanna go off with them alone. I'm going home. We shouldn't go off with them at all. Do you trust them? Do you trust Abdul? There's nothing going on with Abdul, okay? Her face suddenly turned very serious. And I'm really into this guy, I'm telling you, he's cool. We'll have a couple of beers and we'll leave. It's still early! We'll be home by nine thirty, ten tops. Come on, let's go!

Lasme stomped her foot, pouted. It was like facing down a toddler throwing a tantrum.

The things Abdul says aren't true, she said, coming up very close to me. He's constantly joking, he's all mouth. Don't pay him any attention, okay, Nanda? Right, let's go! Her enthusiasm was contagious. We'll go home at ten at the latest? Lasme celebrated her victory with a little jump. Sure, babe, of course, we'll be on our way home at ten. You'll have a good time, you'll see. You've gotta relax a little, hey?

In the end, I let her talk me into it. Was it that big a deal? It would only be a drink and the guys weren't exactly ugly. They didn't speak Spanish, so we communicated in English, except for one of them who spoke French. He and Lasme understood each other perfectly. He was the one she liked.

They made a good first impression: funny, polite. One in particular caught my attention, he made interesting comments. We asked them questions with genuine interest. They were twelve years older than me, maybe eighteen years older than Lasme. They looked so young: smooth skin, perfect hair, in good shape. They told us they were from Dubai, they'd known each other since they were kids because their families had been friends their whole lives. They were just taking a vacation, an "insanity trip" from which they would return worn-out to their routine of business deals and work. They didn't say whether they were married, whether they were fathers; we didn't ask, either.

Would it have made a difference? Would they have been honest with us? They didn't ask much about us. Lasme lied about her age and then we each shared a few personal details.

They were surprised that, as a Latina, I wasn't voluptuous or sassy. They spoke about other places they had visited, their favorites: Tokyo, Sydney, and Costa Rica. You could tell from miles away that they were wealthy: the clothes they wore, their designer accessories, their way of ordering. They dressed impeccably and smelled good; their hands were clean, their nails shone, their beards were perfect. They were handsome men, we couldn't deny it.

After the first beer, I relaxed and little by little became chattier. Lasme also let her guard down. For a second, I became paranoid: did Lasme want to rob them? No, no way. She really did like that guy. I put the idea out of my head. She would have told me from the start. Lasme and the guy were getting closer and closer, their heads brushing, whispering to each other, giggling. Asim, the quietest one, tried to make conversation about any old topic and Malek, the other guy who was in the middle, also joined in. He would turn and stare intensely at Lasme, as she got even closer to Farid, ignoring everyone else.

Why don't we go to another place? Farid suggested, in English, after the fourth round. Asim and Malek looked at each other, Lasme smiled at me, wide-eyed. Voudriez-vous? he asked her directly. Oui, oui, bien sûr. Allons!

I stared at her, trying to communicate with her through my eyes, that gift we women have to say everything to each other with a look. I didn't want to go anywhere, it was already ten, time for us to go as we'd agreed.

I'm going to the bathroom, you coming? No, she replied, shaking her head but without dropping her smile. I'm good. You go, I'll look after your bag.

It should be illegal to refuse to accompany another woman to the bathroom. There is an implicit rule in that request: always say yes, go with your friend or acquaintance to the bathroom. It was the ideal excuse to talk to her and debate what to do next. Do you really want to go with them? Wouldn't you prefer to head home? We could ask them to walk us home, they probably wouldn't say no. We could meet up with them another time, couldn't we? Oh, no, of course, they're on vacation, they won't be in the city much longer.

I didn't feel like staying, I knew how the scene would end: Lasme hooking up with Farid; Malek, Asim and I looking at each other awkwardly, not knowing what to talk about. It could be very uncomfortable, it had happened to me with friends before. Suddenly they'd be hooking up with some boy and they'd forget anyone else existed. It was time to abort the mission, but if Lasme insisted she wanted to go with them, I wouldn't know what to do. *Do I let her go? Do I scold her like a close friend and force her to come home with me? I've only known her a few days.*

I left the bathroom and they were already outside the bar, waiting for me. I slowly approached and started saying my goodbyes. Lasme got nervous, asked me to go with her, not to leave her alone, promising it would be fun. Come on, Nanda! How often do you meet such interesting guys? She nudged me with her elbow.

It was Asim who finally convinced me. He told me I could smoke all the weed I wanted because they had recently scored from a cannabis club and it was good stuff, we could even bake brownies, they had some mix. Malek also insisted: the views from the apartment they were staying in were incredible and they had various board games. It all sounded like a riot, even if Lasme hooked up with Farid, the idea of smoking, making brownies, and playing board games ruled.

Okay, alright, let's do it. All four of them celebrated my capitulation. They hailed a taxi and we got in. Farid and Lasme sat in the back and started making out. Asim, Malek, and I were on the other seat, talking about something I don't remember. A Drake song came on the radio; we all perked up. We arrived at the AirBnB up in Sarrià, a bougie area of the city; the buildings weren't so tall, the streets were wider, everything seemed clean and even the glow of the streetlights felt different. They had a penthouse, and just like Malek said, the views were on another level. The apartment was minimalist, a huge vase in one corner, a giant painting taking up an entire wall. Malek and Asim threw themselves on one of the sofas; there were loads of rolled joints on the table, a bong, and a hookah with several hoses. Lasme went to the kitchen with Farid to fix some drinks.

Asim put YouTube on the TV and we started surfing, each person taking their turn to choose a song or a funny video. The bong hit made me melt into the sofa with a dumb smile and I felt completely relaxed. I was genuinely enjoying myself.

Malek put on famous songs from his country and tried to translate them for me. It was a kind of cultural exchange through music, they showed me who Kazim Al Sahir and Amr Diab were, and I introduced them to Tío Simón, Oscar D'León, and Rawayana.

Without me realizing, the time passed between videos, commercials, and songs. Where was Lasme? It was almost midnight, getting back home would be a total odyssey. The metro had stopped running and I would need to catch a night bus. The endless journey home. At one point, it crossed my mind to hook up with Asim. He seemed more and more attractive to me as the night went on, I fantasized about kissing him or getting close and touching his perfect beard, but I only imagined it, incapable of doing anything.

Bored of being alone with the guys, I glanced around, looking for Lasme. But I couldn't see her anywhere, could she still be fixing the drinks? As if I'd conjured her with my thoughts, she appeared and handed me a glass of vodka and grenadine. She was radiant and walked with her shoulders back, showing off her slenderness; she sat next to me on the sofa and snuggled up to me in a kind of hug, grateful that I had come with her. She looked happy. I felt happy too. Farid appeared and sat on the rug, next to Lasme's legs. He put a little bag of white powder on the table and prepared some lines. He inhaled two, sniffed loudly, wiped his nose, and smiled at me. Malek also snorted two lines. Farid pointed to the remaining lines, four of them.

No, no thanks, I declined the offer, nervous. I dunno, Lasme whispered to me in Spanish. Have you tried it, babe? No, never, I replied, best not to try it right now, smoke if you want, but don't take coke. Oh, c'mon, girls! Farid insisted, chuckling. Vous allez l'adorer, vous verrez. Fais-moi confiance. D'accord . . . juste un petit peu, Lasme accepted.

She came down from the sofa and knelt on the rug beside him. She tilted her head and, covering up one nostril, brought her face close to the table and sniffed, just as Farid had explained. She snorted the two lines. Farid gathered up what was left on the table with his fingertips and ran them over his gums. The change in everyone was immediate. They became euphoric, full of energy, they laughed and danced. Asim and I stayed on the sofa, laughing and swaying our arms to the music but not forming an active part of the ritualistic revelry. Asim lit another joint, we smoked.

Time out. From here on, I need a time out because I can't remember what happened without feeling like I'm reliving it, that I'm still there, in that spacious lounge, in front of a giant TV, with total strangers. The memory seems to be taking form and appearing at the same time as everything happens. That's how it feels, as if this narration were simultaneous with the events. And in a certain way, it is. I close my eyes, I remember: everything is happening now.

The music, the smoke from the weed, the tapping of the credit card lining up more white powder on the table. I feel so good, babe, Lasme says, inviting me to dance with her. You sure you don't wanna try any? You feel . . . wow! Better not, I say, brushing it off. I don't want to get paranoid or feel faint. I'm good as I am. Lasme furrows her brow, I don't think she gets it, she doesn't understand my words.

I take another hit from the bong and dance with Lasme, we hold hands and laugh. Farid gets between us and little by little reclaims her attention, separates her from me, and I sit back on the sofa. Farid invites her out to the balcony and Lasme follows him, both are dancing and touching each other as they go. I can't remember what Asim asks me, I think he says to put some music on, but I don't know what to play, we start surfing again. I realize Malek isn't there, where could he have gotten to? I turn my head toward the balcony and see that Lasme and Farid are hooking up, groping each other; him rummaging under her skirt, her engulfing his neck. Farid has his back to me, Lasme wraps her legs around him, they are fused in kisses and wild caresses. Seeing her like that, consumed by desire, made me imagine myself with Asim again. Instead of seeing Lasme with Farid, I imagined myself in her place with Asim; I got kind of turned on. If he'd approached me, I think I would also have abandoned myself to pleasure.

While they are still kissing, Malek appears with a camera, interrupting. I don't know if he's filming or just taking photos. For the first time, Lasme seems concerned. Asim shows me something on the TV, a funny video or a meme, I smile, not paying too much attention, he's guffawing, oblivious to what's happening on the balcony. I start to feel more uncomfortable, to ask myself what we're doing here with these strangers.

I hear a tussle, a shout, and harsh words. Farid and Malek are arguing, or at least that's what I think, I can't understand anything they're saying. I catch Lasme's eye; she seems frightened. I get up from the sofa as a reflex, my alarm bells going off. Asim also gets up, now completely alert to what is going on outside, but not getting involved, just watching. I notice that his jaw is tense, he seems annoyed, his expression becomes rigid, distant. To my surprise, Farid grabs Lasme and they start kissing again, this time roughly, savagely. Malek's camera flashes. I open my mouth in shock when Malek pulls down his pants and starts masturbating in front of them. Farid touches Lasme's breasts; with a yank, he rips open her blouse. Lasme pulls away, pushing him off her and runs to the lounge where Asim and I are still standing, not doing or saying anything.

Lasme? She ignores me, runs to the back of the room, fleeing. Farid and Malek come in straight away, still arguing. They could be talking about anything really, but to me it sounds like an argument, a fight; they speak loudly, brusquely. Lasme shouts something in French I don't understand, and Asim intervenes. He puts a hand on Farid's chest, says something conciliatory, but Farid shakes him off. Malek looks depraved. Asim turns to look at me and I suspect that something is very wrong, I feel an electric current run down my spine, I tense like a cat.

Suddenly, Lasme grabs the decorative vase and throws it with all her strength; the vase travels in a straight line and smashes at Malek's bare feet. He shouts, now truly furious. He steps on a ceramic shard and cuts himself, bleeds lightly, and shrieks even more. He puts the camera down and looks for a Kleenex.

What's going on? I hear myself shout, but no one pays me any attention. Lasme, let's go.

I try to move toward her, but a hand grabs me tightly by the arm, Asim is holding me back. It's very late. Farid pounces on her and, with an ease that astonishes me, picks her up like a rag doll and slings her over his shoulder, she's no more than a sack carried on his back. Lasme shouts and hits that back which a few minutes ago she was caressing. I shout too, in English and in Spanish. Asim blocks me, I think I hit him although now I don't remember it clearly. Lasme is still sobbing and writhing, like a woman about to be abused, destroyed. Farid goes down a corridor, toward a bedroom. Malek appears again, picks up the camera and takes a few steps in our direction. He leaves a red footprint on the floor; he seems to notice me for the first time. He says something to Asim, points to me. Asim squares up to him and at the same time turns toward me, worried. Go. Go home now. He is serious and determined. He has his hands on Malek's chest and whispers to him, like he's trying to pacify him. No, no, I splutter. Lasme. I won't go.

Malek raises the camera and I feel the flash hitting my face. Asim shouts at him more forcefully and Malek only laughs, a laugh that makes my hair stand on end. I see them exactly as they are. What happened to the charming and interesting men from the beginning of the evening?

I hear another shout. Malek also hears it and turns toward the corridor down which Farid disappeared. I make a move to go that way too, but Asim restrains me, he's between us now. Go now or you're next, he commands.

Malek cackles again. I'm next? The next what? On autopilot, knowing the response and not wanting to accept it, not absorbing the truth because to do so would be like swallowing acid and feeling my esophagus dissolve, I pick up my bag and stand there, static. Asim and Malek are shouting at each other now, Malek shoves him and comes toward me. I see it in slow motion: his greedy eyes, his open mouth, his exposed teeth, how he licks his lips. Asim yanks on his back.

I run, looking for the door, I feel disoriented. *Where did we come in?* And for a fraction of a second, I see her. Lasme is lying face down on a quilt, Farid on top of her, totally naked, grotesque. Lasme has something in her mouth, I don't know what it is, maybe a rag, but her mouth is swollen and open, she doesn't make a sound. I see the tears on her cheeks, for a fraction of a second, we make eye contact, but she doesn't seem to be there.

I run out of the apartment, follow the long corridor, not knowing exactly where it will lead me, *how do I get out of here?* I can't see any elevators and I keep running, I'm scared that Malek is following me or that he'll appear around a corner. I find the door with the symbol for the stairs and open it; I jump down the stairs three at a time. While I descend the staircase screaming and crying for help, I think that someone will appear and will help me, that gives me hope. The lobby is empty, I press every buzzer in the building; no one appears, no one talks to me. I push the door to the street and run again.

I run and run and run because running keeps me concentrated, one foot in front of another, hands moving at my sides; breathe through your nose, not your mouth. Running is salvation. I notice a strong pain in my chest and I stop. I'm crying, I'm struggling to breathe; there's no air. I try to calm myself and control my breathing. Inhale, exhale. Inhale, exhale. Lasme spread face down, her mouth stuffed with something. Her eyes looking at me without seeing me. Inhale, exhale. *Where am I?* I look for my phone in my bag, my hands are trembling so much that I drop the phone and it takes me what feels like an eternity to realize that the battery is dead. *Shit!* Inhale, exhale. Inhale, exhale. Calm down. *Now you just need to get down from Sarrià, because you were in Sarrià, weren't you?* If you go down and keep going straight, eventually you'll reach the center, the sea. You have to go to the police. *Calm down.* Inhale, exhale. *Yes, go to the police.* But where was I really? What was the address? I don't remember the road name, I don't think I ever asked, or even thought about it. I don't know the name of the building either: I only remember the view of the city. But I can't go to the police and just describe the view. *Think, Nanda.*

Nothing. All blank. Lasme spread on the bed with her mouth open and her eyes lost; Farid destroying her body.

I don't have Lasme's number, we never swapped them. I could call 112. *No, my battery's dead.* Idiot. *Idiot!* I force myself to keep walking, with no plan, just downward. *I'm trash.* I abandoned her. I left her there with those men. I didn't shout enough, I didn't ask for help. I could have done more, I could have faced up to them, grabbed a shard of the vase and cut them, wounded them. I could have grabbed a knife and threatened them. I walk blocks and blocks, always straight ahead. *I'm the worst person on the planet.* There's no one on the street, every-thing is deserted, no drunks, no noise. The silence hits me like a stone, the silence screams at me for doing nothing, spits my inertia back in my face, my selfishness. So what if I would have been next? I should have stayed with her, shouldn't I? I should have let myself be destroyed, let myself be devastated, but with her. *Look. You're not alone. We're in this together, don't cry.* That's what I should have done. I cry. *Why are you crying, you trash?* I feel the rage running through my hands and slap my face until it burns and I feel the fire in my cheeks. I need to hurt myself to feel something that takes me out of this torment. I keep walking, pinching myself now and then, punching myself in the stomach, pulling my hair in a kind of nervous mania. Then I see them: there's a group of boys with square, yellow backpacks. They're talking and laughing. They see me and fall silent, watching me. I tense, freeze. I'm scared. I mutter something, possibly a please, no. *Please, no.*

Hey, you okay? one of them shouts. They're wary, looking at me askance. *Why are they looking at me like that?* He shouts again, you okay? But they stay back. Maybe they can feel my fear. I take a few steps toward them, uncertain. I mentally prepare myself to run if necessary, even though they have bikes and could easily catch me. I look at the adjacent streets, searching for possible escape routes.

Hey, hey, are you okay? Do you need help? The men get closer, and I shout. They stop, startled. One of them says I must be on drugs, just look at her, he says with a scornful tone. The one who asked me if I was okay comes over, hands up in a sign of peace.

Chama, are you okay? His accent makes me feel less nervous, but I don't let my guard down. It doesn't mean anything, hadn't that just been made abundantly clear to me? How small we are, how alone, faced with a pack of hounds, and how their howls camouflage our voices. I let myself fall to the ground and break down, finally.

What's wrong? he asks, worried. What's happening? Do you feel okay? Have you taken anything? Do you need help? Some water? Hey, give me some water! he shouts to another member of the group.

I nod. Yes, help. *Help*. He crouches down to my level, and I let everything out. One rider after another approaches cautiously, trying to listen. No one remarks that our accent is the same, that comment repeated every time someone hears an identical pronunciation of Ss and Js. He doesn't reply straight away, looks around in silence. I catch something about calling the police, yes, yes, I nod, the police. Even though I instantly feel another wave of fear. Won't the police be worse? Aren't they rapists too, just in uniform?

Are you okay? Did they do anything to you? I shake my head. *No, I'm okay.* They haven't destroyed me, not in the same way as Lasme. No, they didn't rip my shirt or put anything in my mouth. *I'm okay.* I cling to this thought. *I'm okay.*

The other riders leave before the police turn up, they don't feel safe near those blue lights that tear at the sky. They take a while to arrive. The boy stays with me the whole time. He smokes a few cigarettes before the squad car appears. I'm scared. There are no women, just two male officers. I feel worse, distrustful.

The officers get out of the car and come toward us. I listen as the boy explains to them what little he knows and that I've told him; they nod. Has she taken anything? Drugs, alcohol?

I shake my head, not thinking in the moment that marijuana is also a drug. Can you explain what happened, ma'am? I tell the story again, although I think I'm leaving details out, mixing up the order, the scenes are jumbled. They listen, stone-faced. They take my details. Do you know the details of the other girl? I feel ridiculous, I only know her name. Do you know the address? The name of the road or the name of the building? I shake my head again, tears sting my eyes. They say something over their radio. The rider leaves, he's got nothing to do with this. I explain to the police that I don't know much about her, that I've only known her a few days. They ask me if I work in the street, if I'm a prostitute. I feel venom in my chest. No. What about the other girl? No, she doesn't either.

We're not prostitutes, but what if we were? Does it make a difference? I'm crying, my nose is snotty, one of the policemen offers me a Kleenex and some water.

This is how it goes. Unfortunately, if you don't have the address or the names of these men, we can't do anything. The only option is for your friend to file a report. Do you understand? Your friend has to report what has happened. She's well within her rights. Do you have any way to contact her? I shake my head again. My battery's dead. I don't have her phone number. I feel frustrated. Listen, we'll go to the station, where you can give a statement on everything that happened, as a witness. But you must understand that if your friend doesn't report it, there's nothing we can do.

I want to tell them that either way they won't do anything, that these are rich men, tourists on vacation who tomorrow will probably carry on as if nothing happened. I want to call them incompetent for not going to rescue her, but then I wouldn't even know where to start looking. I hear them talk as if I weren't there: you have to be very careful, you can't trust strangers, much less go to some foreigners' house alone, when one of you is so young and vulnerable.

I feel guilty. Guilty for not having insisted more and convinced Lasme that we should go home. Another car turns up with a paramedic, I don't notice but he's checking my eyes with a light, asking questions, I reply on autopilot. I hear him say that I'm okay physically, in shock, but I don't have any wounds or contusions. I'm perfectly fine. That's what he says, perfectly. Don't they see that I'm having a breakdown? I want to go home, I tell them. They repeat the point about the report over and over. Your friend has to report the incident, she mustn't feel embarrassed or ashamed, these things happen. That's what they say, these things happen. I feel sick. They offer to take me home. I don't have a report to make, and I don't have details to add, they can't help me. They can do a follow-up and go looking for *this* Lasme in the coming days, but they don't sound very convincing. They write a summary of what has happened, read it to me, but I don't understand them, it suddenly seems like we don't speak the same language.

I get into the patrol car. The whole journey is made in silence, the blue lights are off now it's not an emergency. When they reach my building, they pull me from my torpor handing me a sheet of paper, it's a copy of the summary, with that I can go to the police station to file the report with my friend, as proof. I get out of the car without saying a word. They wait for me to go in and they drive off.

When I get home, I go straight to the bathroom and turn on the shower, still dressed. The cold water makes me react. When it warms up, I feel more awake than ever. *This is real, it just happened. This is real, it's still happening.* In this moment, it's still happening to her. *What could they be doing to her?* The vision of Lasme, spread face down, her mouth and her eyes.

I put my clothes in the washing machine. I steal some cigarettes from my roommate and smoke out the window, watching as the sky turns purple and pink; a beautiful sunrise, oblivious to the tragedies that the night conceals. I wait until it gets very late, time to go to work, I get dressed and leave.

In the metro, faced with curious glances, I realize I haven't brushed my hair or my teeth. In the tunnel, when the train windows turn black, I see my reflection and I'm shocked. I tame my damp hair, hold back the urge to cry. In my pocket, like an amulet, is the useless piece of paper the police gave me.

I reach the store, my seventh day of work. Lasme is not there. I feel like I'm going to vomit and run to the bathroom; I do vomit. I'm afraid. Abdul asks me if I'm okay, I ignore him.

There must be a virus going round, Abdul says, bursting into the bathroom, looking at me with disgust, because Lasme called early saying she couldn't come in. That she's not well. And now you too! Just what I needed, fucking hell.

I can finally breathe again. The brick I've been carrying in my chest disappears. Lasme has called. She's alive. The cramps come back and I feel acid burning my throat, I haven't eaten anything, even so, I vomit again; a green and bitter slime, bile. Lasme called. Lasme is alive.

I rinse my mouth and wash my face. I look in the mirror, don't recognize myself. Who is that looking at me from the mirror? *Not me*. That other woman's eyes are flooded with shame, with guilt. I grab my things and leave. Abdul shouts something, probably asking where I'm going. I make eye contact with Débora, she's organizing the products; her eyes remind me of Lasme's empty stare. I shudder.

Where are you going? You can't leave if Lasme's not coming in! Fuck me, do you think you can just do whatever you want? You're all the same.

I keep ignoring him. I leave the store and head back to the metro. I need to take refuge in my bed, under my sheets, stay like that for days, weeks. Until Lasme's stare stops following me, stops making me feel guilty.

That will never happen.

I do not see her again. She doesn't contact me and I don't seek her out. For months, I pay attention in the metro and at Fondo station, I keep my eyes peeled to spot her in the crowd, but I never see her. I visit La Maquinista, the place with the skaters and the clothes stores, no luck. I don't receive a call from the police telling me a report has been filed, one similar to mine. As for the store, in the end they didn't even pay me for the days I worked.

Sometimes I walk up and down that street outside Jaume I station, I pass by the store hoping to see her, to find myself again in her eyes, to find relief in her forgiveness. But I never find her. I do see Abdul, who has already forgotten my face and doesn't recognize me. I think I've forgotten my face too. But Lasme's face, her open mouth and vacant eyes, are tattooed on the back of my eyelids.

EUROLOCO

El Loco's menu was as follows: marijuana, hashish, sound-cloud, yellow pharaoh, green pharaoh, punisher, silver, stars, microdots, hofmann, wonder woman, 2C-B, molly, and that's it. Ten euros for ecstasy or paper. He could do mates' rates, and if he didn't like you, he could put the price up. He could also get hold of coke.

What El Loco liked best was selling weed. Cheo understood that his contacts were some Argentinians who cultivated an incredible plant. Some strains were also from Colombia, but nobody knew how he had so much merchandise or where he got it from. The important thing was that El Loco had contacts, he moved his people.

El Loco lived in Madrid and had a lieutenant in Barcelona. He had to delegate, he couldn't keep doing everything himself, even less now that he was an international phenomenon. That's where Keiber was, in the lieutenant's apartment. He was the only one of our group who had a genuine connection with El Loco; they'd known each other since they were kids, joined by friendship and by their childhood in Casalta.

Right then he just wanted to get more weed and maybe some pills. Ricardo, who was in charge of Barcelona, showed him where and how they hid the drugs all over the renovated apartment. There were two indoor grows in one bedroom, but Ricardo insisted that the weed didn't come from there, that he kept those plants for his personal consumption, though in fact he didn't need to.

Dealers, even intermediaries like Ricardo, rarely admit that they use their own products, but that's how it is. He liked to party and spend money, so did El Loco. And they could afford it. They both also lived with a ton of paranoia and anxiety. Ricardo had a daughter, a baby only a few months old, *I screwed up*. He didn't live with her, but he sent money to her mother every week, so she don't give me too much shit, he said.

They had to tread carefully here, little by little, making contacts. Neither Ricardo nor El Loco was sure what the scene was like, but they did know their market was loyal. If you're looking to score in another country and a supplier is a compatriot, it feels different. Besides, his fame preceded him. Any acquaintance would ask after him; it was a matter of spreading the word and giving it time, the customers took care of that.

The idea of using riders and introducing *drugs to your door* was a good one, they could grow their market. But it was also more dangerous. It was a somewhat slow process and they wanted—they needed—to move money now. They were hemorrhaging money. Going to Europe and everything that involved was draining all their cash. El Loco had to jump through a ton of hoops to be allowed to leave the country: paying for a passport, then a copy of his birth certificate, criminal records, a letter of invitation to Spain, and a ton of other bullshit. Paying a "vaccine" to the soldiers in the airport, outside the airport, everywhere. Money moves mountains. He needed to work hard with all this and right away. *Sell to anyone, anywhere, anyhow.*

The problem was that, as a recent arrival, he didn't know the setup; if areas were already worked, who controlled certain places. He didn't have the information and his people couldn't tell him much more because, when it came down to it, he didn't deal heavy drugs; for many he was just a simple weed dealer. In his insecurity and lack of self-confidence, he felt like he was throwing himself with open wounds to the sharks.

Another part of him said it was all in his head, that zones didn't belong to anyone, that everyone was free to sell wherever they wanted, you just had to be on the lookout for the cops and that's all. There were cannabis clubs where members could buy legal weed, they were probably the biggest competition. But, of course, they came from the city of chaos, where things aren't so easy. Over there, everything is controlled by someone, that person has someone else keeping tabs on them, and so on in a human matryoshka reaching to the moon, *you gotta pay a vaccine just to breathe, an' the biggest thieves, the most corrupt, are always, always, always the witches, the cops.*

In Caracas, El Loco was known, he was a somebody, he had made a name for himself. Though as a child he spent most of his time staying with his grandmother in Casalta, when he was older Baruta and Chacao were his turf. Coming of age moved him to the other side of the city. The students at the Universidad Central and the Católica were valuable clients; if they didn't pick up from him directly, they would have heard of him at least. Cheo, María Eugenia, Nacho, Diego, and many others sometimes took the trip from the university to the McDonald's on Avenida Francisco de Miranda, near Chacao metro station. He always sent them there; they went together in someone's car, ditching some class, thinking about a joint before the midterm. They ended up eating somewhere, arriving late to classes on literature, calculus, or penal law. Other times, they were like a marijuana school bus and circled around the city giving each of their buddies their respective grams. On the way back, they got stuck in traffic on the Francisco Fajardo highway and, in those moments, the radio saved them from boredom and the fear of bikers.

What almost nobody knew was that El Loco earned his fame through punches, pistol-whippings, and kicks. He had to make people respect him because, if not, someone who thought he was tougher would come along and try to trample him. Keiber once recounted—and he knew this because someone else had told him, what with oral tradition and all—that as a kid El Loco carried a gold chain with him everywhere; that metal was all he had left of his father. The only thing people knew, which is the same as saying the only thing they didn't know, was that the dad was involved in some weird shit with shady characters and that he just disappeared, from one day to the next, when El Loco was only six or seven. Neither his mom nor his aunt told him anything, but he did find out that letters from the DEA arrived at his house. The body was never found, and they didn't hold a burial or a funeral, but everyone knew that he was dead, and it was a taboo topic, you didn't talk about it.

The chain became a sacred symbol. As a kid he didn't need to be that smart to put two and two together and, as an adult, to understand what had happened: why his father was always armed, that time when they had a sudden bonanza, the fact that he was almost never at home and always working, why he never went to his school ceremonies and why they didn't talk much either. His father was someone else in his memory; he would never know who he really was. They made him disappear. As a teenager, dragging around his ills and emotional traumas, falling into clichés, he also fell into drugs or at least got started with them. There was a time, he remembers with vertigo, when he wandered the streets stoned, crazy, and lost in his euphoria. He wouldn't let anybody help him or love him. He shied away from his mother because he was ashamed of himself, he couldn't be near her without feeling like a fraud. Little by little, he pulled away from everyone and from himself. That was when the nickname El Loco was born.

It was just another Caracas afternoon: sun, crowds, and a racket. He was relaxed, walking along not thinking about anything more than the piece of ass he was hooking up with: a fifteen-year-old who was totally in love with him. She said she was a virgin, but he was one hundred percent sure she would still open her legs for him if he said some pretty words, gave her some chocolates and a stuffed toy. Something happened to him with young girls; it must be their tenderness or the light in their eyes that turned him on. *The innocence that's stirring, knowing that she'll never fuck me over because she really loves me . . . besides, all the girls think they'll marry the guy who takes their virginity, right?*

That afternoon he was on his way to his grandma Mencha's house in Casalta. It was a pain in the ass going all the way there because he had to take the bus and then another minivan that went up the mountain. But it was worth the effort for his abuelita. Mencha had practically raised him: ever since he was a baby, she came to collect him and took him home; she cooked, cleaned, ironed his school uniform, and helped him with his homework. At snack time, she filled him up with a slice of canilla with banana and a powdered Toddy, she bought him Frescolitas at the kiosk, she let him mix sugar with powdered milk and she always had ice-cold maltas. His favorite brand was Regional, just so he could sing, after the first sip, *maaaalta regionaaaal, vida y más ná, vida y más ná!*

The bus dropped him at Propatria and from there he had to take the Casalta 3 minibus. The buildings were right in front of the mountain, he had to go to Block 1. He remembers how, when he was a boy and his dad took him to his grandma's, he used to sit him in the window and they stared out at the mountain together.

Sometimes there were chases like out of a movie: someone fleeing and jumping from rooftop to rooftop, the cops hot on his heels, hiding in corners, rapid fire. People shut themselves inside; windows and doors locked, the mountain was empty, hushed. All the paths that were usually filled with people ascending, descending, coming, going, a giant anthill, fell idle, vacant. His grandma, or his dad, took him down from the window and made him play in the corridor, safe between two walls, with the sound of the bullets in the background.

A few stops later, he jumped off the minibus to smoke a joint and walk for a while. He liked to cut through the baseball field. He always went down there to buy tamarind tits or Tang from Dario, a bespectacled kid from the Andes who greeted him with a 'sup? and when he gathered up his wares to leave halfway through a match, any time EL Loco asked him, Where you goin', Gocho?, he replied, To the grave.

And so, walking along distracted, remembering things, he didn't even see them. A group of glue-sniffing street urchins.

A gang of kids armed with knives. He wasn't armed, he had no need to be, he was a minor-league dealer, just getting started in the world, in life. They went for him immediately.

Just at that moment, there wasn't a soul in the street, and if there had been, it wouldn't have mattered anyway. They surrounded him like hyenas, they even seemed to make the same sound, letting out terrific howls; pretending to be hard to scare off their own fear. One jumped him and he reacted fast; he punched the kid in the face and knocked him to the ground. His hand hurt. Right then another stabbed him in the side, catching him off guard, and a third whacked him on the head with something hard; he left it like that, those psychos could beat him to death.

The youngest are the nastiest, their minds aren't yet conscious of what it means to kill. Or maybe they are, but they don't care. Death is already a habit. Kids who become immune to everything and as they grow up stay just as merciless, with that childish perspective of believing their actions don't have consequences. Brutalized and humiliated; the streets teach them how to toughen up. *Either you toughen up or they fuck you.*

Gimme everythin' you got, man, gimme all your shit or I'll cut you, cocksucker. I'll cut you. They took his wallet—he was only carrying a few notes. Worse than losing the money was having to get a new ID card and all that bullshit. They pulled a ring off his finger and he put up some resistance; he felt his stomach tighten when the sharpened metal cut his hand. Pain and blood. He kept still, pressing his left hand to his abdomen, and they ripped off his chain.

Run!

Another blow to the head and a stampede. He tried to keep up with them, but they disappeared up the mountain like goats. Motherfucker! Blood was gushing from his hand; he took off his T-shirt and wrapped it, applying pressure. It didn't seem like a deep cut, but hands cause a scene when they bleed. They were some little local street rats who robbed at knifepoint. El Loco was pissed. What infuriated him most was not knowing what to do, how to move, where to find them. He didn't know the area intimately; in fact he didn't know it at all except for the route to his grandma Mencha's and the area surrounding her building. He arrived at her house fuming and, grudgingly, let her treat his wound.

What happened to you, mijo? Mencha asked calmly. She had applied hydrogen peroxide and was now dressing his hand. I was robbed. Straight up. Mencha gave him some pain pills, warning him not to mix them with drink or take any shit. El Loco made a couple of calls and spoke to old friends, persuading them to have his back in exchange for whatever they wanted. *I'll get it for you, bro.*

Oh, mijo, don't get like that on me, it looks real ugly. Fuck, woman, those shitbags stole my old man's chain. Now we're gonna fuck 'em up. So they learn an' get straight.

That night, Jeferson came to pick him up in a burgundy Chevy. They were going hunting. They'd been tipped off about some places where the kids hung out. He wanted to find them before they sold the chain. This time he was carrying a gun, a gift from his godfather, Blas. *I wanna fuck that cocksucker's hand up.* A hand for a hand. He had an aluminum bat too.

They were circling in the car, not taking their eyes off the road. At the baseball field, he thought he recognized two of the kids moving fast in the darkness. They jumped them. He had them in his sights and, to stop them running away, Jeferson and another friend backed him up. They put the boys in the trunk of the car and drove off toward Lomas de Propatria. When they found a quiet spot, El Loco struck them several times with the bat. One of the kids was the one who shouted during the robbery and El Loco took most of his rage out on him.

The boy cried at first. After the second blow, he was unconscious. El Loco concentrated on his hand, hit it so much that it became an amorphous mass. Every bone crushed. The other kid sobbed in silence, covering his mouth; the tears cleaned his cheeks.

Where's the chain? He put the barrel of the gun in the kid's mouth, inventing a thousand things that he was going to do to him, to his family, even though he didn't have a goddam clue who they were; pure intimidation and psychological bullshit. He wanted his chain and he was going to get it, whatever it took. In that moment, he was like one of the kids, but with more powerful weapons. In the end, the boy gave in and confessed that El Nico had it. Who the fuck was El Nico?

They'd exchanged it for weed and food. He hit the boy with the bat and closed the trunk again. They drove to La Yaguara and dropped them at the side of the highway, by the Guaire River. The kids ran away crying. El Loco got to the task of finding out about this Nico; he'd never heard of him.

A friend from school, Maikel, gave him the intel. There was some petty thief in Casalta known as El Nico. Apparently, he also rapped and had more than one fan in the neighborhood. He was just another street kid made good, who made money and could sing every now and then to polish his style. They said he was pretty good, but El Loco couldn't give a shit and only wanted to get his chain back. Nico spent most of his time in Palo Verde doing freestyle and battle raps in the metro stations, side streets, and boulevards. According to Maikel, some kind of battle was organized for tomorrow and Nico would be there. El Loco was agitated; it drove him insane that he couldn't go find him straight away. If he didn't get the chain back, he would never forgive himself. It wasn't just his amulet; it was the physical manifestation of his best childhood memories.

He began to plot what he would do to him.

Maikel was going with him; he warned him that Nico had some dangerous friends, referring to some serious criminals. I'll wipe my ass with them, he hissed. Anyone who gets in my way better watch out.

That night he didn't sleep at all. He snorted some coke, called some girls and other buddies for some company. They all said that Nico was a son of a bitch. The gang of kids who went around the neighborhood robbing people were under his protection; they took him the loot and he gave them drugs, alcohol, or food.

Just before dawn, stupefied by all the visions and memories of his father and the blessed chain, El Loco made a decision. Spending all night ruminating had hardened him and he felt there was nothing he wouldn't do to get it back. Rescuing it was rescuing himself. At once, the whole situation took on a more personal, almost spiritual, aspect; a new opportunity, a message from his father shouting at him to act, a sign of some kind. He wanted to cling to something. Waiting until the rap battle would be unbearable. He stood up and mobilized the others, unwavering and authoritative. Fuck this, marico, it's too long. Find out right now where the motherfucker is, I wanna destroy him already.

When he got that strange look, it was frightening. He set everyone running, asking around all over. To alleviate the hangover from the night before, he downed an ice-cold beer for breakfast. The cold woke his brain. He took another line to get himself going again and not feel the comedown; later he remembered that when he snorted coke he could drink and drink without getting drunk. His hand didn't hurt, and even though the bandage was stained red, he was sure that he felt better thanks to the mix of pain relievers and antibiotics with all the other shit he had taken, completely ignoring Mencha's warning. It wouldn't be the first time. His mind was going a thousand miles an hour and his heart too.

Ready. Nico was staying at his girlfriend's house, right there in Propatria, another kid from the gang had squealed. El Loco had some friends up in Casalta scouring the terrain.

Let's go, let's go. Another line. And another.

The sensation, now so familiar, seized him; the speed with which his body reacted to stimulants, his scattered mind jumping from one idea to another, never staying too long on anything other than the chain; the vision of his father smiling on the beach with the chain at his chest. The same emotion that he felt as a child when he heard from his lips *Someday it'll be yours, when you're a man* overpowered him now, and the effect was so intense that he didn't know whether he wanted to cry or to kill. A current ran through him, head to foot, making him scream and stick out his tongue, open his eyes wide to release the adrenaline that was consuming him.

Some of them went by motorbike, he went in the Chevy with Jeferson and Maikel. They parked by a kiosk right at the base of the mountain and started climbing steps. It was very early in the morning and most people were still asleep. Just a few were heading down to work, half asleep, but alert nonetheless. They moved out of the way and let El Loco pass; not only was he moving fast but he had the silver clip at his waist. People sensed something was coming, they didn't know for whom, but they were looking for someone and judging by El Loco's face, things were going to get ugly.

Up to the right, bro, that red door, Maikel signaled. A bare-brick shack with a sagging red door. El Loco looked at Maikel, communicating with his eyes what would happen next. He kicked down the door, they stormed in, and the shouting began. The entire house was one room: kitchen, dining room, and in one of the beds, Nico was sleeping with his young girlfriend. Toward the bathroom wall was another bed with an older woman and a baby, her grandson. The old woman was the first to raise the alarm. At first, she shouted nonsense, overwhelmed with panic, then you could clearly understand what she was asking: Get out, what was going on, what the fuck was this, what the fuck was happening? The baby started to cry.

The noise made El Loco nervous. He looked at Maikel, who went straight over to the grandma and slapped her; the old woman shut up, she got the message. She held the baby tight and the two of them kept quiet. The girl was whimpering, covering herself with the sheet. Nico looked confused and furious, but they had a gun pointing at him and he couldn't do a damned thing. El Loco pistol-whipped him on the forehead, there were more drowned screams.

Motherfucker, goddamned thief.

They got him out of the bed at gunpoint, made him put on whatever clothes he could find and quickly walked him down to the car where they put him straight in the trunk, repeating the same MO in view of some pedestrians. Before closing, El Loco gave Nico three more blows to the head; he didn't know if he lost consciousness, but his forehead was bleeding. El Loco yanked the chain that hung at Nico's chest. He'd seen it as soon as they got him out of bed. He was euphoric about recovering what was rightfully his, about taking justice into his own hands.

To redeem himself and demonstrate that he was worthy of the chain, convinced that it was all no more than a test, a sign, now was the time he should give him what he had coming and set a precedent.

They drove him around for a few hours, distorting their faces even more with the artificial poison they sniffed. After a while, they decided to head down to La Guaira. They reached an empty plot where there was a minuscule shack, beyond Los Caracas.

El Loco opened the trunk and gave Nico a few blows with the bat. He wanted to keep hitting him, take out his frustration on the cannon fodder before him, but instead of mashing him, he struck at a tree trunk that protruded from the ground; at times he felt like he was hitting himself, to wake up, to react and free himself. But from what?

The others watched him while they inhaled nicotine nonstop, nervous. They didn't understand why he didn't let Nico go if he'd already got his chain back; nor did they understand why El Loco was hitting the trunk in such fury, until the aluminum bat bent. Only then did he stop, panting. El Loco was really messed up. Nobody could have imagined, nor understood, what a deep and delicate cord had tightened within him. The avalanche of memories and words that were making their mark on him; buried for years, dormant, they were now erupting in violence and rage. He couldn't control himself. Was this the test? Being cruel and merciless? He could be that way, he could pass the test and do it without crying, as he'd been warned since he was a boy, *in this house, men don't cry, you hear me?* Marico, why don't we throw him out here in the bushes an' forget about him? No. He wanted to teach him a lesson so he wouldn't go around robbing and fucking people over, especially not the neighbors. An' you ain't gonna use kids no more, you son of a bitch.

With the warped bat, he pulverized one of Nico's hands. Another hand added to the list. Nico was crying, but they had stuffed a rag in his mouth, and he couldn't shout; he only let out dry, hoarse sounds. He was drowning in pain. El Loco left him alone for a while. Then he approached, removed the rag from his mouth and offered him a shot of anis.

Word is, you like to rap, right? Spit lyrics an' whatever. Nico nodded. Show us your freestyle then, he pointed his gun at him for the first time, meaning business. You're gonna rap for me or Imma bust a cap in your face, see how you rap then.

Nico's crushed hand trembled, he was trying to control himself, to bear the pain and turn to stone. He flipped between the burning in his hand and stringing together coherent phrases, blocking the urge to scream.

El Loco gave him some time to think, watching him unblinking. They were the same age, he realized, both around nineteen, twenty. Maybe they could have been friends, but he decided to be a thief. El Loco sold drugs and was involved with shady people, true enough, but he had never stolen and would never steal. He couldn't stand people who fucked over their own.

So, you gonna rap or what? Everyone else watched, no one spoke. Maikel, put down a beat for this shithead then, let's see what he's got.

Maikel improvised a track, inflating his lungs and making an echo with his hands. Jeferson accompanied him with whistles. They went on like that for a few seconds, leaving room for Nico to get used to the rhythm. He nodded slowly, feeling the melody despite the state he was in and, with one eye almost shut, he started to rap.

Early one morning came the crazy man
With his rabid dogs seethin'
Invade my home while I'm sleepin'
Eye for an eye, tooth for a tooth
With a borrowed piece, and your lowlife crew
An' your nose full of coke, the vice got your head spinnin'
For your vengeance an' murder,
You gonna burn forever
But take it easy man
Coz I'll kill you with more hate
I sing rage coz you know I ain't afraid
I'd spit on you but ain't no one gonna care

I understand you coz I've been there
But if we're gonna throw down then you'd better prepare
Coz whoever fucks with Nico better beware
Make you eat your own teeth, wash 'em down with blood
Takes more than guts to face the reaper, bud
I smell the stench of a chicken shit
Dragging hisself through life, can't quit
You can run but you can't hide from yo self
No doubt I'd cut your tongue out,
See if silence stops you frothing at the mouth

El Loco burst out laughing, and a second later, out of nowhere, shot him in the left hand, the same one he had smashed with the baseball bat. Two fingers disappeared. Nico started screaming, Maikel moved quickly to cover his mouth with the same rag from before. Silence. Maikel and Jeferson exchanged looks; they didn't know how far this was going to go, but they were in it up to their knees. They couldn't show any weakness now.

You rap like a three-headed dog, you goddam cocksucker, El Loco sighed as he pulled out the knife he now always carried with him, his mind full of evil, twisted ideas. Would he feel remorse later? Hold him tight, he warned Maikel.

Jeferson came over and helped to restrain him. Nico opened his eyes wide, understanding what was about to happen, feeling the ground tremble under his feet; his own trembling, his frenetic movement to avoid what was coming.

If you try anything, asshole, I swear I will blow your brains out. Open your mouth. He didn't want to, resisted. El Loco whacked his hand. Open your mouth already. As soon as Nico parted his lips, El Loco's fingers went straight for his teeth. It was difficult, with a ton of wriggling and kicking, blood and drowned screams. In a few slices, he finally hacked off part of his tongue. The texture was like chewing gum, he was surprised how easy it was to cut. He looked at it for a moment, almost in admiration, and then threw it into the bushes. Nico was drowning in his own blood; he didn't understand why he'd done this when he had rapped like he asked.

Did anything make any sense?

Vengeance was served and what pleased El Loco the most was that Nico would never be able to sing again, or at least not in the same way. Without doubt, that had been the best lesson for him, the most significant part of the whole godforsaken test that only existed within the walls of his own skull. Now he was worthy of the chain, it was his medal for earning a new name, for redeeming his sins with a human sacrifice.

They got in the car quickly. Drive! They reached a hillside with a view of the sea. They picked him up between them and threw him over the edge, making him run. He ran and rolled until he came to a stop, coughing and vomiting blood. Before him, the giant and majestic sea, with its frenzied motion, hungry for the offering, for this poor devil, victim of circumstance and of his own fame.

On the way back, nobody spoke. It was as if they were returning from a funeral, long faces, serious expressions. Out of nowhere, El Loco started laughing; there was something in his laugh that made your hair stand on end. Fuck, he was onto something with that crazy man. I like it. His new name. The others laughed too—they couldn't help it. But deep, deep down, they were afraid; they had just seen that person for the first time. Who was he really? They couldn't say. They were all still the same kids from school, lifelong friends from the barrio, but at the same time they were different, other people. This monster committed to violence was nothing like the kid they ate ice pops with while watching baseball matches. He baptized himself before the world as a man who could be merciless and cruel without showing any sign of repentance, stone-faced.

And what about him? Did he recognize himself in that new face? Did he really believe that the only way to confront evil was with evil?

No, over the years he would learn, would internalize it to the point that he felt bad even wearing the chain. Might his father have done the same? Might someone have done the same to his father? People asked about his nickname, playing it down: *How crazy can he really be?* Guilt made him invent new stories, recount what happened in other ways, forgive himself through the infinite possibilities of the imagination and the realities created through language. There wasn't a day when he didn't question his own sanity, when his tongue didn't weigh him down.

Or at least that's the story according to Keiber, who has a loose tongue.

I ALREADY KNOW

I miss you more than I remember you.

OCEAN VUONG

Margot slaps her arm, a few gentle smacks, the ritual before the fix of instant happiness that's coming, nearly, in a moment, now. As she removes the needle, a red dot appears and disappears, like a tear wiped away in annoyance or irritation with her fingertips. Her mouth opens a little, her eyes go blank, and the void is filled, or she is filled with the void, and I see her project herself into everything, but she doesn't know that I can see her, in the middle of her most blind and isolated intimacy, as she really is: a fragile and abandoned child. And it's just a premonition, a feeling in my chest that creates this imaginary sequence in my head, a scene I know but have never witnessed, which makes me question our relationship: what is this bond, this shared connection that allows me to sense her and feel her even in her absence?

I know she's doing it: succumbing to the delights of self-mutilation and that maybe I can help her to change; or accompany her rather than change her, because even before I got to know her I knew she was the most unchangeable person, and also the most brilliant, the most articulate, the best at expressing herself and the one who understood everything. *Margot, what could you be doing?* Although I already know: fading away, wanting to disappear.

I already know, that's why we're here. Because I know everything and don't know what to do with that information. At some point, I'll have to let it out and I'm afraid that it will be catastrophic.

Can I take photos? I ask, my phone already in my hand, as she walks from one side of the room to the other, looking for somewhere to dispose of the coffee dregs. There's no trash can to be seen, but there's a ton of stuff everywhere. I don't even move from my floor tile. There's a strong smell in the air that I can't identify.

Yeah, of course, she responds, distracted, she's not paying attention to me because she's still looking for somewhere to throw out the coffee. She opens the dilapidated wooden door and shouts toward the center of the building, calling a name I can't remember right now. Malen? Something like that.

I seize the opportunity to take photos while she's not watching and move to the other end of the room, where there's a sink, full of junk, in the middle of the wall. Hidden behind another wooden door, I see a cat's litter tray and then understand the smell, now much more specific: ammonia and shit. Margot comes over to me, turns on something on the floor, which I had thought was a badly damaged Roomba; it's an electric mini oven, and the kitchen for the seven other people who live in the block. Margot gives up and throws what's left of the coffee onto the only plant in the space: an aloe that has been cut without rhyme or reason, I imagine she uses it on her skin. She gets water from God knows where, maybe the sink, and puts the coffee on. Then she crouches and stays very still, contemplating the coffee pot.

She's changed so much since we met. I don't think I've changed much at all. I'm still doing what I always did, in the same house, with the same job, the same crowd, and the same hobbies. By crowd, I mean the only other two women I know and consider my friends here in Barcelona. It's so easy to feel lonely in this city.

But her . . . oh boy. She's another person. She fascinates and disturbs me in equal measure. Her beautiful blonde mane is gone; I look at her shaved head and it seems like her hair will never grow back. Her tired face, bags under her eyes. She's much skinnier, emaciated. It's unbelievable how much the hair has grown on her legs, thighs, armpits, back. She *is*, and nothing concerns her except being. The coffee sounds and Margot grabs a red mug, the only mug. You take milk, right, Nanda? No, thanks Margot, I reply, I'll take it black. I need to prepare myself for what's coming. If I was free of coronavirus before I came here, I won't be much longer. No going back now. I still don't understand how we ended up here. But that's Margot's specialty: pushing me to the edge of my abilities, my phobias, and my prejudices. She does it not long after we see each other, as if it were nothing; I'll get to that.

We meet outside the metro at Plaza Catalunya, just at the top of La Rambla. She sees me and starts calling me; I don't know how she recognizes me straight away when I'm wearing a mask, or maybe that's why, because I'm the only person in this crowd wearing one. By contrast, I have trouble recognizing her. I see a girl with a shaved head waving her arms and shouting my name. I smile under my mask because I know it's her, even though my eyes take a little longer to believe it. Then when we're together and we hug, of course it's Margot; her smell, the softness of her hands in mine, her eyes that glitter with joy. The most genuine person I know, the most fun and cunning, who always has a plan and words of comfort, who makes you belong: the friend who touches you deeply.

We're running late, as usual. We don't know if they'll let us into the museum. No one cares, so we take shelter in the cool air. This is the best way to spend the summer, taking advantage of the air conditioning, even walking around Mercadona to cool down. We spend two and a half hours looking at paintings by Picasso, burst out laughing at his study for Las Meninas. They're all so current, like atemporal memes. Seriously, he went to shit! He was doing better with the First Communion stuff than this, I mean it, she exclaims.

As we laugh, I forget everything else for a moment, her invitation that I don't know how to refuse, and instead of saying something I just go blank, wanting to let out a guffaw, but nothing happens. So, are you still living with Abi and your other roommates? I ask without really thinking about it, one of those questions that come out uncontrolled, like a reflex. Abigail is her ex-girlfriend, but they ended on such good terms that they kept living together as roommates with two other girls. And a bunch of cats.

When I first visited her apartment, it was a little messy, but it was incredible. One of those big, old apartments in the upper end of Gràcia: spacious, multiple bedrooms and bathrooms, a large and comfortable kitchen, and two terraces that ended up being one giant terrace, enough to make you die of jealousy. It's absurd someone can have a terrace that big with rent at only four hundred euros between four people. Margot decided to move in with Abi when, at some point, the relationship started to get serious. She managed to secure this apartment because it belonged to the aunt of one of her best friends from university. The aunt only cared that someone trustworthy was living there. For a time, it was their love nest. Those were the best times for Margot, no doubt.

No, you know I'm an okupa now, that's how she blurts it out. No, actually I don't know that. I let her speak, maybe she's talking about something else. You know that, deep down, I've always had this feeling, she touches her chest, about living in a commune, like a hippy commune. Well, now I'm doing it. I'm with an organized group protesting property speculation. We're occupying a beautiful old building to stop them turning it into a tourist block. The building must be about a hundred years old. Mm-hmm, right, okay. So how did you end up with this group? Through the community garden, the one I told you about when we last saw each other, remember?

I have a hazy memory of a garden. We last saw each other just over a month ago. Yes, of course, she'd casually mentioned something about a garden run by okupas. It was where the bank had obtained land, also in Gràcia, toward the mountain, and demolished the old house that was on it. The idea was to build a block of tourist apartments and this group of okupas took it, moved in, and created a sustainable garden. Ca la Maduixa I think it's called, something like that, though I don't know if that's the place or the group itself. Or both. Pff, that's right, she had mentioned it, that she went to public meetings.

Oh yeah, yeah, I remember. It's the place you volunteered, isn't it? Yes, well, the truth is, it's a collective and the people I'm with have quite a structured dynamic, the movement demands proper commitment. So it's not really volunteering, you have to respect timetables and follow certain rules. But yes, that's what I was talking about. I met them there, in the meetings about the garden and other issues.

She follows this with a spiel I don't even bother listening to, I nod, but I'm watching the horizon, I already know the speech. Margot always comes out with her socialist theory, she repeats the same discourse over and over, but from the comfort of the first world. I contradict her. It's just discourse, Margot. In the real world, it's no more than a beautiful utopia. If it worked and its followers weren't corrupt trash who only look out for their own interests, I wouldn't be here, you and I would never have met, and right now, one hundred percent, I'd be having coffee with my mom or beers in a Chinese bar with my friends.

This time Margot has gone too far. Her family paid for her degree in Anthropology, her brother is outside of Barcelona studying music, her paternal grandparents live in an enormous apartment in El Eixample, and her maternal grandparents live easy by the sea, in Blanes. In other words, she has no needs, wants for nothing, it seems like they all love her to the extent that they accept everything and let her do whatever she wants. *I know Margot, it would be impossible to force her to do anything she doesn't want to do or that goes against her principles.*

And what do your parents say about this? I interrupt her, not knowing what she just said. She furrows her brow and screws up her mouth. Aha, I've hit a nerve.

Well, you know, they don't agree with me. I knew it. They tell me I can protest and be an activist in other ways. You know what they're like. Yeah, like from the sofa, I said to them. I laughed despite myself. She goes on another rant about socialism, the bucolic life, and so on. I bury the whole matter at the back of my mind and, for the time we're in the museum, try not to think about it, or at least not bring up the subject. I just want to spend time with her.

The plan is to have a vermouth and some snacks after the museum, on a terrace with enough breeze to combat the heatwave and the thirty-six degrees. But she has other ideas. You're not in a rush, are you, Nanda? She looks at me and I feel lost. No, why? I feel like I sigh. Come back to mine, we'll buy pastries and make coffee. We can drink it on the terrace with the views and that way you can meet my flatmates. *Shit.* Okay, let's do it.

I try not to overthink the matter or come across as uncomfortable, even though in reality I'm already feeling anxious. I don't want to start imagining things because I don't want to be prejudiced or fall into stereotypes.

We leave the museum and walk to Urquinaona. We change to the yellow line at the next station and get off two stops later, at Joanic. The whole of Gràcia seems so colorful and pretty to me. We're talking in a very animated way and then, just after we leave the station and turn the corner, Margot stops at the entrance to an apartment block, in front of a metal door. There's a guy talking to an older woman. Why don't you go ahead and buy the pastries, Nanda? That's Marc, she points to the guy. Okay.

I go to the café just across the street and realize that people are watching them, watching us. I order several croissants, some butter, some chocolate. Margot comes over and contributes a few coins. I thought something was going on, but it's just a neighbor who wants to talk, she says.

When we go back to the entrance, I see that the woman is still there, and also notice the giant banner hanging from the building. *Ca la Maduixa som al barri*. We are the neighborhood. Occupy and resist. Next to this banner, there's another one, also hand-painted and all in Catalan, with much smaller writing: We announce that this building is occupied by CA LA MADUIXA. After almost five months since our eviction from Ca'ls Miralls, we return to the neighborhood with renewed strength. The speculators and landlords want us to abandon our neighborhoods and give them to the rich, but we will not give away BCN. We will defend our spaces. Others are painted with messages like: Occupy a space. Create a home. Resist with it. Build your life how you want to live it.

It becomes clear that they're a kind of group whose slogan is occupy, create, and resist. The neighborhood for the neighborhood and tourists go home.

I look closely at Marc and he's just as I imagined him. Yes, I admit it; there it is, I said it, go ahead, throw the first stone. His head is shaved at the sides with a crest of long, straight hair in between. He's wearing a long T-shirt with the sleeves cut off in such a way that I can see his boobs. I wonder if he's in the process of transitioning to a man or if he just identifies as male, anyway, what does it matter. Everything is valid. He is barefoot and his feet are dirty. There's something attractive about Marc, his face is pretty and tanned, tons of sex appeal. I go over with Margot, and we stand next to Marc and the lady, a graying woman wearing a floor-length red dress.

I see you girls don't shave, she says, pleased. I don't either, you know? she prattles, as if this were the only requirement for her to fit in. Well, everyone should do what they choose, Marc responds. His voice is raspy, like those women we say have a smoker's voice, even if some of them don't smoke. Hey, Marc, we're going in. Sí, home, clar. Marc moves away from the metal door and lets us pass. I see the panic attack coming: my OCD getting out of control, the stress I feel at finding myself in enclosed and not very sanitary spaces; the anxiety of socializing with new people, insecurity about not being nice or empathetic enough. All of this added to the spiraling fear of an unknown virus on the other side of the world that will arrive at any moment. *At any moment.* That's how Margot takes me to the edge of my limits: serving up on a plate a hundred situations that make me feel uncomfortable while she, at the same time, stoically tries to show me that there's nothing to feel uncomfortable about. She takes apart my myths.

Behind the metal door, there's a narrow staircase with things piled on the steps: hammers and other tools, baskets full of glass bottles, boxes full of plastic; they recycle. The first thing that hits me is the smell: armpits and sweat. I relax because I thought it would be much worse. Here's my room, I'll show you in a sec. Let's make coffee first.

Margot points to a wooden door, the only one on the first floor. We go in; we have to walk carefully along a path between the chaos of objects piled around us. My fingers twitch. We reach a kind of living room with a beautiful stained-glass window, blue, green, yellow, and red; the light hits it straight on and the colors fill the floor. There's a table covered with stuff and in the middle a square loaf of bread and a knife. Where's the coffee pot . . . ? Margot walks from one side of the room to the other and I look around, processing the disorder. There's a noise and Margot jumps like a cat. She shouts a girl's name—now I do hear it clearly, it's Malen—she's chubby, tanned, and blonde. She greets me with two kisses and shows me the cat she's carrying in a backpack. *Xurri*, the coffee pot's up in my space, she tells Margot. Do you have coffee? Malen nods and heads down a corridor, disappearing to the back of the apartment. I don't see her again. We go up to the second floor.

Margot wasn't lying; the building is so old that the wooden stairs creak under our weight. The decorative wallpaper is pretty and stained, and all the furniture, though covered with dust, shines with that vintage charm people crave.

Was all this here when you moved in? Yes, everything is from the building. We've cleaned up some pieces and we're using them. But you can't even imagine, pff. Before, we were on the main floor, ground level, but the police got in a few days ago at six in the morning and moved us out. We didn't realize what was happening because they turn up without any warning. We had all the furniture and everything on the first floor, where I sleep now. With the eviction from the main floor, we had to rearrange all the furniture to make more space. The neighbors told us that about twenty years ago an old man lived here who had Diogenes syndrome, you know? You can see he brought everything into the flat. You can't even imagine the shit we threw away. There was a layer of papers and stuff ten centimeters thick. You couldn't even see the floor.

The next floor is even worse: mattresses in the corners without even a sheet or a pillow, dirty and weathered. I feel short of air and fan myself with my hand. Written in huge letters on a wall: Affection is a revolutionary act. I don't realize I'm still wearing my mask until Margot tells me to try the coffee. She offers me the solitary red mug. What about you? She shows me a mayonnaise pot that still has its label. Where can I wash my hands? She looks at me like she doesn't understand. Margot, where can I wash my hands? Hello, coronavirus. She smiles. Oh, over there, see? and points me to an old basin full of transparent containers. I squeeze out some dish soap and rinse my hands several times, scrubbing well between my fingers and under my nails. She washes her hands too, more to keep me happy than anything else.

Unable to put it off any longer, I remove my mask and try the coffee. No sugar, how I like it.

Despite my fears, it's good. Delicious. There, you see. Margot wiggles her eyebrows, proud of her coffee. Grab your things, let's go up. I pick up the mug and follow her. The staircase seems to get narrower and the steps taller; it's difficult to walk with so many things lying around. We go up two more flights and I'm getting tired when at last we exit onto the roof terrace, gigantic and just as run-down as the rest of the building. At one of the edges, there's a couple sitting on beach chairs, naked. The girl is inspecting the boy's head. Margot greets them and introduces me. I hang back, taking in the scene.

The girl stops looking for lice and comes right up to me; I try to focus on her eyes and smile. She hugs me tight and I can feel her tits on my neck; she gives me two kisses. I forget her name as soon as she says it. The boy follows her, I force myself to keep eye contact and not let my gaze wander downward. Adam, he says, and plants two rough kisses too. My head itches, that's how squeamish I am. I stare daggers at Margot and move to the other end of the terrace to look out over the city. The view is great.

I can see Torre Glòries and, very close by, the Sagrada Família and the giant cranes that surround it. From the opposite side there's the mountain and Tibidabo, perfectly visible. The kids go back to what they were doing, removing lice. I don't have a hair tie to fix my hair back.

Hey, what's going on with the hippy, has he got lice? Margot asks, as if I were another one of the group. Well, I suppose in this moment I am. The hippy always catches lice, you know, babe. He picks them up from girls at work. But I'm not removing lice from Adam, just some fluff in his hair. We're going in a minute anyway, so keep your hair on, Adam says. If I catch lice, I'm never talking to you again, I whisper to Margot, and she laughs. No way, if that happens, I'll help you remove them, don't worry. Shall we sit? She points to a pallet in the middle of the terrace. Around it are some slim mattresses and a black sheet, one of those big ones people take to the beach. Okay. No, that isn't what I wanted to say. I don't want to, I'd prefer to stay standing. It's pointless. She arranges the pallet and the mattresses, then places the sheet on top and sits down. I straighten my skirt and stick it to my buttocks as best I can; sit on a corner. I grab a chocolate croissant; Adam and his girlfriend don't want any because they're vegan. It's sickly sweet and I don't want to drink coffee. Well, I do, but I can't stop thinking about the mug and the possible germs. I ignore that small, tormenting voice and swallow the coffee.

Just then Marc arrives, with his long toenails. He throws himself down on one of the mattresses. I don't know why he's holding a lighter with his feet, gripping it with his big toe; with the other foot he turns the wheel and sparks the flame. He leans forward with a joint in his mouth and lights it. Smokes without offering any to us. They talk in Catalan about a book Adam's girlfriend is going to lend Marc. Her favorite book, the one that changed her life . . . and it's called Walden because he went to live on that lake, away from everyone, communing with nature, she says. Fuck, you're all so intense talking about this Thoreau all the time! Marc exclaims, amused. Okay, you'll have to lend it to me. It's incredible! It explains how to return to the essence of what's human, and to find the social and the emotional there, Adam explains, wide-eyed. Shush, no spoilers, Adam, his girlfriend warns. He even recorded what he harvested down to the gram, details like how to do it on your own, all thoroughly explained. You'll see how my copy is full of notes and underlining. What's it called again? asks Marc. Eugh, home, I just told you! Walden. That's the one.

They keep talking as if Thoreau were the Messiah. They're talking in Castilian now, looking at me and involving me in the conversation. I don't say anything, just move my eyes from one speaker to another. They repeat things like death to capital and that the only way to defeat the system is by not being part of it; as simple as that.

It's around five thirty, the sun is starting to disappear. From the terrace, I can see the sky turning orange in the roof tiles and then becoming darker and darker. The roofs give the impression of a piece ripped off the giant paper that is the sky. Adam and his girlfriend are still naked and unashamed, in fact I've even forgotten their nudity. They are against the light so I can only see their silhouettes and behind them, the last colors of the sun. I want to take a photograph because it's a beautiful image.

I don't, of course.

There's just no other way, we must resist and rebel. Civil disobedience. Yes, and devote ourselves to the bucolic life, the countryside, and nature. Capitalist life makes you sick. Hundreds of things run through my head. What does occupying the building have to do with defeating capitalism? Is it an act of civil disobedience and nothing more? Are there other ways to protest, and, if so, what are they? Why not hand this occupied space over to people living in the street? Why not clean it up properly and set it up as a cultural space of protest? All I see is a group of young kids, some of them from good families, living a dream of empty protest, waiting to be run out of here to go to another site and make banners and paint slogans, and so on forever, making the same speeches, but not doing anything. All mouth.

And that's how many people, though not all, are consumed with this lifestyle, not achieving anything in practice, not making a noticeable change, not changing the perspective of all the people who thought and think like I do.

Yes, it's very nice and magical, but it needs some modernizing or seeing how it can be transformed to apply to the here and now, right? Because that book is from what year? The eighteen hundreds? And being here in the city isn't exactly living the bucolic life that Thoreau hailed, or is it? This could be playing at life instead of living it. And what about everyone else? I ask. We mustn't wait for the majority to change, it's urgent that we act in a radical way, Adam replies. We've got food, shelter, and clothes. Everything we need for a simple and spiritual life, the girlfriend adds.

So living as they live is the radical way to act and to protest? I feel irritated because I don't understand it fully. I'm incapable of being empathetic and not judging them. Couldn't you give this space to people who really need it? I ask Margot in a whisper. Anyone who becomes an okupa is doing it out of necessity. The personal is already political, that's her response.

Need or protest? It's not clear to me.

Some people have no other option but to squat and I'm not sure if those people, who do it out of genuine need, are aware that their action is at the same time a form of political protest. For them, maybe it's just a question of survival. But others, like Margot, are people who, even with money and opportunities, choose to live like this. You can't say they're not involved in the movement. Could it be a kind of cult? I get carried away with this idea because their lifestyle clashes so much with mine that it's easier to see it as a cult.

Adam and his girlfriend leave and the three of us stay up on the terrace under the full moon and the lights from a few surrounding buildings. Marc says something to Margot in Catalan, I don't pay them much attention, I'm too focused on looking out over the roofs of Barcelona . . . Avui l'he vist i m'ha dit que el Pau i el Jordi sí que hi van sempre, que està molt content. Però de tu m'ha dit que no et passes molt per l'hort ara, I listen hard hoping for the words to translate.

Oh! Ha dit això? Quina pena, Margot replies, twisting her whole frame. Li he dit que això justament ho hem parlat a l'assemblea d'avui, sobre la implicació i que cadascú s'implica fins on pot, no? Que també tenim altres coses a fer i potser no sempre es pot anar a l'hort. Ja, és que aquí no hem parat de fer coses. Entre la neteja, els pamflets i les pintades, preparar el concert de dissabte, cuidar de les nostres coses i tal. Ja clar, però sí que intentaré passar-me per allí aviat, més sovint, vull dir. És que estic molt emocional ara, també és que estic premenstrual. I don't know what Marc replies, but I give her a few pats on the back.

Margot smiles at me.

Marc gets a call and moves away to talk on the phone. Come on, I'll show you my room. Okay. I have to go soon anyway, it's after eleven, the metro closes at twelve.

I use the flashlight on my phone to go down the evil stairs, I'm scared a rat or a cockroach is going to emerge from a crack in the steps. We reach the second floor, go in. A corridor and some wooden doors, white, with windows, there's Margot's room. A mattress on the bare floor, at least it has a cover, pillow, and sheets. It all looks clean and tidy. I notice some paintings on the wall. Do you like them? I did them with my period. Seriously? Well, yeah, they're pretty. Do they smell? she asks, bringing her nose up to the painting. I copy her and sniff. No, I don't think so. This one does, a little. We sit on her bed.

Right next to it, like a bedside table, there's a pile of books on feminism, anarchism, Marx, Engels, Thoreau, Rosa

Luxemburg, Tolstoy, sociology, and a few on anthropology. I pick up a small one by Simone Weil. Keep that, it's yours, and she pushes the book to my chest. You're painting then? I think that's great. Have you got any more? Yeah, I'll show you. She hands me a book of watercolors she pulls from a black backpack. Pretty watercolors: vaginas, plants, more vaginas, a dining room, a window with a purple chair that seems familiar. Your house! Where she lived with Abigail. She lies back on the bed and turns on the bedside lamp. She already explained to me that they steal electricity from the street. I look at her in the dim glow and she seems strange, a different Margot. Look what I've got, Nanda. She takes out a pipe and a clipper. I'm so surprised because Margot never smokes; in fact, she doesn't really get on with drugs. She smoked marijuana for the first time at my place and had a terrible whiteout, she said her aorta was going to blow. I laughed at her thinking she was joking until I realized she was serious, and we had to do breathing exercises until she calmed down. After that, she never wanted to smoke again. I've got weed. And I've got this, she forces a smile like the Cheshire Cat. She's holding a small clear bag with what looks like a miniature quartz. I look closely at the pipe, a clear glass pipe, with a fairly long stem. My heart sinks.

Is that wax or something from cannabis? No, it's much, much stronger, do you want some? No, not now, thanks. Margot puts it away, but I can see she's anxious. She scratches her arms unconsciously, bites her nails. Have you spoken to your grandparents? I ask. I know she has a very close relationship with her grandparents and visits them often.

No, they don't know I'm here. I don't know if my dad has told them. How are they, have you been to visit them? She distracts herself ripping a scab off her knee, avoiding my gaze, or at least that's the impression I get. No, it's been a while since I've been over there, with Covid and everything, I don't want to expose them to anything, you know they're already quite frail.

Margot stares into space. I think about the disorder on the other side of those curtains she closes to forget that everything else exists.

We should get together one day; we can paint and drink wine, what do you think? Or I can come and lend you a hand, if you want, we can tidy whatever needs it or clean or something . . . Yeah, yep. I hope another month doesn't go by without seeing you again, okay? she laughs. Oh, give me a hug! But a real one, for more than twenty seconds. Any less and it's not real.

She wraps her arms around me and I do the same; at first I'm like a standoffish cat, she keeps saying I have to hold on for the twenty seconds. I relax and let myself be enveloped by Margot and her smell. Strong and sweet at the same time. We start talking about her paintings again and Margot lies back, takes out the pipe and smokes some of that shining quartz.

The effect is immediate. Everything in her relaxes, melts, a dumb smile appears on her face, her eyes half close. Now she's not listening to me or looking at me or anything. Then she opens her eyes and is awake, active, energetic.

Out of nowhere, Marc comes into the room, coughing, and I can't help but think of coronavirus. *Seriously?* Margot offers the pipe to him and he sits on the floor to take a hit. Margot, I have to go now, will you come with me? The metro is about to close on me. Don't go, stay! I insist as best I can. Okay, come on, I'll let you out. I wave goodbye to Marc, he nods at me and keeps smoking. I turn on the flashlight on my phone again and follow Margot. She's talking quickly, I don't know what about. We reach the metal door and she removes some hollow bars that lock it from the inside. Let's meet up soon, okay? Maybe you could come to one of our meetings, they're open to everyone. I'll let you know. Take care of yourself, please. We hug each other tight. She closes the door and I hear the bars slotting into place.

I walk quickly to the station, feeling like Margot is adrift and nobody is helping her: that we should do something before it's too late. *Who?* Before seeing her shoot up something stronger than the shiny quartz. It's now or never. How is it possible that her parents let her act like this? I scold myself for having such a backward mindset when it comes to this. *There's nothing wrong with what Margot is doing*, that much is clear. The problem goes much deeper than throwing herself into the adventure of living as an okupa and fulfilling the fantasy of belonging to an organized protest group; the problem emanates from her guts, from her chest. I feel like there's a void she's trying to fill, but what is she missing?

I remember the times we spent with her parents who, though they divorced many years ago, still get along well enough and are always there for her. Her relationship with her brother has deteriorated since she decided to become an okupa—she told me that in a delicate way, maybe because it still stings. It's hard to believe that someone with a good family, friends, social and economic privileges, could feel so deadly empty and alone. *And yet, we're all depressed.* Is Margot sad? It's very possible that under that facade of joy and anarchy there's sadness. I want to get inside her head and see what she really thinks, rummage in the depths of her triggers, her reasons, if there are any.

But no; Margot shows people what she wants them to see.

And who doesn't? I realize that there is a chasm between my perception of her and her experience of life; only she knows her suffering, shames, and regrets. I know almost nothing about her childhood. *When did you ever ask her?*

But I don't have time to ask her because a few days later the quarantine comes in hard and fast. *I knew it, the virus would arrive any moment.* Locked up and alone. She doesn't reply to my messages or calls; I write to her dad, but he doesn't reply either. I'm stuck here with all this information I can't share and I'm afraid it is going to be catastrophic.

And that's how I spend my days, asking myself every so often, *Margot, what could you be doing?* But I already know, or I think I do.

DAMP

Lucía lives in a very small old house, just behind a convent, near Plaza Catia. Before, it was a nice, quaint neighborhood, mainly inhabited by foreigners: Spanish, Italian, Portuguese. Lucía has been living in the same place for almost a hundred years. Her parents moved to this house when they migrated, she was just a baby. She grew up here with her two older brothers and enjoyed moments of infinite happiness, and here she remains. Watching how everything deteriorates over the years. Little by little, the area has lost the charm of back then. I must have met Lucía when I was born, but I obviously don't remember her; my grandparents also arrived in Catia when they migrated. And when my parents got married, they bought an apartment in the same development as my yayos. I mean El Chavo, a two-story building, with apartments following one after the other in a snail formation leaving a central patio, shared by all the neighbors, as well as the roof terrace. Lucía lives next door; she is the small separation, the comma, between the residential building and the convent.

Calle Ayacucho was quiet. On Sundays, children would go out to play in the street: baseball with broomsticks and bottle tops, or tag. There was always movement. When Lucía was young, she found work as a secretary and helped support the family. She did it because she wanted to, her parents already had money and the twins, her brothers, also brought in money through their businesses. Later, the twins married and, in 2000, they returned to Italy. Lucía didn't want to leave. She never married, although she did live with some men. She was a woman who knew how to enjoy herself and have fun. With the death of her parents, she inherited the house. She got into the habit of having many parties, gatherings with important people from Caracas society at the time: painters, writers, architects, actors, and impresarios. Her house was almost always full. She was a beautiful and vivacious woman. She left her job as a secretary and went to work at the art gallery in the Chacaíto mall, a place with French cafés, bookstores, people with innovative ideas, thinkers, visionaries. It was the era of Saudi Venezuela and the oil boom, in the seventies. People with money were everywhere. Lucía liked to surround herself with influential and famous people. In her house, she has a pile of photos with various celebrities and, if you ask her, she will explain to you, pleased with herself, who that blond man is and where they were in that other photo, dressed so elegantly, raising a glass.

Now her street has really gone downhill. La Cortada de Catia became a violent place. The residents of Calle Ayacucho changed drastically. The former homes were modified, bit by bit, by their tenants, people made divisions to bring in relatives or friends and everyone lived crowded together like sardines in a can. Lucía kept her little house; she received good offers for it and everything, but no, *I can't leave.*

Leaving means accepting, once and for all, that those glorious flashes of the family past, sparked by a fleeting glance at a window or a wall, will not return, not even in memories.

Lucía collects her pension, but as for all senior citizens, the money doesn't cover anything. She survives thanks to a monthly transfer from her brothers. She hasn't spoken to them for some time, nor does she know whether they are still sending her money because, what with the problems with the electricity, everything is complicated. She knows that they give euros to a friend and that friend transfers bolivars to her. Years ago, the process worked well: Lucía went to the bank and took money out or paid for everything by card and that was that. But for some time now—she can't even remember how long—she can't do anything, not a thing, *honestly, she doesn't even try.* Paying by card is torture, the signal is too weak. *If it's not the electricity, it's the internet.* People prefer to make transfers over the phone or online, they do it as soon as the electricity comes back on. But Lucía doesn't know anything about that, she's never got on well with technology. She has her landline attached to the kitchen wall. Nobody calls her because there are problems with CANTV. Sometimes she even forgets she has a telephone.

She does feel lonely and talks to herself more and more often. She replies to herself and gives herself a fright. *Who said that?*

At what point did she end up so alone? She forgets things and then has sudden, vivid memories of bygone years. She doesn't understand, she time-travels between the folds in her brain and a present that is increasingly blurry, less real. She catches herself by surprise. Out of nowhere, she's on the patio, not knowing what to do or why she's there. She goes out onto the street and gets lost, lets herself be carried away by some glimmer or familiar sound, like a child.

Pedrito, a neighbor, says he's going to teach her how to use a Huawei, but first she has to buy one. The prices of those gadgets seem ridiculous to her.

No, son. Where do you think I'm going to get that kind of money from? From your family in Europe who send you euros, of course. No, don't be silly, it's not like that. I wish they sent me euros. They give me bolivars and every day they're worth less. Well, you know how it is. Ask them for more then. Lucía laughs.

No, no. They do enough already. More than enough, they're older than I am and they still provide for me, go figure. And can't you do some odd jobs, kill some tigers? Forget about tigers, I'd end up killing myself! Hey, you're still strong, Lucía, Pedro says. It's just that you've been spooked since that time and now you don't wanna do anything, you don't go out anymore. Being cooped up is bad for your health. Oh, shush, foolish child. Don't you talk about that.

There's truth to Pedrito's words. Two years ago, some guys broke in to rob Lucía. They tied her up and left her in the kitchen while they went around opening all the drawers, emptying cabinets, nosing everywhere. They took all the valuables they could carry: jewelry, money, antiques, tchotchkes. One of them was a hefty lump, Lucía remembers the acrid smell his body gave off. That man raped her. Old women turned him on because they were defenseless, fragile creatures, feeding his megalomania. When he saw Lucía, so well preserved, so refined and modest, he ignored his friend's warnings and did as he pleased. Lucía felt a terrible pain. It might have been a blow to the head, she can't recall. She passed out.

Gladys, another neighbor, was the one who found her; the wrought iron reja was open, odd because Lucía always closed it. And there she found her, as she had entered the world: in a fetal position on the rug in the lounge. They called the police. The door hadn't been forced, it opened as normal. She will never know how they got in, everything is very confused in her mind, the events succeed each other, not in a linear or consecutive way, they are moveable stains outside of time. Maybe they pushed me while I was taking out the trash, that could be it. I don't know. She was bleeding from the vagina. Gladys accompanied her to the doctor, she had tearing. How crazy is this, dear. You're telling me . . . having an STD test at my age. What can I say. She had to wait a few weeks for the results. They gave her a prescription for an ointment, but she didn't buy any medicines, everything can be cured with chamomile baths, so she said.

At that time, Pedro was already looking out for her, but not as much. He was still going to university, so in his spare time he kept her company, helped her with her shopping or spent some afternoons with her watching TV or drinking coffee. Those men were ignorant, son, Lucía repeats when she dares to remember the incident, I have so many paintings here and they didn't even take one. Philistines is what they are.

She's not lying. The walls of her house are draped in paintings of all kinds. Her favorites are the ones by Vigas, gifts from the artist. She also has some by Luisa Palacios, watercolors by Trino Orozco, framed poems by Emira Rodríguez, a big one by Mauro Mejíaz, and, facing her bed, a canvas by Francisco Hung. They really are ignorant.

As a result of that experience, Lucía became wary and with increasing regularity closeted herself away in her house and in her world. She sent Pedrito to buy some huge padlocks and put one on the reja and another on the door, then she couldn't remember where she left the keys and Pedro had to calm her down from outside. Lucía felt so much loss for her stolen belongings that she didn't eat for a few days, then later she would forget those objects. Symbolic trinkets that evoked another time, another life: jewelry, almost the only thing she had left of her mother; watches, her accessories that she wore throughout her life; more jewelry, and even shoes.

Well, okay. Now she doesn't leave the house. For any chores, she uses Pedro. She gives him money and sends him to buy what she needs. She gives him her debit card too and her PIN so he can withdraw money for her. Lucía has a small reserve of food because she also barters things with her neighbors, gives them a trinket for a bag of pasta and so on. The truth is she still has a ton of stuff in the house, even after the robbery. Side tables, stools, standing lamps, hanging lamps, lava lamps, paintings, hundreds of books, clothes she doesn't even remember, and an absurd number of ornaments. Unlike her neighbors, Lucía's family never sold land for others to build on, so the house still has an intact patio where Lucía grows a ton of plants. She loves being there, sitting in her rocking chair and telling stories to the shrubs. Some neighbors, feeling for her after the robbery, keep an eye on her and shout from their roof terraces every now and then to see if everything's alright.

Lucía is more and more unkempt and dirty. *What happened?* She can't remember the last time she bathed, or if she has already eaten, what she ate, where she left the keys to the padlocks, where she put her glasses. Sometimes she catches herself talking to her brothers or her father, replying and laughing quietly. At least once a week, Pedro takes her out to the patio and throws buckets of lukewarm water over her, she scrubs herself as best she can, with a housecoat stuck to her body to protect her modesty. She gets grouchy, she's increasingly senile.

Either you let me wash you or you and I are gonna have a problem. You know I don't like filthy old bags. Rude child!

Filthy old bag, my ass. Then she bursts out laughing, a full belly laugh, and Pedro washes her.

No one can be sure of Pedro's real intentions with all of this; nothing is free. But at least he understands the old woman and takes care of her. In fact, Pedro looks out for several old people in the area. He sees some more than others, depending on what state they are in. That's how he kills tigers. But for as much as he makes ends meet in this way, looking after old folks in his free time, it's not enough. There's no such thing as spare cash.

It's already midday, the time when Pedro goes to Lucía's house. He shouts from outside until she appears at the reja, like a ghost in her old-lady robes. As soon as Lucía gets close to the door, he's hit by the stench.

You stink, Lucía, I'm not kidding. Woah! Did you shit yourself or have you just quit washing? Lucía can't help laughing. No, son. I think I have a problem with my wastewater. The problem is your ass, sweetheart, you smell like crap.

She has a stain on her butt, the robe doesn't hide it. Stop it, now. Don't you have any respect? I got dirty all over because the patio filled with muck, look. Come on, come with me. They remove the padlocks, open the reja, and Lucía drags Pedro inside the house. The stench intensifies. The patio is flooded with mud and other foul-smelling substances.

What a mess, alright. Something must have burst, Lucía. A pipe or something. Sure, but I don't have any money for that. Sweet Jesus, what could have been damaged . . . This is unbelievable, look, do you see? If we cover that drainpipe on the wall, over there, maybe it won't get so full of gunk. It's because of the rains. Those downpours weren't normal. And you're covered in crap too, Lucía. You gotta clean yourself up. I know, I'm going. I'll throw out this robe right away too, who knows whose shit this is.

Lucía is angry at life, she walks about brooding and muttering, blaming everyone for the situation. Pedro helps her to clean the patio; they pour out some of the water Lucía has been collecting in tubs and clear the mess from the floor, it doesn't smell so bad now.

Lucía, look at this. Pedro points to the patio wall, the one that backs onto the convent. There's a huge stain here, it's waterlogged, can you see? Maybe this whole mess is from that leak, from the convent. You think so? Lucía comes over and looks at the stain on the wall, up close. Sure enough, a nauseating smell is coming from the stain. No, son. I've never had any problems with the nuns, they're good people. Well, what's that got to do with the price of fish? It doesn't matter if they're good or evil, it's not about that, it's about them having a serious leak and now they have to take responsibility for their mess. That's what's important.

Lucía isn't entirely convinced, she doesn't want any problems. Her father always told her that it was best to be on good terms with the nuns. And in all those years of parties and commotion the nuns never complained. In fact, until Lucía became insolent they got on well.

Fuck me! It smells even worse over here, Pedro says, moving away from the wall. Lucía, listen to me. You have to get this checked out because it will fuck up your house. This wall could come down any minute. Listen to me, old girl. Old girl! I'm not your grandma. Stop with the stubbornness and come here, I brought you food. What food? Food, just food. You're like a little kid. Plantain, rice, and some beans. Come on, then.

Pedro stays with Lucía for a while, then in the midafternoon goes over to an old man he's also fond of. Homero and Lucía are his favorites. Homero is more fun than Lucía because he drinks and smokes a lot, he's almost always drunk. Pedro takes charge of feeding him and keeping him stocked up with rum and tobacco. He keeps him happy. The old man is generous with him, treats him like a son. Pedro also brings over hookers now and then, when Homero is depressed and asks Pedro to bring him a babe. Even though he's tough and robust, he can't achieve anything without Viagra. Pedro has to get some for him so the old-timer can run the race. Other times, when he's struck by nostalgia, he takes to drinking on the balcony, until he collapses like a sack of cement. Pedro doesn't know much about Homero, only that he worked like a dog his whole life, his wife died fifteen years ago, and his sons emigrated, leaving him alone and in squalor. Though he lives this way because he wants to. When he gets drunk, he tends to cry and tells Pedro that he was a bad father, that's why his children abandoned him. That he deserves it.

Homero has dollars and euros saved up. *He could live well and buy himself whatever he wanted.* But he lives like a lowly animal. He's happy with rum and tobacco, he's not interested in food unless he's hungry and then anything will do to satiate him. Homero doesn't understand people who go to restaurants to spend money. He gives Pedro a few dollars a week and Pedro buys food to fill the old man's cupboards and his own. From what his mother cooks, he takes meals to Homero and to Lucía.

In other words, the old man more or less provides for all of them. Pedro would like to introduce them, but Lucía has really gone downhill, *really aged.* Plus, after the robbery, she has become even more nervous and men make her uncomfortable; she doesn't worry about Pedro only because she knows him from before.

Pedro's friends don't understand why he spends his days with these dirty, crazy old fossils, nor will he explain himself. It's a good business, end of story. Anyway, these old-timers don't have long left. And he's the only one there for them. The whole thing was the idea of his mom Inés. You get in good with them, bit by bit. You'll see, they won't last long and they're real grateful. It wasn't too difficult to ingratiate himself, it turns out they were in need of human warmth and some affection. They were more than willing to accept anyone who offered them a little of their time and some attention, no matter their motives.

Pedro lives alone with his mother. It's always been that way, just the two of them. He doesn't know his father and grew up overprotected under the maternal yoke. Now he can do his own thing and, as he always gives money to Inés, she leaves him alone. With the old-timers or without them, he has to make money somehow; everything can't fall on Inés' shoulders and Pedro's no longer a boy, he's better off getting productive. Pedro went from studying two degrees simultaneously at the Universidad Central to taking care of two senior citizens. He opened up with them. Better than any friends his own age, Lucía and Homero have thousands of interesting and funny stories, plus they spoil him whenever they can: they give him clothes, shoes, more money, trinkets, you name it. They treat him like a grandson.

That night, while eating some arepas Inés cooked, Pedro tells her about Lucía's patio and the fetid, damp stain on the wall. And the whole floor's overflowing with this dark black, rotten liquid, I swear. You'd say it was shit. Poor woman, repairing that'll cost her a heap. And for what? The whole thing seems to be the nuns' fault coz the leak's coming from the convent wall. Aha, that would not surprise me. What d'you mean? Well, they gotta turn up somewhere, right?

Pedro doesn't understand and Inés doesn't bother to explain any further; she clears the plates and sets to ironing some shirts she has to return in the morning. Nuns are slippery. Even if it is their fault, they won't take responsibility for a damned thing, you'll see. They'll make her pay for everything, the repairs and the wall, the whole lot.

The following day, it's the same. Pedro takes food to Lucía and as soon as he reaches the reja he's hit by the smell, even though they cleaned the patio the day before. Lucía has candles and incense all over the house, some old incense sticks that have been in a drawer for years. Pedro doesn't know which smell is worse. He's worried that with so many candles, something will catch fire, he'd better blow them out before he leaves.

Jesus Christ, woman. Listen to me. Someone's gotta break open that wall and see what's happening. Then it's fixed and that's that, the wall will still be there. Lucía shakes her head, obstinate. You gotta complain to them, they have to check out this wall. No, no, no. I've never had any problems with the nuns, and I don't want anything to do with them. But Lucía, why would you have any problems with them? If it's their fault, they have to take responsibility. Responsibility, my foot! Look, stop this nonsense now, foolish child.

Pedro teases her a little more, makes jokes or yanks her chain and laughs under his breath to rile her up. Lucía gets mad and tries to whack him with some dried branches that hang on the key hooks. It's a habit she picked up from seeing her parents and aunts and uncles doing the same thing so often. When she was a girl, they would scold her and the other children by swatting their legs and arms with dried branches. Whenever they went to the country, they gathered a bunch and hung it from the key hooks. If anyone was insolent or misbehaved, they grabbed the sticks and whipped them all over. Lucía remembers it stung like hell and left her skin red, bleeding, leaving scabs that she would pick off later. As she doesn't have anyone else to hit with the dry branches, she threatens Pedro when he won't stop teasing her.

After a while, Pedro says goodbye and heads straight to Homero's house, about twenty minutes' walk away. He already knows what's waiting for him: a few good shots of Santa Teresa or Pompeo, the old man doesn't drink anything else.

Homero doesn't take good care of himself either and Pablo has to wash him and remind him of things; he forgets to eat but never to drink or smoke. What intrigues him about Homero is he almost never speaks about his life and getting information out of him is like pulling teeth. Unlike Lucía who remembers everything, or at least that's what she thinks, and whose eyes light up when she reminisces and talks about her life. Pedro only knows that he worked as a fisherman for a while in Portugal, that he traveled through many countries before meeting his wife and getting married. Nothing more. Homero's house is austere and contains only the essentials. No ornaments, nor paintings, nor sculptures. He does still have his children's belongings, but he's never bothered to check them or look through them.

And so months go by in this way, Pedro looking after the two old people every day. It was as if the fetid smell of Lucía's house were a reflection of the state they both were in. Pedro noted the degeneration, especially in Lucía. He couldn't believe it because he was sure that Homero would be the first to cash in his chips what with all that liquor and tobacco. *How about that, those who fuck around the most last the longest. They're hardened and death can't take them so easily.* One of those afternoons, Lucía didn't recognize him. She screamed, pulling her hair out, hitting the rejas, scared to death. Finding herself locked in with the padlocks that she herself had put there only made her situation worse. The neighbors came running when Pedro asked for help, who knew what the old woman could do in her desperation. After a while, they managed to calm her down, and little by little she started to recognize people, she was ashamed, it was the first time she had a fit like that. From then on, she always wore the keys around her neck, Gladys' idea.

I'm going to leave you my house, son. So you can find yourself a wife and become independent and get away from that mother of yours. What are you saying, Lucía? Have you lost it again? No, asshole. I'm leaving you my house, I'm serious. You know I don't have children. My brothers must be dead by now because it's been so long since I last heard from them . . . I barely know my nieces and nephews, I don't even know their names. I don't have any friends. Look at me: I'm alone. No way, don't say that. You're still tough, Lucía, more than most people. Don't go thinking about these things. Come on, let's dance.

He turned up the volume of the merengue on the radio and led her in a dance, which seemed more like a bolero because Lucía moved slowly, so slowly. The old woman meant what she said. She was so set on leaving her home to Pedro that one day she cleaned herself as best she could, dolled herself up, and left her house for the first time in years.

Outside, she was blinded by the sun and deafened by the sounds of the street: the shouting, the cars and motorbikes, the music coming from windows, the drunks. She made a superhuman effort to concentrate and, walking like an insect clinging to the walls, went straight to where she remembered the notary being. She wasn't sure if she needed a lawyer, so much bureaucracy overwhelmed her, but it seemed like a notarized will was more than enough. The notary was still in the same place, but the whole route seemed dirtier and uglier: unrecognizable. The building, the streets, and the corners were a shell of the city in her memory; the sidewalks, where she biked with her brothers, were gone. The shops that had always been there were closed.

Where am I? Her reference points were rusty, as was she. For a minute, she feared she was having another fit of forgetfulness, as she repeated to herself to prevent the word "dementia" from crossing her lips.

Pedro didn't know what to do with himself, felt ashamed. He would keep looking after her until the end, even if she didn't leave him anything. But that had always been Inés' idea and she was bursting with joy. She couldn't believe her son's good luck. Pedro felt a slight remorse, but then he weighed it against his genuine affection for the old folks and felt better.

His concern for them was honest; without thinking about it, they had become the grandparents he never had.

Giving away the house was like signing a death sentence and, as Lucía said, ended up killing her. A few days later, Pedro had to call the neighbors to help break the padlocks. Lucía wasn't responding. It took them a while to cut through them with shears and when they finally got in, they found her lying in the kitchen, pale, with a halo of blood spread over the tiles. A chair nearby. First came shock, sadness. Second, trying to understand what had happened. Lucía had climbed on the chair to reach something above the cabinet. She fell and, though the fall wasn't fatal, she had bad luck and struck her head on the edge of the marble table. She died of a cerebral contusion. Pedro got up on the chair to see what Lucía was looking for above the cabinet and found an envelope with the convent's logo, full of dollars. Hundreds and twenties. How they got there or what Lucía was going to do with that money was a mystery.

According to her will, she wanted to be buried in the same plot as her parents, in the Cementerio del Este. Pedro used the money to cover the funeral and burial costs. He contacted her family in Italy; her nieces and nephews were very surprised by Lucía's death because the twins had died not long before: Jorge around a year earlier and Guillermo just a few months before. They all went together, at least. Pedro paid extra for the coffin to be well reinforced.

Even though Pedro published a death notice in various newspapers, nobody went to her funeral. After spending her youth surrounded by illustrious personalities and great minds, having multiple lovers and confidants, she died completely alone. Forgotten. The only people who came to pay their condolences and to look—out of pure morbid curiosity—at the coffin and the old lady were those people who took advantage of anyone's death to ply themselves with coffee or tea in the funeral home. They didn't have an ounce of shame, going from one cubicle to another with a sad face and a sorry for your loss; then they went back for more coffee or juice.

Pedro was distraught. Lucía's death affected him much more than he imagined it would, the old girl wasn't a bad person, it wasn't fair that she had ended up like this, alone, abandoned. Homero had to cheer him up and drown his sorrows in rum.

The envelope full of money with the convent's logo ate away at Pedro and kept him awake at night. He was irritated by his own curiosity and having no way to unearth the truth. He even went to the convent's entrance and rang the doorbell insistently, but they didn't want to receive him. The Mother Superior came out and gave her condolences for Lucía, promised to pray for her soul, but they would not let him in. They were cloistered nuns, they couldn't leave the enclosure. Could Lucía have been a nun at one point? Anything is possible under the heavens, but a habit didn't exactly go with the lifestyle Lucía maintained.

Well, that's it, don't stir the shit anymore, Inés said. You gotta get to work on that house, it's about to fall down. She helped him to clean and tidy up, to remove all the things that betrayed Lucía's time between those walls, which were as neglected as she was. They gathered up a mountain of stuff and old clothes, gave it all to the neighbors. Inés wanted to sell everything, down to the last pin, but Pedro wouldn't let her.

When Inés saw the leak in the wall, she realized it was something serious. Gross, and there was me thinking that stench was a dead animal or something round here, she said, getting closer to the wall for a better look, but covering her nose. No, I told you it was a nasty leak. Fuck me, what could be leaking? Coz it stinks like you're shitting yourself.

With Lucía's dollars, Pedro said he was going to get to work on the pipes and bring the house into shape. Fix the problem with the leak once and for all. He called Ernesto, a neighbor who worked in construction. He made ends meet doing odd jobs in the area, whatever he needed to do to eat. He turned his hand to everything, didn't say no to any work. The years had made him an expert bricklayer and an all-round handyman.

Ernesto entered the house and immediately wrinkled his nose. Bro, is that the stench you told me about? Yeah. We don't know what it is or why it smells like that, come, look. Yeah, gotcha. They went through to the patio and when Ernesto saw the wall, he brought his hand to his neck, between pensive and shocked. Oh yeah, it's ugly alright. Someone shoulda looked at this a long time ago, jeez. The wall's about to go, we're gonna have to be real careful, but I'm not making any promises, man. We gotta open it up an' see what's in there. Go for it. Whatever you gotta do. What do you think it could be? Fuck, there must be something blocking the pipe and water's draining out. Stagnant water stinks real bad, but it could also be something else there or between the walls. An animal that got stuck an' started rotting, we'll see.

Ernesto hit the wall a few times with a hammer, taking care. The idea was only to open a small hole and see what the problem was. But the wall was pretty weak and, on the fourth hammer blow, it came down completely. Ernesto moved away just in time. The smell worsened, it stung when they breathed. Pedro wanted to vomit, bile burned his throat. A section of wall toppled and along with the bricks fell a pile of strange objects. They took a closer look; yes, there was something there.

At first, Pedro thought they were rocks. Getting closer, he noticed they looked like ears, but bigger and meatier. He looked more attentively, realizing. Horror clouded his face.

They were fetuses. Some were black, amorphous blobs of putrefying flesh, others had a blue tint; a few were still reddish, rosy.

Pedrito, you seeing this shit? Ernesto was in shock, squawking like a parrot. He couldn't believe it. Pedro didn't know what to think or say; nothing went through his head in that moment, he was totally blank. Impossible to put words to what he was feeling. But, how . . . ?

Ernesto let out a snort, outraged. Oh, bro, you shitting me? Those fucking nuns, man, and he pointed to the convent.

It was like a spark in his brain. What Inés had said about the nuns and their crookedness, that they had to turn up somewhere, how weird Lucía got about the whole issue. But what was Lucía's role in all of this? Did people know about it and just leave them be? Surely because they didn't have rotten fetuses stuck in the walls of their houses, that's why nobody complained. *They're all a bunch of bastards.* No, it was impossible that Lucía knew about this. But what about the money in the envelope?

If they're living there bringing in girls, saying it's for religious shit . . . they can blow me; Ernesto pointed to his crotch with his thumbs. They go there to empty their bellies, lighten their guts. All those rich bitches, all knocked up. An' they think that way they're helping them, enablers, motherfuckers.

That's how they kill their tigers, Pedro replies.

TRUTH OR LIE?

A conversation begins with a lie.

ADRIENNE RICH

In September, I had to go to Madrid for some paperwork at the embassy. There isn't a consulate in Barcelona, so I had to buy a train ticket and decided to make the most of it to see some friends. There are too many Venezuelans in Madrid. I didn't think it was true but it blew my mind, left me speechless. If you decided to save a euro for every Venezuelan you hear in the street, the minimum wage would seem like chump change.

Madrid is chock-full, as a former coworker said seconds after meeting me and learning my nationality: What's with all you Venezuelans? Jesus, you're a plague! Uncomfortable laughter, trying to be nice. How much do you want to bet that the person who serves us is Venezuelan? Flavia asked me, sucking her teeth. We went for a walk and our current game was to say "clibo" for every Venezuelan we found. If there were more than three you could say "family-size clibo" and you earned more points. We spent a few hours that way until the game became tedious from so much shouting clibo! or cliiibo familiaaaaar!

I stole the word "clibo" from a game I used to play with my parents when we were on the highway; when we saw a Volkswagen, the first person to shout "clibo" got a point. Now I was doing the same, but pricking up my ears to see what accents I caught, in which words I recognized myself.

The friends who were hosting me in Madrid didn't smoke and I wanted to score. Let's say I was having a minor meltdown about the status of my papers at the embassy, because I didn't know if the application would go through or if I'd wasted my money traveling there. I needed to relax to be able to read and write calmly first thing in the morning.

In Barcelona, Cheo was my connect with a friend of El Loco, he was the go-between so I was never in direct contact with any dealer. I gave Cheo the money and he brought the weed to my house. Simple. I always heard about El Loco because, in Caracas, my friends from university scored from him in Chacaíto. But I never saw him. I only knew some stories and the reputation he had won for himself: that he was paranoid, mistrustful, and that he had been inside a few times, making him even more evasive and suspicious.

Here, though, I didn't have anyone to score from. Cheo sent me El Loco's number, or the number of one of his friends, no one was too sure. Did he even exist? Write to him, he's in Madrid. I'll tell him you'll be in touch. *Go on then.*

Writing to a dealer, and the whole process involved, is the most awkward thing in the world. There are many gaps in communication and everything is open to misinterpretation. You don't understand if they mean yes or no, whether you're being very nice or direct, if he'll be there at a given time or not. The whole thing is exhausting. El Loco's messages were brief and unpunctuated, making him even harder to understand. He never said yes or no. Most things you had to work out or just guess. He replied to my message with a Hey bud, without explaining if he was holding, what he had, the price, the place, anything. Is that a yes or a no? He only replied: Yeah estrecho. Estrecho? Did that mean anything?

I showed the message to my friends, we debated it a while until Flavia came to the conclusion that it was an address. And yes, it turned out to be a metro station. We worked out that he meant we should meet there. How much? Five for twenty. Okay, sounds good, sure. What time? About six. Great. I didn't have any cash so I had to stop by an ATM. The metro station was about forty-five minutes away. Flavia went to work at the café and I was left alone in the intimacy of her home.

It's a strange but also pleasant feeling being in the personal space of a friend you haven't seen for years. That complete trust floating in the air like static. I lingered over her books, arranged by color, her plants, some paintings and posters on the walls. Everything around me had Flavia's touch. Isn't it incredible how our home becomes a reflection of us, how we can feel like it's ours through how it's decorated, the condition it's in, its smell. And this small, open-plan house was Flavia all over.

I made tea and read; I wrote a while, probably about everything and nothing. I amused myself watching the cats across the street, jumping and pirouetting, and the woman next door hanging out her washing, in no rush; the white sheets gave me a feeling of freshness on that hot afternoon. Go out for a walk, don't stay shut up in here! Flavia's words were boring into my head like a woodpecker. I decided to listen to her and, mainly to be contrary and not find myself obliged to admit that she was right about me being a hermit, I got dressed and left the house.

Walking alone in a bustling city when you suffer from social anxiety is overwhelming. Especially because I feel like people look at me strangely when I sit out on a terrace and order two or three beers in a row and do nothing but read or write in a notebook. *What's a pretty girl like you doing all alone?*

I went to La Latina and got lost in those picturesque alleyways, which seemed much cleaner than those of Barcelona. I walked in a straight line until I reached the Prado. I saw it from outside because I couldn't afford the entry fee. Luckily, the Thyssen had free entry, I don't know why, so I went in and killed some time looking at paintings, moving closer or farther back by instinct, watching out of the corner of my eye what other people did in the presence of art, how they consumed it. One man took selfies with every one of the paintings, copying some pose or expression. When he caught me watching him, I couldn't help but giggle.

In the end, I rushed through everything because time was getting away from me faster than I thought, that's the problem with getting so distracted. Back outside, I headed to the 100 Montaditos opposite Plaza de las Cortes and had a couple of beers. I felt more relaxed and decided to risk a short stroll through El Retiro. The park was very large, I could easily waste the whole afternoon if I didn't pick up the pace, so I walked straight to the pond and spent a good while there, watching the people in boats, struggling to go in the right direction, crashing into each other in some cases, kissing, sunbathing, or just reading. That image: abandoning yourself in the boat like someone giving in to the tide on the high seas, dedicating yourself to reading with the soporific rocking.

I tried to draw what I could see but gave up and lay back on the grass, under the shade of a tree. Time seemed to be passing very quickly, and suddenly, it was almost time to meet El Loco.

Shit, shit, shit.

According to Google Maps, it would take me an hour to walk to Estrecho, which is what I'd been planning from the start to get to know the city a little more. Now I had no choice but to take the metro and hope that the red card Flavia gave me still had rides available. If it did, I could keep spending my travel money on beers.

When I'm on the metro, I prefer to read, that way I avoid looking at the people glued to their phones like automatons and the journey goes quicker too. If I'm paying attention, I focus on everything that's happening around me, the stories on people's faces. Here and in every corner of the world, the metro is the frontier between reality and fiction. The womb of its own magical realism. I didn't feel like reading and concentrated on the people around me. The carriage was different from the ones in Barcelona, it seemed a lot smaller and we were all closer together. The journey passed in a flash, intent as I was on watching a guy covered in tattoos talking to and kissing his girlfriend with the unbridled passion of young lovers in the honeymoon phase: lucky them.

At last, I got off at Estrecho. The platform was tiny, making me feel stifled, as if I might suddenly fall on the tracks. Was that where the name of the station came from? A long and narrow platform, with a train passing close by and people moving slowly toward the stairs. Tons of Dominicans got off with me, or at least that's what I thought, thanks to the stereotype we all carry of a Dominican or someone from the Caribbean: jet-black hair tied in a ponytail, diamond earrings, gold rings, baggy clothes, and a leisurely gait. If you're careful with your stuff, there shouldn't be any problem, Flavia had said. Of course, like anywhere else. *It's not true that a Latino is going to come rob you at gunpoint, if you ask me.* Theft works differently here.

As soon as I left the metro: torrential rain. But how? Moments before, I'd been watching people sunbathing and reading in boats on the lake, now the sky was gray. I didn't have an umbrella with me, I never imagined it would pour down like this. *Well, now what?*

It was almost time to meet and I had an impossible mission: find an ATM and reach it without getting soaked. I walked under the sliver of protection provided by the offices, fighting other pedestrians for the right to the tiny strip, not budging, forcing them out from under that minuscule shelter so I could continue on my path, my feet already sodden. *Shit and of course I put on my stinkiest shoes.*

I found an ATM that didn't charge too much commission. I always get nervous when I have to use a machine, as if it were a video game where I only have one life and anything could go wrong. I expected the instructions to be in Catalan but it was all in Castilian and my brain sighed in relief. The system was running slow, a few seconds to process the PIN, the amount, the PIN again. I don't know if it was because of the rain—I guess so—but the light blinked just as I was about to get my hands on my cash. The screen went black, I was left with my fingers outstretched, waiting for my money, my card still inside.

No card, no cash, and nothing to smoke. Six p.m., the bank had closed hours ago. There's no one to talk to. I panicked. Brute force doesn't solve anything, but I still gave the ATM a few well-placed blows to see if it would sort itself out. I reconsidered and asked it nicely, stroked it just in case it took pity on me and spat out what was mine. Nothing. The machine was slower than ever and some strange hieroglyphs appeared on the screen. Try hitting it again, said a woman who had somehow gotten close to me, watching the whole scene, protecting herself from the rain under the same ledge as I was.

In the middle of all this, El Loco sent me a text: Dude i got bad news. *More bad news? What can be worse than this?* I went to koko yesterday & it was off the hook. I sold all my stash & im only carryin 3 but they r gonna bring me more. Dunno if u want 3 of weed + 2 of pollen or i can sort u out later. I replied that it didn't matter, *absolutely fine*. Give me a minute coz the ATM ate my card. He didn't reply.

I didn't get my card back no matter how many times I slapped the machine. The woman with me even tried to help by putting a wire in the slot but there was nothing for it. We were minutes from trying to force it open, until it started blaring a shrill tone, as if it knew we were trying to thwart its plans.

Now what do I do? I opened the bank app and canceled the card, *now I'll have to get another one*. Where are you? At the KFC on the corner. On my way, I wrote. I moved quickly, no longer trying to stay close to the buildings or avoid the loose paving slabs that vomited dirty water; I was already drenched from head to toe.

As I got closer, I started to rummage in my wet bag for loose change. I didn't even want to look at the notebook or library book I was carrying. *If I get to ten euros, it'll be a miracle.* I gathered all the coins in a little pile in my hand. I cant see u, ive got a skateboard, he wrote. Nearly there, I replied. I saw the KFC, as well as the skateboard at the entrance and a guy in a blue sweater and shorts. He had his hood up, which made sense because it was still raining; I wanted to wring myself out like a dish towel. I waved at him, said hello, and he came out of the KFC. I went over to him and we started to walk.

Hi, nice to meet you, he said. Likewise. I'm Nanda, I added my name in the hope that he would tell me his real name, but he only said Loco. Sorry, bud. Last night got away from me, I'm still half drunk. He had a vacant look, it was hard for him to focus on anything, though his eyes were wide open. He didn't make eye contact with me.

Where are we heading? It was still raining, although by then it was more like drizzle. His clothes slowly darkened like mine, absorbing raindrops. Suddenly, I felt his hand delving into the pocket of my pants and I stood still, looking at him, ready to howl if I needed to. He burst out laughing.

Gimme your hand, then. I grabbed his hand in a very indiscreet way. Even though it was raining, there were still people in the street. You got two, did I give you two? He had a brief anxiety attack. Yes, yep. I've got two. Look, I've only got ten euros and all in small change. I could do a transfer or something, it's just the machine ate my card, but we could . . . No worries, babe, we'll sort it next time, chill.

I gave him the coins, so many of them. Looking at him properly for the first time, I was surprised by how young he was. *We're the same generation, we might even be the same age.* He had a scar across his left eyebrow, reaching all the way to his cheek, *but it's old now and not so noticeable.* His eyes were the color of honey. We observed each other for a few seconds, the kind that seem eternal because you really take in what you're looking at. Alright, well, thanks so much. Great to meet you.

We had clumsy goodbye kisses on the cheek, one of those times where you start kissing just one cheek and then, out of habit, move to the other one, but hesitantly, resulting in a half-way kiss, a kiss with some lip involved. My cheeks were burning under that cold rain. *Later, Loco.* I noticed he was much taller than me. I also noticed his scent, a hint of perfume, probably just deodorant. He certainly seemed messed up, his eyes were very wide, surprised. You could tell he'd been out partying: his face looked tired, there were bags under his eyes. I felt his hand on my lower back as we said goodbye, that pacifying gesture some men do unconsciously, and though he was a stranger, I liked it. I saw myself reflected in those yellow eyes, vibrating with life, though the rest of his face and his body told a different story. *He's just doing his job.* In the end, the meet wasn't too weird; *it could have been worse, I thought it would be worse.*

The almost kiss went no further, the looks were just looks, and I hurried back to the metro, retracing my steps under the narrow shelter, though I was so wet by then it didn't matter, I could feel my feet going numb. After descending the stairs to the center of the earth—*show me mercy, Estrecho station*—I discovered there was a delay of more than thirty minutes because of the heavy rain. Of course, the line I needed was the one suspended. *Now what? At least I didn't swipe the card, I didn't lose a ride.* The bus system wasn't running either. Torrential rain in Madrid: total collapse.

Think, think, think.

I consider whom I could go to in the area, but frankly, my contacts are limited. I feel anxious because I really want to smoke and in this rain I can't even have a few puffs in the street. I don't have many options. Fifteen minutes of climbing the stairs to the surface and I finally leave the metro and head to KFC, defeated. *At least there's Wi-Fi there*, I can kill time reading or playing a game on my phone. I want to buy an ice cream but remember I've got no card or money. *Fuck my life!* I go in and head straight to the seats at the back, there aren't many people there, but there's still quite a racket, they're raising their voices over the rain. When I go to sit away from them all, I find myself facing him. The same guy in the same blue sweater and shorts, with his skateboard. He's glued to his phone and when I go over he looks up. He doesn't seem to recognize me at first, then comes the hit of that scent, the honey, the hint of lip. He smiles.

Hey, bud, he says, realizing who I am. What happened? The rain, I reply, the metro is over half an hour delayed. He whistles. Shit.

Who would have imagined I would end up sitting with this lunatic in a half-empty KFC in Madrid. Rain buddies. I could pretend we were in the McDonald's in Chacaíto under a downpour forcing us to spend the night here indefinitely; *God, I'd love that.*

So tell me, chama, you live here? In Barcelona. I came here to go to the embassy, I'm staying with a friend. Where's your

167

friend? She went to work in the morning. Now she's probably with her boyfriend. I didn't want to be a third wheel and, well, I really want to smoke.

He laughs and wrinkles his eyes, the light is bothering him. He must still be experiencing the last traces of an intense trip, or the comedown, which is much worse. Or maybe, just maybe, it's me that makes him look away, like when we get self-conscious around someone we're really attracted to. My narcissism in action.

D'ya want an ice cream? he asks. Go on, then. Thank you. I look at him, surprised; I still find it hard to believe he's so young. What about everything Keiber told us? I always imagined him around forty. But this version of El Loco isn't bad, *fuckable even*. A normal guy. If it weren't for the scar, he could even be hot. *Well, I already think he's pretty hot.* Maybe the nickname El Loco comes from his protruding eyeballs, as if he had thyroid issues.

What about all those stories and rumors about him that went around back there? The horrific past that marked him and pursued him and all that? Are you the real one, the man from that story . . . ? *No, it's impossible.*

That other Loco could be my father, when this Loco in front of me could be my age. Why do I find him so attractive? The danger, the legend behind the name, the deep-rooted beliefs that set my adrenaline pumping? Probably because I already had my idea, my version of him, and that fiction lends more weight to the reality in front of me. Nothing more.

A part of me wants to believe all those rumors and Chinese whispers that Keiber told me.

Later, with the downside of intimacy, I would understand that he was indeed crazy, but then, who isn't?

Let he who is free from insanity cast the first stone. I get the impression that he could be a good friend, a better half, even a great lover. He doesn't talk much and when he does, I tell myself not to believe everything, there's always a hint of doubt about his identity, what he's really thinking, his intentions. *Aren't his intentions actually my intentions? Aren't I a different Nanda for every person who knows me?* There are moments when the communication flows without the need to speak. That's his charm, our charm. We discover that we can be anyone, by choice or by invention.

I don't know if he'll play along, but it's worth a try. I'm half-crazy too. Who doesn't have a screw loose?

Hi, nice to meet you, I'm Gala, I hold my hand out just as he sits down and places the ice cream in front of me. Chama, what the . . . You a cop or some shit? he asks with a half-smile. I burst out laughing. Of course not, play along. I'm Gala, I repeat. Gabo, he replies, shaking my hand. I look at him closely, does he look like a Gabo? I eat a few spoonfuls of my ice cream. What's up, Gabo? How're you doing?

He watches me with a strange expression, considering the possibility, for a brief moment, that I really am batshit. He shakes his head, trying to understand, and then loosens up. All good, keeping on keeping on. You? How's Barcelona?

That's true, because I did tell him some truths. Barcelona? No idea, I've never been. This is my first time in Spain. I live in Germany. Shit, you speak German. No, another truth. What about you? Nein, he replies. How old are you?

We carry on like that, answering with imagined lives. The downpour gets worse, denser. Too much water. Thunder and lightning brighten the sky with bluish light. Through the shouts of the people waiting for the rain to stop, he says that his hobbies, Gabo's, are PlayStation, doing tricks on his skateboard, listening to music, and partying. Truth or lie? I tell him I like to paint, read, and write, that I want to be a writer. Truth or lie? But if you write, ain't you a writer already? Or not? The magic of telling total lies always bathed in truth. He says he has a dog called Arya, I say I have a dog called Joey. *They'd probably get on super well.* Truth or lie?

Tell me a crazy story, Gala says. Shiiiit, I got so many, but now I can't remember none. He runs his hands through his hair and smiles. You know what is a crazy thing? he asks, scratching his chin. What? Mules, traffickers. Jíbaros, Gala says. What? Nothing, pushers, dealers. Like you. He nods. People get sick, you get me? Too much shit in one place. I got a friend who worked on a plane, one of them who serves food an' all that. A flight attendant. That's the one. She told me once that on a long-haul flight there was this woman who spent aaages with her baby in the same position. She tries to talk to this bitch to let her check the baby or whatever, coz it's dangerous, you know there's like a gas or some shit they pump out to make people sleepy on planes, they get dopey. Seriously? Yeah, an' that shit can be dangerous for kids. So my friend reports something's up, the woman won't let her check the baby. An' shit, I think her coworkers came an' all hell broke loose coz the kid was dead. No! For real? The most depraved thing was when they landed, they realized the baby was stuffed with coke. That's some fucked-up shit, my friend. A scare story for you to write. The thing is, did they kill her an' then fill her with drugs or did the drugs kill her during the flight? Was that her real mom? What would I know, you crazy?

I finish the last spoonful of my ice cream. He didn't eat his, the ice cream remains untouched on the table, melted, with the spoon floating in it. Now you tell me something crazy. Why? Surely you've got crazier stories.

There's a long silence, he seems to be studying me, arms folded and a mocking smile on the lip I've already tasted. I don't have drug stories, but I did once see a girl get raped and I didn't do anything to help her.

Truth or lie?

Shit, kid. That's fucked up too. Goddam rapists. I also saw rapes and didn't do shit. But then, the person who sees it ain't to blame. Right? You are if you don't do anything to help, don't you think? Then I admit my guilt, he says, raising his hands. Me too, I whisper, copying the movement of his fingers.

We catch ourselves with our hands in the air and bring them together as if we were about to sing one of those childhood songs and play pat-a-cake, clapping in complicated combinations. *¿Quién es Lola? Lo lamento. ¿Quién es mento? Mentolate. ¿Quién es late? Latecoco. ¿Quién es coco? Cocosette. ¿Quién es sette? Se te mete. ¿Quién es mete? Meteoro. ¿Quién es oro? Oro puro. ¿Quién es puro? Puro pan. ¿Quién es pan? Pampero. ¿Quién es pero? Perolito. ¿Quién es lito? Tu abuelito . . .* , palms meeting in an automatic, precise, and ever faster rhythm.

We are the guilty ones who turn themselves in without knowing their crime. We are the stories invented in the reflections in a pupil. We don't know if we are a truth or a lie.

But then, what happens if you can't do anything to help? If doing something means putting yourself in the same situation as that person? If intervening means signing your own death sentence? I ask. I dunno, he replies. Our hands are entwined. But I think watchin' from a distance an' still not tryin' nothin' kinda makes you part of all that shit. Right?

I nod. Who would've guessed we'd end up doing therapy. My nose starts to itch, the irritation that comes before tears, I look up to control the water threatening to gather in my eyes. He realizes and smiles, this time a new smile, different. *Are you a moron, Nanda, what the fuck?* I berate myself. There are very sensitive nerves that, when you touch them, stir earthquakes inside.

We've all seen an' lived through thousands of ugly things, but we've all got, like, the chance to change, at least that's what I think. No shit, if I think 'bout all the shit I did as a kid or how I used to behave, I'd throw myself on the metro rails. But I'm here, tryin', coz I believe . . . I dunno, that you can, like, build a better version of yourself or somethin' like that.

Truth or lie?

The rain keeps coming down, though not as heavy as before. It'll clear up soon and I'll be able to smoke, at last. Hopefully, the metro will sort itself out too. What about him? What's he going to do after the downpour? And what about us? Where are all these stories carrying truths leading? The rain will probably wash them away, cleaning out our demons like it cleans the street, refreshing us on the inside.

Tell me something else, Gala asks. He looks me over, to see how far he can go. He raises an eyebrow; he must be getting over the effect of something and can focus better. Or it's just reality abruptly interrupting our gazes, allowing us to see fully. If there's something we do well, it's looking at each other; reading ourselves in the other's irises.

What d'ya want stories for? For your writin'? I nod. An' what if they're made up? It doesn't matter, who knows what's real and what's not? Us, he replies. He looks down and scratches his ear. He smiles again, I smile at him, we smile at each other. He touches my palm with his index finger. Fuck, the only thing that comes to mind is about Calígula, a neighbor from the barrio who was a real creep. People say he wasn't like that before, that he went nuts overnight.

Dude, no wonder. With that name, it's natural he went crazy. Do you know who Caligula was? No, who the fuck was Caligula? A Roman emperor. A bunch of people ganged up to kill him. He was half-crazy. Once, in the middle of a battle, instead of fighting, he ordered his soldiers to collect seashells. And I think he raped his sisters, or pimped them out, something like that, I'm not too sure.

Fuck me, that shit, like, comes with the name then, he shows his teeth, a little twisted. One of the first real smiles that I see from him, that I can feel. The sound is accompanied by him banging on the tables, the banging we do when we're sure of something or to protect ourselves from a truth that seems absolute.

Why? Coz they caught that dude fuckin' a dog an' his sister. What? An' get this, it wasn't even his dog. She belonged to another neighbor. The guy used to go round his house an' disappear to fuck the dog. The neighbor's old man was getting suspicious coz they'd already heard the dog squeal a few times. Then, one afternoon, when they heard the dog squealing again, his old man went in the back with a machete an', no shit, he found him givin' it to the pitbull. He chased him out at machete-point.

And what about his sister? His sister was a little soft in the head, you know, he shakes his head and goes cross-eyed. She never knew what the fuck was happenin', always in her own world. You get me? I think she was two or three years younger than him. One afternoon, their mom found him in the shack out the back an' well, they chased him out an' the punches started flyin'. He got locked up, but that girl was screwed by every boy in the barrio.

I don't know what face I make at him, but he holds his hands up, in a sign of peace, apologizing. Hey, hey. Don't get mad at me, I had nothin' to do with it. You asked for crazy stories, didn't you? Well, there you go.

It's true. They're terrific stories, you've got a ton of friends. You got no idea, he grunts, but *friends* friends, not so many. Over time you, like, lose friends.

We fall silent and he starts to roll a cigarette. He points the tobacco bag at me, letting me know I can take some if I want, so I grab some and roll a cigarette too. *For later.*

You've never seen a dead body, admit it, he murmurs, tapping the cigarette with the end of his lighter. More than one. Truth or lie? He snorts, incredulous.

And have you seen someone get killed? Just once and, funnily enough, here in Barcelona. Bullshit, I don't believe you. I was living in a real nasty neighborhood, a traveler neighborhood, full of Chinese and Moroccans. I became friends with a guy who had a fabric shop under my apartment, I always gave him things to sew for me and paid him in beers. One night we were having a few at his shop, with his cousins, and out of nowhere we heard these awful shouts. We opened the door and an old man was shouting at a boy, all very heated, in a strange language that sounded harsh and, well, the old man pulled out a knife and started stabbing the kid. Over and over, in such a short time, everything was covered with blood and then he ran away. It all happened so fast. Nasty, nasty, nasty. Shit, I believe you. What about you? Hmm . . . I've seen loads of dead bodies, who hasn't? But, let's see, I think the worst I've seen was when a guy shot a man while he was takin' cash out of a machine. Like this, straight in the head, he makes a gun with his hand and touches my forehead. It all went real fast too an' the machine, the floor, everythin' was covered in blood. I remember the man's head was blown apart, but his leg was still twitchin' an' people were screamin'.

Truth or lie?

It's not raining so much now; the background noise has stopped, sudden drops fall here and there. The air is fresher too. The people around us have left little by little. Without realizing, we've ended up alone. Another lingering look at each other, trying to tell each other the mute and secret story just with our eyes. I'm gonna head out before the rain starts again. Okay, chama. I hope there's no more delay on the metro, that's the thing. Oh yeah, hopefully, it's been a while now, right? Bye, Gabo. Thanks for the ice cream and the weed. He's surprised.

Truth or lie? Who knows, maybe he gave his real name. Maybe he invented the stories in the moment, or maybe not. Perhaps we construct ourselves before someone else's eyes, showing only what we want to show, saying only what the other person wants to hear. Or not. There are two options: trusting what we told each other or trusting that the whole thing was one big performance. And something tells me that his eyes weren't lying, aren't lying. In the same way that I tried to be sincere with this stranger who will take charge of throwing out my mental trash and my share of guilt, beyond my limits.

Are we what other people think about us? Are we those stories our names carry around and we don't even know where they came from? All I can see here is a guy my age, making a space for himself, fighting to bring to light his own story, his truth. Don't I do the same thing? Don't we all, in fact, do the same, try to show our truth, our history, our origins? Gabo, Gala, Nanda, or El Loco. Who are we? Who were we? *Whatever we want.* What we ban and forbid, what we renounce or accept.

Can I give you a lift on my wheels? he offers, chuckling, pointing at his skateboard. I shake my head, no, no worries, there's no need. I watch him skate away along the wet street with raindrops still falling from the trees. I feel like he's taking with him my secrets that don't know they're secrets.

I hit quite a delay on the metro. It took me a long time, but I got back. Once I was at Flavia's house, I went straight to the shower and then rolled a giant joint. It kept raining and that night various parts of Madrid flooded, the videos reminded me of the Vargas tragedy: streets blocked with mud, enormous rocks falling and taking everything in their path, cars floating like boats, lost puppies, people in flooded houses and their drowned histories. Nature returning to its course, treading firmly on the land it knows to be its own, despite progress, development, and technological advances.

The brown rivers appeared on the news carrying cars, animals, and containers. Emergency zones were decreed. Loads of people went on TV with downcast faces sharing how they had lost their homes and belongings. Various stations were still closed in the morning, covered in debris and full of dirty water. Things you believe would never happen here, in this shining present, so full of opportunities, so different from the world we left behind. But here we are: Madrid under torrential rain was no more than a painful and distorted reflection of that Caracas collapsed under the downpour.

I'm on this side of the pond. Truth or lie? Then why does it feel the same? Why do I still feel the same emptiness I felt leaving behind the Carlos Cruz-Diez mosaic on the airport floor? Watching the havoc wrought by the rain and the sad faces of those people, I thought that a feeling of belonging doesn't come from places or geography, but from people. And El Loco, Gabo, or whatever his name was, had taken me to that land which promised us belonging through language, through jokes, through acceptance and the understanding of someone who knows himself to be both—victim and culprit.

Truth or lie?

It depends on who tells it; it depends on who hears it.

INSECURITY4U

The pandemic really knew how to fuck with Nacho. And with so many others. The world came crashing down around him when, overnight, he couldn't ride for Glovo anymore. He couldn't even work anywhere else, because everything was on hold, frozen in time. The Monday of the week when they closed the schools, before they implemented the State of Alarm, he received his temporary NIE through the asylum process he started two years earlier. Finally, he was someone: a laminated piece of red paper certified that, in the eyes of the Spanish state, he existed. No more miserable, illegal jobs, no more pedaling beneath the merciless summer sun with sweat stains at his armpits and his T-shirt glued to his back. At last, he was a human being and not one more sudaca, now he really was one of those coming to steal the Spaniards' jobs. But what good did it do him?

With this lockdown, he couldn't even look for another gig, a legal one, where at the end of the month the bosses didn't play dumb and he wasn't left without pay because he had no way to report them. He was stressed, losing his mind. Those months of total lockdown had eaten his nominal savings, the money he was going to use to bring over his girlfriend to keep him company at night. He couldn't help his parents with the monthly groceries that he always used to pay for; they'd have to make do with the little they could afford. His priority was getting a hold of medicine for them, and they'd have to deal with everything else themselves. *I can't do any more, for fuck's sake. Goddam shitty virus.*

Cheo, María Eugenia, Keiber, Nacho, and all the other worker bees were having a tough time. They were a bunch of undocumented immigrants with no savings, and they couldn't even do bullshit jobs like pedaling until they could no longer feel their thighs. The virus and the lockdown had taken away their only means of self-worth, their only way to feel human and part of society, for as much as they were at the bottom of the pyramid. Other people, those with papers and Spanish citizens, at least had the right to furlough and could stay calm because, sooner or later, they'd get their paycheck, but what about them? Despite their university degrees and their ability to speak English better than most people, they were nobodies, and no one cared about them.

When safety measures were relaxed and you could invite friends over again, Jordi told Nacho that he might be able to get a gig through a contact who was looking for people for something to do with security. Perfect. Nacho sent his résumé and they interviewed him over Zoom, easy. The stasis of the city, the halting of the economy, the closure of bars and museums brought him something he didn't suspect at all. Before they called off the State of Alarm, even before the third phase of de-escalation began, the company called him; they were already up and running and needed people hungry to work.

Come on. The only thing Nacho had in excess after three months of biting his nails was hunger to work.

Like everything in life, it's all about who you know; *that's how it works back there, over here, everywhere.* Living here means realizing that it's true, these were our conquistador forefathers and that's why we are who we are today; that's the root of all our ills: our drunkenness, the insults, the ridicule, the camaraderie, and the corruption; they are our reflection, with a first world label.

And so, before everything returned to the new normal, Nacho was already out and making money. He didn't know what racism was until he started installing security alarms across Catalonia. There isn't any racism in Venezuela, he used to say, offhand. Then he would think about the Country Club people, who lived in their own bubble and looked down their noses at sweaty morenitos like him; everything else gets hazy. Classism, racism, and machismo coexist in harmony, holding hands and dancing like the three Disgraces. The eternal party of the Caribbean. But Nacho wouldn't know how to explain the difference between classism and racism. *Is there a difference?* He had buddies of all colors and he himself was kind of Black, well they sometimes called him Black affectionately, but in reality he was more like cappuccino. He never felt like he was treated badly for being darker-skinned, although he'd never really stopped to think about it. What would be the point?

This is Latin America, baby, racism doesn't exist.

Aha.

He was unaware that he had, on multiple occasions, been the victim of a racism so disguised and accepted by society that not even he noticed it happening; in fact, no one seemed to notice, or at least they didn't point it out. White privilege? Now he did notice.

Sure, as a delivery rider he already felt the contempt in the way people looked at him; he noticed how some people edged away from places packed with riders, like him, because they were all illegal immigrants who could rob you. He attributed it to the fact of being a rider, rather than his physique, his hair, or the color of his skin.

He started to work at the security camera company and was apprenticed to Montesir, a Moroccan with an even darker complexion than his, who didn't speak Spanish very well. The first few days, when they arrived at the houses, the clients would not speak to Montesir directly, addressing Nacho, who was white next to the Moroccan. Nacho didn't know anything because he was just learning, so he stuck to listening to the client and then looking at Montesir, who responded through his mask, and the clients kept looking straight at Nacho, not taking on board that the explanation came from that other dark-skinned individual with the strange accent. Nacho didn't know him well enough to know or to guess what expression was hidden behind the mask, and his eyes didn't say anything, they were completely neutral and inexpressive. Why didn't Montesir get mad? *Mm-hmm, and what could he do about it anyway? Nothing, shut up and put up.*

Montesir became nervous in front of people and his Spanish got worse. Nacho was obliged to interpret. Dammit, Montesir, you speak Spanish well when you talk to me. Montesir was also excessively delicate and careful with the objects around the homes. If they needed to move a table, he would rather contort himself than touch or move anything. He walked around on tiptoe putting back every item that Nacho moved. No, man, do not touch anything, he said in his strong, guttural accent. Learning was complicated because Montesir did everything so fast, without explaining what he was doing. Nacho settled for watching him press buttons here and there, setting up this and that. You see, you see? But Nacho did not see, he just followed him like a dog following a scent, eyes wide, as if that way he would understand what Montesir was doing, as if he could absorb the information directly through his corneas.

He learned everything on the manual side in no time: how to install the cameras, how to adjust them on the walls, which angles gave the best coverage, how to make holes with the electric drill, and how to connect the current; but the most fundamental thing, how to make the cameras work and make the images reach the control panel, that was a total mystery. He would only get two weeks of training, and with Montesir, he was better off teaching himself, keeping himself busy.

While Montesir set up the cameras, Nacho got ahead with admin, filling out payment forms and all the necessary paperwork, he spoke to the homeowners and accepted everything they offered him: water, coffee, Fanta, beer, whatever. *Yes yes yes yes yes, yes to everything.* Montesir wouldn't accept a thing, he didn't even eat or drink during the day. All he did was chain smoke, one cigarette after another, like a chimney. Nacho felt sick imagining how his mouth must taste when he swallows, having spent all day smoking without drinking a drop of water; raspy throat, bitter saliva.

The best thing, the thing that made it worth tolerating Montesir's smoke and the scornful looks from clients, was traveling around Catalonia and getting to know places he would never have been to on his own. Incredible houses in the mountains, beautiful landscapes; the air felt fresher, his nose cleared, and he felt that he was getting more oxygen into his lungs—when he got away from Montesir, of course. Nacho carried around a weed pipe to smoke over the course of the day and Monte never said a word.

He left the house at seven thirty sharp each morning, and returned late, sometimes after nine. They had to go to far-flung locations and, as there were only four technicians at the company, they shared all the work between them, sometimes doing five or six alarms in one day. Yes, they were earning more money, but Nacho soon understood that Montesir was the company's slave because he never said no to anything. If you're one of those people who doesn't know how to say no, you'd better get used to being someone's bitch. Another friend worked with me, he stopped coming to work on Saturdays, tired of working Saturdays. Bam, goodbye. No more work. Less alarms each day. And then no more work. Bullshit, my friend, Montesir repeated over and over.

He spent all day in a mood, moaning and doing things begrudgingly, which meant their work took even longer, because Montesir would make mistakes or get confused and it was a whole mess. Nacho tried to calm him down, but Montesir didn't know how to dial it back, constant stress. He didn't know how to use the GPS either. He got lost often and was too stubborn to take directions from Nacho. No, man, no. We are better going this way, that was always the answer.

By Friday, Nacho was already stressed and losing his hair from pulling on it too much. The other technician only did four alarms a day and didn't work weekends. Montesir, on the other hand, did six and, in some cases, they had to install up to twelve cameras. Install, set up, and then test them all one by one. They arrived on time to every appointment but wasted a lot of time between jobs because Montesir kept getting lost and going the wrong way.

Eight wrong turns in one day: Nacho counted every one of them. It was too much. Some were even in central Barcelona, unforgivable for someone who had been living there so long.

Nacho couldn't control himself any longer and grabbed the GPS, started telling him exactly where he had to go. Take a left at the street that's coming up. Okay, after the roundabout, you're gonna go right. Aha, that's the stuff. Right, goddammit! Montesir smiled, he couldn't help it, Nacho was funny and, deep down, Montesir was happy with him. He could see that he wanted to learn, and he was sharp, he got ahead with things without Montesir having to ask him, he put the tools in order and prepared the cameras so that all he had to do was install them; he was a good helper and that meant they finished earlier.

Nacho noticed that the Catalans, at least the ones they dealt with that week, were unfriendly and persnickety people. The most distrustful: they asked about everything, checked everything, always wanted to force their opinion on them, often making them install all the cameras how they wanted and not how they should be done. *That's their problem.* They never said a word to Montesir, ignored him entirely. The majority were older people with a backward mindset who never spoke anything but Catalan, even if Nacho spent fifteen minutes trying to understand them; they were unwavering. If they had to repeat a thousand times vull que la càmera estigui damunt de la finestra, they would. Until, from hearing it so many times, Nacho's brain would spark, or Montesir, who was more used to Catalan, would intervene.

Sometimes, when they traveled from one installation to another, Nacho listened to podcasts. Cheo said it was self-help nonsense, but it helped Nacho to see things from another perspective. Then he'd try to explain it to Montesir, unsuccessfully: . . . it's talking about how we've all had racist, classist, abusive thoughts, but life itself is a path of constant learning and you have to rebuild yourself. I think that's what they say, do you know what that is? It's when you bombard yourself with questions, when you realize the prejudices and beliefs you have deeply engrained from childhood, from society, from your parents, you get it? The idea is we're all ignorant fools. Man, I am no fool, eh? If you want to be a fool, that is your business, not me. Nacho would sigh and they would end up laughing. You keep listening to your thing, I will listen to my music, man.

The most shocking moment, the thing that woke Nacho from his mental lethargy, was when, after a two-hour drive to a village seventy miles away—in the ass end of nowhere—they had to turn around because the owner refused to let them into the house.

They called their boss from outside the house while the old man shouted things they didn't understand from the balcony and a crowd of people gathered at their windows to see what was happening. Moro de merda, go back to your own country! shouted a chubby old lady with lilac hair, from the safety of her balcony. Sí, home, i tant! They wanted to come in and rob me, they are all thieves. Pocavergonyes! Call the security company immediately. That's the kind of thing the neighbors shouted from above.

Shit, sorry mate. They're a bunch of tossers. Of course, come back, come back. So they went back. Why did they have to be like that? There's no need. Nacho got into the van, his stomach was in knots. He had never felt like such a pariah. Nothing new, man. Always like this or worse, Montesir seethed while he lit another cigarette. This and all the other similar experiences he'd been having finally pulled Nacho from his cocoon of privilege and forced him to see the plain and simple truth, with no filters to disguise or soften it. He took two hits from his pipe and offered it to Montesir, knowing he'd refuse. This will help you unwind, trust me.

That's how they spent the day, or the day passed, going from one place to another in the van, installing a ton of cameras, their arms stiff, deafened by the drill, watching the countryside go by, with a lump in their throats when they arrived at a new installation because they didn't know if they'd be allowed in or told to eat shit. There's a Catalan proverb: De qui no et miri en parlar, no et fiïs en obrar, don't trust the actions of someone who won't look you in the eye when they speak. Clients never looked at them when they spoke to them; they were a thing to which people refused to turn their gaze.

By the second week of training, Nacho had met Xiomara, Montesir's Puerto Rican wife. It was common for Xiomara to call Montesir, well into the evening, furious and spitting bullets, to find out where the fuck he was, when was he coming home, the kids hadn't seen him for days, he said that he'd come home early to spend some time with them, but all he ever cared about was fucking work. Shit or get off the pot, eh? What are you thinkin'? I see right through you, yo te conozco bacalao.

Nacho didn't understand half the things Xiomara said, though the substance didn't escape him. We have three children, you know, and this one never sees them coz he's always workin' too much. I feel like I'm the only one raisin' these kids, you know? Days can go by without the kids seein' their dad. It's not how much, it's how often.

When they sucked him into the conversation, Nacho tried to tread lightly and say something funny that would diffuse the tension; most of the time, he just laughed and took Xiomara's side to pass the buck, saying things like: Jeez, Montesir, you're being a bad boy. Sometimes, joshing or lighthearted comments weren't enough, and Xiomara gave him a dressing-down in a tone that permitted no reply. Montesir hung up as many times as was necessary, and kept smoking, unfazed.

Nacho knew that Montesir needed money, and he also got the impression that he was sick of his family, given how he avoided them through work, that's why he spent so long on the installations and tried to spend the best part of the day away from home, even working weekends, though he complained about it afterward. Nacho didn't know anything about his kids, not even their names; Montesir never spoke about anything other than work. His kids must have really missed him, or maybe they were used to his absence.

Tuesday, they had to install alarms in a house where an elderly couple had died. Their children were securing the home because people had already broken in a couple of times when the parents were still alive. Nacho was in superstitious mode and didn't want to touch anything, he had a strange feeling about it and wanted to get out of there as soon as possible. While he made the holes in the walls where Montesir indicated, he couldn't help daydreaming and imagining the poor old couple who used to live all alone in that huge house. Totally morbid. Who died first? Did they get sick at the same time or even share a cause and moment of death?

Everything was intact, frozen at the second of death: objects don't miss anyone, they don't have memory, they only collect dust and wait.

The two siblings were in the living room, the sofas still had blankets that their parents must have covered themselves with for their siesta or when they watched TV; on the side tables next to the larger sofa lay an open book and a forgotten mug. The daughter picked up the book and started to talk in Catalan, to no one in particular.

How strange they left this book here, who could it belong to, Ma or Pa? I suspect Ma, you know how Pa preferred to watch television or listen to the radio. And what shall we do with these paintings? Aunt Ana wanted to have this one, she pointed to a large canvas in the middle of the room, a kind of still life with a bottle of wine and two very realistic fried eggs, the one Ma painted that summer when we all went to Ca'Julia, in Palamós. Do you remember? Of course I do! The summer when Pa stood on a sea urchin and his leg swelled like an Iberian ham.

They both burst out laughing and Nacho smiled too. He didn't understand what they were laughing about, but he saw them there, happy in their parents' inner sanctum, remembering things, and he couldn't help but smile as well. After packing up and heading back to Barcelona for the final installation of the day, Nacho half-listened to Montesir's conversation with his wife. If anything was certain, it was that they were going to be thrown out of their home and needed to move right away. Maybe their rental agreement was already up, and *you don't mess around with that*. There's time until the exact day, no more, no less, you can only stay if you accept the new price the landlord imposes.

They arrived at an incredible house in a gated community. It belonged to some Russians who treated them very well, offering them snacks and beers. Nacho had begun to think of foreigners as nicer, friendlier people than the locals. The Russians even gave them chairs so they could be comfortable while they set up the equipment. That was unusual. Nobody did that. Usually, they'd do the configuration while standing or crouched on the floor. Nacho glanced around the house: spacious, double-height rooms, classy furniture and interior design; *these Russians are loaded*. He noticed a monogram,

MAZ, on different objects: on a commemorative plaque, a kind of small statue, *he obviously has connections. What is going on with the Russians?*

He realized that he'd had several Russian clients recently, all very wealthy and welcoming, buying whole blocks to turn them into tourist apartments.

Wednesday afternoon, he electrocuted himself. Jesus Christ! he shouted, waving his hand to air the pain. He managed to separate himself from the lethal suction by kicking against the wall. Two fingers were cut, ugly wounds that needed to be seen by a doctor, he was shaking. And all because, to save time, Montesir hadn't cut off the current. The owner of the house—an older lady with all the space-age apparel of the new normal: face mask, gloves, protective screen, and a spray with which she spritzed everything every other minute—showed genuine concern. If the current had run through you and out your other hand, completing the circuit, you'd be dead, eh? You'd kick the bucket, she said trembling, you'd better go to a doctor, you might feel alright now, but it's best to get these things looked at, there could be delayed symptoms. She wasn't making him feel any better, that's for sure.

They took the autopista to return to the dirty air and sky of Barcelona. That's how he knew he was home, when he had trouble breathing again. Before dropping Nacho at his house, so he wouldn't have to take the metro with his hand in that state, Montesir confessed, half-kidding, half-serious, that he was thinking about squatting. *Thinking about squatting?* Not long ago, the word didn't mean much to him. A school friend had people take over his dad's apartment and he spent years trying to remove them; he knows it was an intense fight for his friend, but nothing to do with him. Now the word squatter is charged with new meanings and images: on the street where Diego, one of the gang, used to live, there were men living in the lobbies of office buildings. They were always wasted, drinking in the street, pissing and shitting in the entrances to the parking lots on the block because they didn't have any toilets, and being offices they didn't have occupancy certificates so the water and electricity could be cut off. You had to be careful with bikes and motorbikes because the men often went out stealing. People hated them, and with good reason.

Then they were moved on. One day, six patrol cars turned up and they spent hours clearing them out, the rambla filled with people and all the neighbors went onto their balconies or out into the street to witness the spectacle of the quarantine. One of the men was strong and tall, he must have been six foot six. It took eight police officers to bring him down, beating him. The guy had enormous strength; when they managed to lock him in the patrol car, he destroyed it from the inside, silencing the street with his cries, CHRISTIAN BASTARDS. They removed the whole group, eight men in total, living cramped in two office lobbies, with no sinks, no showers, no space, nothing. The problem got worse because they found drugs. The solution proposed by the police? They captured the one with superpowers by force, then told the others still resisting, and the minors, to gather their things and move on. Where to? Wherever, far away from here, come on, get going.

What more, what else? The Pakistani under Nanda's house. That is, my house, when I lived in the low-income housing in Santa Coloma. Nacho spent so much time at my house and with another friend who lived in the area that the Pakistani who ran the phone store knew him.

One afternoon, on our way to the beach, Nacho got the urge to buy a new cover for his phone and we went to the Pakistani's store. He asked us, without much preamble, how much rent we paid. Nacho looked at me and I told him what I paid for my room, some 350 euros. Oh, too much, my friend, too much. I have a flat for you, cheaper, much cheaper.

To this day, we couldn't say how we agreed to view a large apartment where we only had to pay the bills. This is weird, something doesn't add up. How much? Let's just take a look, see what it's like. We agreed to meet at ten that evening on Plaça del Rellotge and walk to the apartment from there. In the end, I flaked and told Nacho it was his problem, who asked him to be so reckless? They met on time and went up a few steep streets. Nacho lagged behind. They turned right and down narrow side streets. He'd never been around there before and was afraid after everything he'd heard about La Salut and La Pau.

They reached a building where most of the apartments were in darkness, but with a spacious sidewalk, lit by two tall lampposts. *At least it looks decent.* The Pakistani opened the door and led Nacho inside, in the dark. They went up to the third floor and he opened one of the doors. In the dimly lit living room, there was only an old sofa. The walls were stained with damp, peeling, and some of the windows were boarded up. The bathroom was a toilet in the middle of a tiny room, and a pipe hung off one wall in the guise of a shower; a small hole in the floor was the drain. The bank takes these flats and then they leave them empty. Nacho opened his eyes wide, understanding the situation at last. Aaaaah, of course. There is electricity and water, you only pay bills, no more. It was a wretched place. And no making noise, so the neighbors are not annoyed. Who lives here? *Fuck, you idiot, people who can't afford to live in this goddam rich people's city. Like you, for example.*

Then the Pakistani took him to the apartment next door, proud of himself because it belonged to him and his wife, a Spanish woman who was always with him in the store. The woman smiled while he showed off the apartment, the same size as the previous one, but better cared for: painted walls, a lamp, some furnishings.

With effort and love any hole can become a home. Nacho told him he'd think about it, that he'd talk to me, but, to be honest, he was planning to move in somewhere else, with some friends, thanks anyway, he had been very kind to show him the apartment.

He hurried away feeling strange. He used to think that squatters were all the same, like the social misfits who pissed and crapped in the street, but there were the Pakistani and his wife, business owners who anyone would think lived in a decent apartment, nothing out of this world, but in habitable conditions at least. And now Montesir, who had a job where he earned up to three thousand euros a month, well above the average salary, was considering squatting too. If he wasn't already. Could Montesir be living in the same conditions? A hole for him, his wife, and their three children? *Who knows.*

Following the electrical accident that could have killed Nacho, the head of his department, a tall and stocky man, called and told him he should be checked out by a doctor, but he didn't say when he should go, and because they didn't cancel his installation schedule, he went to work with Montesir the next day. His hand hurt, he couldn't move his fingers and he had suppurating blisters. He was using a cream that he bought at the pharmacy, but it didn't bring him any relief at all. That day, he was slow and awkward, he didn't help much, he couldn't. Now the first thing Montesir did was cut the current. I could've died, dickhead, he said, and Montesir chuckled by way of apology.

Slow and unoccupied as he was, Nacho realized that Montesir was eyeing up both the houses where they installed cameras and the surrounding areas. He leaned out, went up on the roofs, and spied around, no shame. Nacho couldn't believe it, he thought about all the prejudices people had toward Montesir, could they be right? *Well, there he is, looking for ways he can get in, isn't he?*

What if they've got cameras? Nacho asked. Montesir waved, swatting away flies. Ah, do not worry. All this is Security4U, Tyco, Securame, or Insel, no problem. What about electricity and water? The owner has to keep paying services, then later they cut it off, but much later, years later.

Incredible. He had everything worked out. Unstoppable and frightening: Montesir, master of security camera installations. Any building, apartment, or house was powerless against him. When they reached Barcelona, Nacho's hand was worse, the blackened skin was separating. My friend, you should go to the doctor, that hand does not look good, hey?

Nacho went straight to the walk-in clinic where they treated him as an emergency and signed him off work for at least three days. Uff, at least he was spared his last few days with Montesir.

Maybe he could finish his training with Óscar, the other technician, a Venezuelan who could do up to six installations in a day without finishing after nine, but who preferred to do only three and spend the day with his family.

At the walk-in clinic, they gave him a prescription for antibiotics and painkillers. A fat spliff and three pills later, he slept like a log. He still woke up early; dazed and covered in drool, but early. His body clock was now used to starting the day at the crack of dawn.

Later, while he was lying on the sofa smoking and watching podcasts on YouTube, his phone vibrated, Montesir was calling him. He waited until it stopped; missed call. Then a message: Bad day, explain later. Tools stolen. Nacho replied straight away. What happened Monte? Fuck, what a nightmare! How? When? Where? At night, they stole everything from the van. *Jeez, that's bad luck*. How was that possible?

Nacho sent a message to Óscar telling him Montesir had been robbed. It's the third time he's been robbed in under six months. Coz he leaves things in the van, coz he's a jackass, he replied within minutes. *They've really got his number*. But then, what could they do with all those tools and cameras that only people who work with them know how to use?

A light bulb came on, a cliché, but that's how it was.

Nacho's face lit up. *He robbed himself. Of course. Monte robbed himself. One hundred percent, he turned himself over.* Nacho's spite intensified. It's too much of a coincidence: he's being run out of his home because he's squatting and who knows how long he's already been there, he's looking for another house to squat again and now they've stolen his tools for the third time in six months. *Suspicious.* It could also be an act of personal revenge because the company fired Montesir during the pandemic. The truth is they had always treated him badly and taken advantage of him because he worked and followed orders like a donkey, never standing up for himself. I have had it up to here, man. This is bullshit, man.

Nothing happened. Nacho's sick leave came to an end; it had been more like a long and restorative weekend. Monday, when he woke up, he went with Montesir to Mataró, where they kept the vans and materials. Montesir once again collected everything he needed without asking anyone, keeping a record, signing anything, or telling a soul. Nobody asked either. Nacho couldn't believe it, they made it too easy, not just for him, but for anyone who wanted to make some extra cash at the expense of the warehouse. The boss hadn't even called Nacho to tell him which would be his van, or to give him his login details to activate the alarms on the digital platform.

Montesir told him to take any van, whichever he liked, and materials. The more, the better. He did as he was told. A while later, the secretary who booked installations called and told him he had three alarms for that day. Nacho had to leave right away for Gavá or he would arrive late to his first solo installation.

He didn't feel prepared at all. He tried to remember all the buttons Montesir had pushed frantically as he trained him. You see, you see? He was nervous and didn't take the usual two tokes of his pipe on the way, he was scared of fucking it up from being high.

He spent all day coming and going, from one end of Barcelona to the other until nine at night. He took his time, but managed everything himself, with no help from anybody. It was a real baptism by fire: learning for himself, but always, always cutting the power before touching any cables.

The week was uneventful: he concentrated on doing his installations well and spoke to Montesir when necessary, video-calling when he had doubts, though Monte got nervous and spoke faster than usual; Nacho couldn't understand him and preferred to look on Google or, when he had time, watch a YouTube tutorial.

About three weeks later, Montesir invited him over to celebrate San Juan. The house was in the suburbs of Barcelona, around Sant Cugat del Vallès. Nacho arrived in his work van and was shocked. *No fucking way.* He even felt awkward getting out of the van and going in.

The house was large, with parking, a pool, and a small garden. There were various houses in a row, like a gringo neighborhood, very pretty and quiet. No neighbors were staring out their windows giving them dirty looks and Nacho relaxed. He could see they needed to repair some leaks, change lightbulbs, fix some windows, but nothing major.

After several beers and smoking some hash in the hookah, Nacho looked him straight in the eye. So, all this then? Did they have Security4U? He waved his hand indicating the whole place. They both laughed, full belly laughs. No, my friend. I paid a friend who is an estate agent. I gave him six hundred euros and he gave me the keys. This way is even better. *Fuck yeah, it sure is.* That was a whole business Nacho had been oblivious to until then.

Cheers to that, and they clinked bottles.

DRYAS IULIA

Julio is now Julia. In process, in an intermediary state, transforming into Julia. I can't say I'm surprised, not really, although it's not every day your ex tells you they're now a woman. It was a mixture of surprise, joy, and curiosity, all at the same time. I asked all the indiscreet questions you're not supposed to ask, but she accepted them all with no problems, no misgivings. We are apprentices at life and, curious, we discover ourselves in front of each other, as if trying to copy the movements of a shadow, with a second's delay, with clumsy and sometimes abrupt fluctuations. Neither of us knows much about this game of shadows, but we know each other from before. Hey, I know you. I recognize you as a fellow woman. Friend, sister, and lover.

Julio is still Julio for many people and probably will be for some time. He's shy by nature, a little lackluster. Julia, on the other hand, is garnet, sensual, delicate, voracious. I don't know . . . , she writes, I don't think it's dysphoria because I'd be in agony, and I don't feel like that. At least not now. A few years ago, he started to think about it and feel it more intensely. He mentioned it to his girlfriend at the time, but it was just a comment, he filed it away, not paying much attention to it, as if he'd kept a pretty pebble to stroke and admire in the right moment and the right moment never came.

That's how Julia told it, playing it down, although I know that for Julio it was something much more profound than just packing it in a box and putting it away. What transition isn't frightening? What abrupt change doesn't make us tap our foot or bite our nails subconsciously? So it's not something you take lightly, you know? It's not like I woke up one day and said, right, now I am a woman. No. I think that seed was always there, but the fear was stronger than the desire, I dunno if I'm explaining myself very well, Julia confessed in a voice note one afternoon when we shared our break online. I understand, I'm trying to, and I accept you and celebrate you just as you are or might be. Sticker of puppies play-fighting.

He broke up with his girlfriend, but says it wasn't because of that. We already had a ton of differences and we saw that we weren't heading toward the same place, we didn't have the same interests. We both wanted something different and we decided to call it a day. I do think it had something to do with it, though he denies it. She told me she isn't into women, that she's one hundred percent straight. My callousness makes me ask things like: Will you get rid of your love giraffe? Giggles. No, no, for now I feel good with my love giraffe, GIF of a giraffe poking out its tongue.

It was a very personal language: years ago, Julio gifted me my first vibrator, which came wrapped up in a plush giraffe. But, who knows, maybe the next time we see each other I'll have a pair of tits. She doesn't laugh, or I believe it's rather him who laughs. We start to read things together, to instruct ourselves and deconstruct ourselves, not our bodies, but our concepts; it was an escape valve: letting off steam, commenting and questioning, being able to talk about the most intimate things, without shame, without panicking about causing offense or falling into prejudices for lack of knowledge. We made arrangements to watch documentaries together, her over there in the Southern Cone and me here, facing the Mediterranean; later we discussed them, we took them to pieces along with our beliefs and ideas. We recommended books to each other, so many books, jotted down on Post-its and stuck to the walls to remind us, to have them present, sacred books of magic and transformation. It was intense, starting to see things from another perspective and not understanding how we didn't reach this revelation sooner. Why did we never talk about this? Why was this topic thoroughly absent from our chats and our flings? You never talk about it until it happens.

I also had no intention of talking about this and especially not back there, you know what people are like. If being gay is frowned upon, imagine being trans. Did you know anyone trans there? I ask because I didn't know anyone. No, no one. But I do know several people who started their transition once they left. Why do you think they're transitioning abroad? Why did you decide to do it now and not before?

She takes a while to respond though she's online, I start distracting myself with chores while I wait for a reply: I wash some dishes, sweep the kitchen until the table vibrates. I can't generalize, you know everyone experiences it in their own way, but it could have a lot to do with being on our own and independent. Plus, now that I think about it, not only did I not know anyone trans in Caracas, but I bet that hormone treatment doesn't even exist over there. People don't even contemplate changing gender, it would be like, I dunno, signing a death sentence.

Julia still doesn't take hormones, but she's mulling it over. I discover that social security here covers hormone treatment for trans people. I think that according to the new law they also cover voice treatment and any genital surgery, Julia says. Does social security cover it over there too? I'm not too sure, but I would guess so. From what I understand, you have to go for a psychological evaluation where they basically say you have dysphoria, they make you sign some papers as if you were crazy and suffering from a mental illness, then they require you to live as the opposite sex for some time, and after all that they agree to give you hormones. It's a pretty complex process, but I don't know if the laws have changed or anything . . .

Not everyone took it well, many people were fine with it, but not really fine. Many friends stopped being friends, some didn't even say anything, they maintained a silence that was as if they had disappeared. I kept asking her the typical questions of curious minds, not worried that I would hurt or offend her, because I was shielded by our trust and friendship. When did you realize? How did you realize?

Julia is writing.

Since I was little, I've been curious, I remember playing with my big sister's clothes and dolls. I don't know. As I grew up and saw that I liked girls, I tried not to worry about it because I wasn't gay, and it was like, if I'm not gay, then what's really going on with me? It's like, at that age I didn't even know being trans was an option, you know, no one ever spoke about these things. But it wasn't until a few years ago that I really saw myself and felt that I was a woman and decided to live in a more, I don't know, feminine way, as a trans woman. It was like, I don't know, suddenly everything seemed to fit together and make sense, at least for me. When I accepted it, I felt good about myself, as if I could breathe fresh air again. I don't know how I realized exactly, it wasn't something that happened from one day to the next, in my head I always had a suspicion. I felt that, in part, I was tricking myself and I was sick of pretending, even to myself. It was simply deciding to live in a more feminine way, but without the crushing dysphoria, I think. Not all trans people experience dysphoria. This seems incredible to me because I always thought that trans people felt super uncomfortable in their bodies or hated their genitals. Look, it does happen, there are people who suffer a huge amount and can't live with that anxiety, but that's not the case with me. Representations of trans people tell us that's true, that all trans people suffer from dysphoria, but it's not necessarily like that.

If Julia hadn't left, this awakening would never have happened, it would have been the decline of Julia. The freedom she got from being alone in an unknown country allowed Julia to rediscover herself and to exist in the world at last, to show herself. Yes, totally, one hundred percent. If I were still there, I don't know, I'd surely still be Julio and that's that, I wouldn't even have thought about doing it, though it would have been awful. Sticker of a girl drowning in toilet paper. We spoke a few times about the confusion that still overwhelms her now and then; waves of feeling that she couldn't control because she didn't know what they were or where they came from. Because I couldn't name it or talk about it in a natural way, it was as if it didn't exist and I felt like I was going crazy, that there was something very wrong with me.

What we do not name does not exist.

Julia's style is different, but in keeping with her essence; dresses and overalls are her favorite outfit. I think this knot you have at your chest is meant to be on the back, tied in a bow. The color is divine, it suits you so well. Garnet, red light on her bedroom walls thanks to the curtains she was so excited to buy. Cats, so many cats. I haven't got a handle on these things. *Yet.* Everything needs time and patience. In pandemic times, the mask makes her feel protected because all you can see are her eyes, with purple shadow and eyeliner;

the moustache and goatee are hidden, and eyes just are, a look doesn't have a gender. The rest doesn't either, but this way it's easier for people to see me in a good light. I don't say anything, but I sense, I imagine, how difficult it must be for her when she goes out and people only see him.

Julio let his hair grow out and I discover Julia dying it burgundy. There are rings on her long, pianist fingers; there are black and pink striped socks, or patterned with bows and kittens. There are also bones, less meat on that five-foot-nine frame. You're skinnier, I blurt out; *you shouldn't talk about people's weight, Nanda*. A slip of the tongue. I couldn't help it, I said what I saw. Julia took it well. Julio says he's the same as ever. But no, Julia and I know that he is lying and that there's hunger behind his words. Anyway, you're beautiful, that's the truth. Sticker of a puppy covering its face with a paw in the middle of a heart made of purple flowers.

I was afraid you wouldn't be attracted to me anymore, now that you don't see me as, like, so masculine, she lets slip when I in turn let slip that we're all a little bisexual. Well, you won't be so masculine, but what's wrong with that? I like you, not your masculinity. *Really?* Yes, I didn't fall in love with Julio's masculinity. And that seems very sexy to me. Are being attracted to and finding sexy the same thing? Julia's sensuality is, more than anything, in her attitude, but I didn't tell her any of this. I don't tell her anything.

Julia sends me photos of her outfits, of the new clothes and accessories, that's how our get-togethers started, sending each other snaps of combinations: Do you think these high-waist jeans suit me? Wow, I love how you look in yellow! Lace panties, black and ruby, fishnet tights, embroidered corsets, long skirts, cropped tops showing her belly button, her abdomen, bras in an intense purple; under my questioning, she admits that yes, yes, she stuffs them with cotton wool or socks, for now. Now watch out, she is and was much more than all that, much more than putting on heels or lipstick. But that's how Julia started out: with clothes, with accessories, physical changes, and play, yes, through that dynamic and play, with me and in front of me, she started shaping her personality, rediscovering herself. That's how we all start out, isn't it? She experienced her authentic initiation, her second adolescence.

I still don't feel very confident going out like this. There's no problem at home, especially because when I'm working they can only see my face. But you can't imagine how frustrating it is feeling free at home and having to change to go to the supermarket or buy food for my cats. I guess that's why she doesn't shave off the moustache, *keeping up appearances*. I send her an emoji of a mustachioed man. Hey, don't be mean.

A few days ago, she posted some stories of her nails painted blood red, showing off her crop top with her head cut off, out of the frame, just a body. A GIF of both genders mixed together. He/She. I reply with the heart-eyes emoji. We talk, she is beautiful.

I like her because I know that she's still him, well no, not him. Let me rephrase that: I like her because I know that she's still the same fun, lighthearted, and warm person; I can't resist her charms and at the same time I question myself, I can't help that either. Am I a lesbian or just bisexual or what's the difference? Trying to give myself a label to feel like I've got a grip on things just makes me feel more fragile.

What the fuck does it matter? How does she feel?

She doesn't talk about this much, ignores certain questions. I learned that the term transvestite is offensive and to not even mention it. The first and only time I did, she replied: I think it goes far beyond just dressing up as a woman. It's not a trend or a game or something fleeting. This is who I am.

Julia mentions it to her godmother, the only person in her family she dares to tell for now. The thing she had most trouble with was the idea that I'm really a lesbian. She struggled to understand that I'm a girl who likes girls and that my penis has nothing to do with how I feel. I'm a lesbian. Period. Did she get angry or anything? What did she say? Not at all, zero anger. She told me that she would understand in time, but that there were a ton of things that made sense now, sticker of an expressionless chihuahua. Like what? Wide eyes. She said I was always a little weird, well, no, mannered, and I always let my hair grow out, painted my nails, and things like that. That she used to think I did it because I was a metal-head or something. In fact, she took it really well. Are you okay, how do you feel? I'm okay. I was super nervous, but I had to do it, showing myself to the people who are most important to me is what will finally consolidate my transition, make it real. Sticker of a stick figure lifting a brick to kill himself.

One afternoon we gossiped about Jon, a friend from university, who, now he's living abroad, has become the drag queen Dulce Concepción, or Dulce Conchita to her friends, and puts on his best Argentine accent, sashaying from bar to bar. Nanda, you would die, I've never, ever seen him so happy in my life. Back there, there wasn't a hint; all toxic masculinity to go unnoticed. It's like, think about it, if even periods are still taboo, saying that you want to change or experiment with your gender is sacrilege, unthinkable, a sin. And people don't even talk about all this, I didn't know that trans or queer or non-binary people existed until I grew up, because we never spoke about any of that at school. Everything would have been so easy and different if they gave us this information when we were little.

Yes, exactly. Hey, do you remember that time at university when I had a tampon in my bag and the professor kept talking about how my cookie was on show and we were all like WTF? What cookie? Until we finally realized he meant the tampon. Yeah, of course I remember. It seemed ridiculous to us that he would get so offended by seeing a tampon. That professor was an old dinosaur. Imagine if he could see me now . . . No waaaaay, he'd die, plus he was a Jesuit. They'd probably take my degree away from me or something. Zombie emoji. We write hahaha though deep down it doesn't make us laugh, but that's what you do when you don't know what to do or say: laugh to pull your mouth upward rather than downward.

Amid all this novelty, we both face up to our desire and do things we never tried before. Sexting makes an appearance, and photos with fewer clothes, suggestive poses, and fingers touching. Desire emerges, pleasure, horniness, and fantasies. We look at each other's bodies for the first time because, back there, when he was Julio, our bodies never met. Sometimes we go days without speaking and others we can't stop writing to each other, needing to hear from one another.

No, my parents don't know. It's better to tell them in person, I think. Wise decision. She doesn't look too sure about this, seems doubtful; she's scared of rejection and that's understandable. That fear of rejection spreads like a cancer, forcing her to keep being Julio in person and only Julia on her phone, only in the virtual world, through a screen. *Julia only exists there*. And not even that, because Julio is still everywhere: the username and profile picture for every account, nicknames, avatars, and email addresses. Little by little, she starts to reveal certain things, but not going too far, not tempting those friends and followers prone to attacking and offending and demanding. Very few of us are going through this transition with her, for now.

She doesn't mind that I call her Julia. You're the only one who calls me that, the name I'd like to have. It's your name. Yours. Other times I forget, or I give in, and call her Julio and Julia interchangeably—most often Julia. Julia seems a thousand times prettier to me than Kima, one of the options she has in mind. Julio has more of a Julia face than a Kima face, and she agrees. Yeah, you're right, I don't feel like a Kima. I've always liked my name. At one point, I thought about having a totally different name to mark the change in me, leave that other me in the past. But I don't think he'll ever be completely in the past or forgotten about because, in some way, he's still me. I'm me. Don't you think? That's what people don't understand, that I'm still me. So yeah, Julia suits me well. And it's a way of, like, making it easier for my parents and everyone, keeping the name they gave me, right?

She sends me her first video walking down a street, at night, just a block, and then entering her apartment smiling and hyperventilating, bouncing. Haha, yeah, at the time I thought the video made everything perfectly clear, then I realized you almost can't see that I'm out *in production*. I went out again and it was much more relaxed, though I was still super nervous. Plus the night gets away from me, I overthink it, and I end up going out real late, which is more dangerous, next time I'm gonna go earlier. Emojis of dancing rabbits and painted nails. Purple heart emoji; tongue, fire, little devil.

Do you have any friends, do you go out and distract yourself? You need to make a group of friends and people you can trust. I have one trans friend, yeah. She's helping me a lot. We go out for coffee sometimes and talk and stuff. I see Dulce Conchita pretty often too. Sticker of a boy walking in heels.

Julia needs friends who keep her company, who give her love beyond a telephone screen, who are really there and can hold her hand and smile at her.

If you were here, I'd take you to my secret bookshop, then we'd go read poems on the grass in Montjuïc and later hit the mojitos and pinchos on Carrer de Blai. If you were here . . .

I feel a shiver down my spine. It doesn't seem real that all these feelings and sensations can flower so suddenly, just from a few messages, some calls. As if this impulse had been dormant, waiting to hear her voice, calling me. Every time my phone lights up and I see her name, the butterflies in my stomach swell.

One afternoon she asks me to do a tarot reading over video call. I grab my cards and think of Julia and Julio interchangeably. *Concentrate*—I give in to that intuition. I draw three cards: The Magician, The Sun, and Judgment. In my mind I see it all clearly, but it's difficult to express it, to put this feeling, this vision, into words. It's a challenge. They're good cards. The Magician seems dead-on, with those androgynous features, where you can't tell if it's really him or her, or both. That eagerness to incorporate everything: the elements, the opposites, the feminine and the masculine. The roses and the snake biting its own tail, the Ouroboros, the circle of life. The Sun, with the smiling boy, his arms open wide, accepting what will come: naked, with nothing to hide or to fear. The sunflower representing the fertility of the spirit. The rays of the sun offering warmth and light for the process of transformation. Judgment is the decisive card, the conclusion. People emerging from tombs, naked and arms outstretched, the angel playing a trumpet: rebirth, acceptance, profound reconciliation. What a powerful message, Nanda. Can you believe that's exactly how I feel? Look, my hairs are standing on end and everything, you're magic, she murmurs, staring into space, lost in her musings. I make a sucking noise and she laughs.

I remember Julia's kisses. No, Julio's. Soft, fleshy lips. Hands that took delicate hold of my head. Hands that grabbed me by the waist, lips that stretched out seeking my lips. I was always so evasive. *Gruff like my cats.* I don't remember anything about sex, because nothing happened. I wanted to, I don't know about him. The rumors and gossip that I considered my sources said that he was a virgin. An atheist teenage boy having nothing to do with sex. I didn't pay it any mind. I was left wanting and we slept in separate beds.

Could that have anything to do with it? Could Julia have anything to do with it? I'll never know because I'll never dare to ask. Julio was special, different. His introduction to music, my initiation into music and discovery of Mogwai and Sigur Rós. I'm only now realizing how difficult I found hanging out with him, the asphyxiating shyness that enveloped me in front of him because he left me speechless: I couldn't express my emotions, no physical closeness, always keeping my distance, never any hugs. Frigidity incarnate. Julio initiated me into the world of affection, of watching TV lying on someone's chest, falling asleep, of giving kisses and cuddles. Jesús, Ángel, Daniel, Sebastián, Alfredo, Matías, and Álex initiated me too. Every love requires an initiation, a similar but different ritual. Sitting on the roof of his house and looking at the stars in the clear sky of the Caribbean until it got too cold and the stairs refused to carry me back down. My fear and his arms, his tall, warm body. Julio still makes me wet even though nothing happened when really everything happened. Those fleeting loves, the ones you don't take any notice of because they begin in such a spontaneous way; as if the magic of the ideal partner carried within it the seed of the break-up. I don't know about Julia. But then she's still that person, that fascinating and stubborn and funny and caring and creative and divinely intelligent human being. Does Julia have a different essence from Julio or is essence something that doesn't change? I feel the same with her, I still have the same fondness and affection.

Yesterday a dress she bought arrived and she quickly sent me a picture of her mind-blowing new treasure, with pockets. A long, strappy dress, greenish-gray. She pairs it with her red Converse. Her hair is already down to her shoulders. She won't take her mask off, why not? *I want to see your face!* It doesn't matter what you look like. I'm really comfortable. You're beautiful, breathtaking.

Our relationship feels like best friends who are in love with each other, best friends who share facial mask recipes while they talk about what they think and feel with no restrictions. If I couldn't express myself with Julio because I felt self-conscious, with Julia it's been an unprecedented unfurling of honesty and authenticity. I think none of my friends knows me like she does and I've never spoken with any of them about the things I talk about with her.

She spends more and more time with Gabi, who in turn has introduced her to other friends, it wouldn't be possible for her to keep going without these relationships. We all need each other. Now she's more confident, more self-assured, she posts sassy stories, she has even spoken a little about what she's experiencing. Every time she shows more of herself, of that new her who has always been there. She takes off her mask for the first time, little by little, and reveals her true self. I watch the transformation of her body like someone witnessing the blossoming of a flower, the budding of fruit; the evolution from pupa to butterfly, a Dryas iulia, *the flame butterfly*. And at the same time as I contemplate the natural course of this change, I dig my fingers into my beliefs and ways of loving, I question myself but don't give myself any answers because feelings say more than any definition. She's still the same person, she's always been her. There is no distinction between them, except for appearances, the shell. You, Julia, are a butterfly with the name of a butterfly. A photo of the Dryas iulia she found on Google is now her screen background.

Julia forwards me a message from her parents. They say they support her and they'll always love her, they need to know if those photos she's been posting, those comments she has shared, and the general change in look are due to: 1. A phase linked to some trend or something fleeting. 2. A change in sexual preference. 3. A total or partial change in gender. And yeah, they sent it exactly like that, because that's how her parents are, methodical, rigid people; they don't have shades of gray, only black or white. She sends this on after a few voice notes I haven't listened to yet and I don't know how to reply. I'm nervous because I know she must be scared to death. I close my eyes with my phone in my hands. I see her mom drinking coffee and painting watercolors out on their terrace—attractive, fun, and affectionate. The similarity to Julia is obvious. I can't fully visualize her father, but I know I liked him, he was funny, making quick and witty comments. She replies yes, it's due to a change in gender. Then they have a long video call, with some tears, and when we next talk, a few days later, she feels light; even her face is brighter. She tells me she's decided to start the whole process to be prescribed hormones; we celebrate. Clinking glasses emoji, chin-chin.

Gabi tells me that some girls have a kind of goodbye party for their former selves, but I don't think I need to say goodbye to myself. I'm satisfied with who I am and that I'm doing this at this moment. Do you realize that the next time we see each other I could well be different? Bomb emoji. Yeah, of course. And it'll be great, like meeting each other for the first time again. Are you happy? Very happy, and also very nervous and anxious about everything that's coming. Flamenco dancer emoji.

I do say my goodbyes, in my head. I remember the times we spent together and I'm back with him at the viewpoint he took me to for the first time, with beautiful, unfathomable views. *His shyness was my shyness.* Seeking me and planting a kiss on me despite his fear. I didn't reach for him because I am evasive, but I wanted him so much. One touch more would have been enough, a hand squeezing my thigh, a breath on my neck. *We slept in separate rooms.* He didn't seek me, I didn't seek him. This weighs on me and I keep it to myself. My adolescent spirit, that internal fire, languished. I lost interest: I wanted something wilder, something that over time would end up destroying me a little. A certain domination, hands on my ass, maybe bondage. All those fantasies hidden in my smile, my acting introverted. Plus, he was leaving. From the start, the rule was to not get my hopes up, to not fall in love, because he was leaving.

His departure hurt me. At least I ghosted him and didn't have to say goodbye. Everyone was leaving at that time, it was the start of our great migration; like the monarch butterfly. It's tough to watch us leave with such fragile wings. I cut myself off from that emotion, the feeling of abandonment; I covered it up with fluids and books. Julio left me small treasures in our language. I left him a painting with a secret message, impossible to read unless you opened the canvas and took apart the frame.

There are so many things from him in me that some-times I feel part of him, well, her. So many memories and objects buried by the yearning for something that eluded me. *Enough.*

It still hurts me that he didn't look for me that night, that he didn't sleep with me. Salt in the wound. More time-wasting. This cold fish can't help asking herself if there wasn't something more. Beyond dysphoria, gender. I know there wasn't, but I still fantasize, what if it were something physical? My morbid side imagines intersex genitals that increased his shyness and sexual inhibition. His abject fear of rejection, of the gaze that renders him invisible. *Why didn't he confide in me?* He probably sensed, felt, my carnal intentions, my hunger for secretions and spankings. *Maybe he didn't even want to do it.*

What Julio didn't give me I looked for in many others, never finding it. We were fleeting. If Julio and I didn't really understand each other, with Julia there's another level of understanding; one that starts from the complicity of being women, the history that joins us and the desire that remains intact despite the years and the distance.

For a few weeks now, Julia has been living entirely as a woman, it's part of what she has to do to access the hormone treat-ment. The changes are notable even without the hormones and, though it's unbelievable, I feel like she's more herself than ever. She doesn't have facial hair anymore, her hair is halfway down her back, she wears makeup and perfume, she changed all her profile pictures, accounts, and avatars, as well as her name and email address, and she even told work that from now on she is Julia.

It's true, we don't write to each other every day like before, but we keep each other in mind. I'm infected with her vibrant joy, her confidence, her decisiveness. Now and then, she goes out with friends and writes to me a little buzzed, the waiters are calling me ma'am, haha. Or sometimes an: I want to see you, I need to see you, I miss you. She says she is going to organize a trip over here, that she wants to spend time with me; she needs to know whether what we're feeling holds up when we're face to face, *we can't carry on like this, I love you.*

So many things shout inside me, so many repressed and uncommunicated feelings. I'm afraid and I write because it's the only thing that calms me down and allows me to be honest. It's only in writing that I can find myself, only words return my reflection. What can I write to her, then? I fantasize about writing something like:

Dear Julia,

Once upon a time, or rather, I was once sitting in an empty park (Los Caobos) opposite the love of my life. I didn't know it then. They read my palm, sliding their fingers along the lines, saying only nonsense. Do you remember? Inventions that I believed in that moment. There are souls possessed of absorbing, magical eyes. I think I remember that my great love had, in turn, their own great love. A very passionate relationship. I wanted to be the great love of my love, but I was afraid to take it on: the quivering in my belly and pangs in my diaphragm. The hunger. The insatiable thirst between my legs. With my great love, I learned to savor the world unsugared, to face its unadulterated flavor, to experience it. (Thank you for that.) My great love took me to the sacred mountain, the highest one, and showed me its waterfalls; raging, rejuvenating water. We drank from that water and explored paths flooded with green. My great love gave me the gift of museums, the Teresa Carreño, and, among plazas and crowds, kissed me. My great love drank cocuy at my side, lighting me on fire with their gaze and waiting for me while I bought books from the stalls outside Bellas Artes. My great love, in the most romantic style and like in the stories, spoke in a voice of velvet and during the protests rescued me from the university, crossing the minefield that was the highway. My great love took me on journeys, with the afternoon in the windscreen, sharing cigarettes in conversations that lasted all day and all night. My great love taught me how to dance tango and read me fragments of Japanese stories. Looked for me in the corridors of classrooms and drew dogs on my exam papers. My great love was already my great love and I didn't understand. Did you understand, by some chance? There was nothing to understand, everything was a question of feeling. I didn't want to feel and I paralyzed myself, frightened to death I distanced myself from my great love, I gave myself over to the emptiness of hundreds of faces. I am sorry.

I'd write something like that, although I'd never show her.

How are you Dryas Iulia? I haven't heard from you in days. I've been low because my mom wasn't all that comfortable with our conversation about changing gender and it bummed me out for a few days. But now I feel better, I think we've both been getting over it little by little. It's understandable. I take a while to reply. Do you want me to call you? Bear in mind that she'll also need time and space, in their own way your folks are transitioning too.

Our conversations have dwindled, we went from long and intense paragraphs to sharing emojis and funny videos. I think that's how we avoid each other, with diversions.

I'm waiting for work to confirm if they'll give me the days off I'm owed, although I can work from anywhere really; this way I'll be totally free. Do you want to see me as much as I want to see you? Of course I do. I'm peeing myself with excitement. Purple heart emoji and the monkey covering its mouth.

In Barcelona I retrace her steps and look for the flowers and cactuses she planted years ago when she lived here, leaving me the exact coordinates for this multidimensional encounter. Years later, she would tell me her tattoo had been for me. Did I get any tattoos thinking of her, in honor of her memory? I got a piercing the day she left me in Plaza Altamira, the last time we saw each other. She didn't know it, I made the decision as I was getting out of the car, with a fish tank in my throat threatening to flood my eyes.

I walked to San Ignacio and on the middle floor, where all the tattoo parlors are, I got my ear pierced. It hurt more than the tattoos. I saw the piece of skin pushed out by the needle. I didn't cry; I enjoyed it.

A strong sensation to get over a crushing emotion.

The need to provoke physical pain to relieve an emotional pain. My tattoos and piercings have the names and surnames of the experiences and people who shape me, she said once, and I agreed with her because it was the same for me. But not even the pain from the piercing could quench my thirst.

After the piercing, I wrote to my ex, who lived a few blocks away. He was home alone. I went over and we fucked. We filmed ourselves with his professional camera from university, I asked him to. When it was over, with a cigarette in my hand and standing butt naked at the window, I was surprised by my animal action, by that impulse that came from deep within me. I felt embarrassed and left. Whenever I touch the piercing, I think about him. *About her*.

That was my goodbye.

She doesn't know about any of this and I don't know if I should tell her. How I felt with him and why I fled. *The fugitive*. The song she would dedicate to me a few years later precisely for that reason, for vanishing, for disappearing. Now I feel like Julia has become my best friend, could we be lovers?

I question myself because my past with Julio constrains me. I give in to desire and to love because I know that she is him and he was always her. Is that wrong?

I can't delete or change my memories; nor do I want to. I love her because nobody ever made me feel this way and even with all this time and the sea and the mountains between us, she still makes me feel the same and even better, and all through a screen. What will our re-encounter be like? My phone vibrates and her name appears. My heart skips a beat and I bite my thumb.

FROM SAVAGERY

As of today, María Eugenia has been in Barcelona for a year. *Already? So soon?* She looks back, thinks about everything that has happened this year, and feels a little dazed. Is she still the same person she was? No. Instagram reminds her what she was doing on this day, one year ago; she doesn't recognize herself in those photos, in that face which has changed so much. *I'm still the same, but different.* How could she be the same but different? She didn't understand it either, but that's how she felt, and that was enough. *Everything that's happened has led me to where I am now, my new me.*

She's sitting out on the apartment's small balcony; spring is crossing the street, and all the balconies are starting to open up along with the flowers. People are beginning to spend time on their balconies, on terraces. She watches the sun set over the city that welcomed her, remembers the prayer on her lips as soon as the plane touched the ground, to not leave, to not give up, *bless you Barcelona, fruitful land which will make me fruitful.*

Her hairs stand on end. In the distance, she sees smoke rising; the city is in a frenzy, as is she. For days now, there have been protests and demonstrations calling for freedom: freedom for political prisoners, freedom for singers, freedom of expression. *We're not so different after all.* She's ambivalent about the protests themselves. Who is she to judge political matters in this country? There's much she still doesn't know and she's not interested in learning, at least not now. What does frustrate her are the limits on movement; streets closed off and Mossos d'Esquadra all over.

She dunks a María cookie in milky coffee, eats with relish, and finishes her drink. It's dawn for her, even though the sun is about to disappear. For the last few days, she has been working from five in the afternoon until the early hours. Last night, she got home at three. She slept a while and woke up at nine thirty to deliver for three hours, until one. She went home, ate whatever she could find, and lay down to sleep until now. She likes the days more and more, thanks to the warm weather and the light lasting until eight at night. The winter had a devastating effect on her mood: alone in an unfamiliar country, without many friends, used to the heat of the coast, to the light that's always the same, unshakeable. Now she has more energy, more will to face the daily grind.

She dresses and leaves at four. Sara is on the sofa, typing at her laptop. Around her are empty bags of chips and chocolate wrappers.

Later you'll complain you've got acne, María Eugenia says, taking a block of chocolate from her. Oh, but I'm leading a campaign this week and it's making me super anxious, chama. What about healthy eating, exercise, and all that? Well, if I screw up once eating crap it's no big deal. It's not like I do it every day.

That's true. María Eugenia fills her water flask, grabs an apple too, in case she has any time to eat it waiting for an order.

You're not really going to work today are you, the day of your Barna-versary? Sara asks, tearing her eyes away from the screen. We've gotta celebrate, even if it's just a glass of wine, right? No way, Sara. Don't be stupid. Celebrate what? Today's just another day. Don't be bitter, party pooper. When you get back we're having a glass of wine and that's final, she says, her voice firm. She types a couple more things. In November, it'll be six years for me. Time flies, doesn't it? Yeah, it's scary, María Eugenia puts on her helmet. Right, I'm off. See you later. Okay, good luck. I'll wait up, I'm not working tomorrow. Cool, bye.

She catches the last glimmers of sun on the buildings, the golden hour. In that light, everything seems special, like on the point of defining a decisive moment, an epiphany. She takes a photo of a balcony, which, in her opinion, has the prettiest windows in the neighborhood; and it's bursting with flowers. *I'd have my balcony as pretty as that too.*

She bikes to McDonald's and stays on the corner, waiting. There's a group of riders at the entrance, but she's not in the mood to go over and socialize or be nice. The sound of money chimes in her hand. She waits a few minutes, giving them time to prepare a burger and fries. She leans her bike on a pole and goes in to collect the bag. Order 1065! shouts a teenager with a greasy face and María Eugenia shows her phone so she'll hand over the bag. She puts it straight in her backpack, which is still over her shoulder. She briefly remembers Diego and his confession: he sometimes steals fries from orders.

Do you think they're gonna notice if you take three or four fries? María Eugenia kept arguing against him, furious. You can't take advantage like that. Oh, please! Don't start with me, you know damn well I'm not the only one doing it, that's how it is. Are you telling me if someone orders eleven nuggets, you're not gonna take even one? Course not, dumbass.

She didn't debate much more. Every rider had their own circumstances and their own demons: delivering all day with a rumbling stomach, for example. Well, you do you, I still think it's totally wrong. She was sore at Diego for a few days until she got over it; she wasn't going to cast aside almost ten years of friendship for some fries that weren't even hers.

The app reveals the address, toward Sants. She doesn't understand how the order came to her when there are other McDonald's near the address. *Could there be too much demand?* She ambles down Avenida Madrid, crosses at Carrer de Galileu, looks closely at all the numbers even though the app tells her that she hasn't arrived yet, that there are a few blocks to go. The address says she has to deliver to number 96 and she's already there, but the app is showing something else. There's probably a glitch. She really doesn't like calling customers, but she's got no choice. She takes a couple of deep breaths before dialing the number. *Okay, enough, don't be stupid and call already.* Hey, how are you? I've got your delivery, I just wanted to check if the building number is 96. Okay, perfect. Yes, I'm here. She presses the intercom; they open up for her, she leaves her bike in the vestibule and goes up to the third floor. The door is closed so she rings the bell. She hears noises inside and waits, lifting her heels a few times until the door opens.

Hey, good evening, she splutters like a recording. A stout woman appears, much taller than her and with a beard. A chestnut beard, thick and well kempt. The woman's eyes are blue, very shiny. María Eugenia hides her surprise, but can't take her eyes off the beard. I've got your order. Thanks, the woman replies. She doesn't seem the slightest bit surprised that it's a girl delivering and not Álex from the photo. I need you to sign here, please. The woman signs and smiles at her. A line of perfect white teeth. Thanks. Thank you, bye. Bye. No tip.

She takes a few spins around Sants to see what happens. More female riders come out at night, the majority on scooters, with their backpacks on their backs too. She doesn't know why there are more women at night, she thinks maybe more than one works during the day and moonlights as a rider, *could be. Maybe they feel safer? No, I don't feel safer at night. Well, there are fewer cars and people, that's true.* She cycles to the station and waits again in the McDonald's; another order comes in and she delivers it a few blocks away. People's laziness continues to astound her. *Why can't they walk a block to get food?* A KFC comes in and she has to go a little farther toward Hospitalet.

Next, she picks up sushi from a Doner Kebab. If she's learned one thing as a rider it's that restaurants are never what they seem. More than once she's looked for the name of a place in the app and the pictures look good, appetizing, but in real life it's another story. She would never think to eat sushi from a kebab place.

The stop light brings her to a halt; she's bored, drumming her fingers on the handlebars, hoping she gets a good order or at least that someone gives her a tip. At the pedestrian crossing she sees a woman who seems familiar, *where have I seen her before?* A short, white woman, maybe in her forties or fifties. She flicks through her mental archive until she comes up with the information. Cristina? Is that you, Cristina?

The woman, with thinning hair tied in a ponytail, turns toward her. María Eugenia is still pondering the name. No, love, she replies, her voice is thick, she's a heavy smoker. I'm Va . . . Vanessa! María Eugenia exclaims. Yes, yes, the woman who was in the ATM in Camp Nou, right? Yeah, Vanessa nods, but I ain't stayin' there no more. Since they attacked me I'm stayin' in hostels or hotels.

What do you mean, they attacked you? I went by a few times to give you food, but I didn't see you again, María Eugenia says. One or two days after I met you, a bloke got into the booth an' attacked me. He tried to do more an' when he couldn't, the right bastard, he grabbed my tin of tobacco an' ran off, that son of a bitch, you know? That dickhead. No way! But are you okay? Do you need anything? Vanessa snorts, indignant. I'm fine, but what really stings is that he was Spanish, a lad who couldn't have been more than thirty, for God's sake.

María Eugenia nods, she knows Vanessa doesn't mean any harm, but then what, the only people who can rob and attack are Moroccans and Latinos?

Can't you report it? Look, I'm done with reporting, she shakes her hands. The police just say I ain't got enough bruising on my neck to prove he was stranglin' me, what about this an' that, I'm done with it all. In the end, they don't do nothin', they ain't got a clue, you know? So, now you're staying in hostels? Yes, love, I am. I try an' get there early so they give me a bed. If not, I stay in hotels when I can. Or at a client's house.

María Eugenia wants to ask her what she does for work, but she keeps quiet. *What clients?* She gets up onto the pavement with Vanessa, the light has already changed. I'm always in the Entre Tapes bar too, you know? Over on Carrer de Sants, right by the Badal metro station. I'm always there. An' if not, you ask for Sandra, a blonde who works there, she's like a sister to me. Okay, will do, she replies. Do you like to read? I can leave books for you, or paper if you like to write, whatever. Sure, love, sure. Look, what I like is action. Any kind of crime fiction, detective stories. None of that romantic crap, okay? I don't care about none of that. Murder mysteries, Agatha Christie style, you know? Yep, got it, María Eugenia nods, smiling. Well, it's good to see you, Vanessa. You too, love, remember the Tapes bar. Of course.

She pedals away. She can't believe that Vanessa was attacked. *What the fuck are they going to steal from a woman living on the street?* She didn't have anything of value beyond a packet of cigarettes. Being a woman and living on the street is like being walking bait. Maybe everyone else thinks she's in the public domain, a common good, that they can try to rape her and nothing will happen. *And it's true, nothing will happen, because she is a nobody.*

One of María Eugenia's biggest fears is ending up homeless. Having to sleep in the street, for whatever reason. That first time must be terrifying; being utterly defenseless, using your bag as a pillow. Every time she sees someone setting up an ATM booth to make it their bedroom for the night, she feels a knot in her stomach. *Any one of us could be in the same situation at any time.* The great majority of the homeless people she sees are men. That's why when she saw Vanessa, disinfecting the floor of the ATM booth where she stretched out her mat and sleeping bag, she couldn't help going over. She knocked on the glass and Vanessa smiled, waving her in; she probably thought that she wanted to take out some cash.

Come in, love, come in, she said as she opened the door. No, don't worry, I don't need to use the machine, María Eugenia said, holding up her bike with a hand. Are you okay? Do you need water or food? No dear, I'm fine right now. I ate at some friends' house, all good. What about tomorrow, do you have anywhere to eat? I don't know about tomorrow yet, she said, half-smiling. María Eugenia saw that her lower teeth were darkened from tobacco. Look, I'm usually here around quarter to ten or half nine. By this time, I'm here, settlin' in. Okay, I can try to stop by around this time and drop off something for you. Thanks, love. I'm Vanessa, pleased to meet you. María Eugenia, and because she didn't know what else to say, though at the same time she had so many questions she wanted to ask her, she decided to say goodbye. Well, see you this time tomorrow. Okay, love, yes, around quarter to ten or so.

María Eugenia had left feeling somewhat satisfied. The next night, she couldn't stop by because she was assigned deliveries toward Badalona and didn't have time to cross to the other end of the city. She felt guilty, and when she returned over the following days with sandwiches and cigarettes, she didn't see her again. Now she knew where to find her. She would try to look in goodwill stores and recycling centers for crime fiction and action novels.

The night is buzzing, unlike the preceding days when she spent more than an hour waiting. The only bad thing is she doesn't get any tips. That's the way it goes sometimes, days and days without tips and then multiple customers on the same day or in the same week spare a few coins.

It's completely dark now, there are fewer people in the street. Her phone sounds for the fifth time: Pollos Ricox. María Eugenia already knows where it is because she's had to pick up food there before and, if she's not wrong and trusts her gut, she also knows where she has to take the order. There are some repeat customers. They're unusual in that they take a long time to serve and they also treat riders very poorly; they don't let them sit outside, they ask them not to gather at the entrance, to spread along the pavement, and all of these commands are barked at them. She takes the opportunity to eat her apple while she waits.

On the corner, there's a small group of riders talking and laughing; they have a speaker and their music permeates everything, a Héctor Lavoe song that María Eugenia hums along to, though she doesn't really know it. At last, they hand over her order and she checks the address. Yes, she does know the place. She has to head toward Camp Nou. Just in front of the stadium there's a very pretty building, with rejas that look like entwined bows, that's where the hookers work. Some of them. Others are set up on the street that leads to the stadium, and many more are spread out toward the university zone. María Eugenia doesn't know if there's any kind of hierarchy, although she thinks those in the building must be the classiest because they don't work out in the street. She assumes clients come to the building and then leave. They're all friendly and they always tip. The vast majority, like those working the street, are Latinas.

When she reaches the building, she gets down from her bike and rings the bell, taking the chance to take out the fried chicken combos. One of the girls opens, she has seen her before, she knows because she wears a white wig, straight hair all the way down to her thighs. She has fake breasts and a waist like a wasp and she always leaves behind a pleasant scent, like lavender. Hi! Oh, check it! You're the same girl from before ain't ya? Haha, what're the chances? she greets her effusively.

María Eugenia is sure she told her her name at some point, but she can't remember it right now. The name that appears on the order belongs to another woman, that much she does remember. Seems like you're the only one deliverin' around here, right? Yep, it's me, it's me. It's a total coincidence, nothing more. She holds out the bags of chicken and the woman leaves them on the stairs. It's one of those duplexes where the stairs to the second floor are right in front of the door. Thanks, hon'. Here, she hands over some coins. Thanks so much, enjoy! She closes the door and María Eugenia decides to bike around Camp Nou.

She goes all the way up Avenida Arístides Maillol and then skirts the stadium along Avenida de Joan XXIII. There's a promenade with grass and flowers; she doesn't smoke anymore, but she used to stop there to smoke a cigarette or have a few tokes on a canuto, as she has learned to call a joint. She doesn't carry anything on her, only water. There, farther along, there's always a man waiting. He's a giant, at least six feet tall. María Eugenia doesn't understand what he does there all alone and she imagines that he looks after some of the girls who work that street.

The avenue is empty and silent, apart from the voices of the women; they laugh and chat, down mini-bottles of alcohol between each joke. She looks to the left, to that green area where she used to enjoy a break, until in the full light of day she discovered it was littered with condoms, tissues with red and brown stains, paper, plastic, dog shit, and human shit. The place lost its allure and not even the prettiest flowers would make her stop there now.

She remembers how naive she was a year ago and can't believe how much she has changed, how much she's been through. *It seems like more than a year.*

This area was her favorite when she started delivering, about a month after she landed. After compulsively sending out résumés and being rejected every time for not having papers, she decided to pedal. She liked the place because it was secluded, there were several in-demand restaurants, and, oddly, there weren't many riders. She discovered that she was most likely to end up taking orders to Hospitalet, which could run into Sant Boi, Cornellà, or El Prat: far away, very far for her.

On one of those first nights, when she felt invincible and safe in this first world country, she stopped right on that grassy mound to her left, next to those flowers surrounded by condoms and those large pines whose branches swung from side to side. It was summer and she was shocked by how hot it was, even at night; the place was refreshing. She decided to have a smoke, send some messages, relax for a while. She was standing, laughing at a meme someone had sent her, when she saw headlights approaching down the avenue; the sixth sense she developed in Caracas made her tense up. She saw it was just a regular car and relaxed for a few seconds until the car started to brake and pulled over in front of her. María Eugenia looked around; there was no one. *I'm so stupid! How could I stand here in this deserted place? I must be an idiot.* She threw the cigarette to the ground and trod on it several times with her rubber-soled bambas.

Hey! a man's voice shouted from the car. María Eugenia leaned over to see better. It was a young guy, maybe around thirty, dressed in office wear. Hey, you! he shouted again, with the tone of a despot who knows he is powerful. Seeing that he was alone in the car, she decided to approach with caution. She didn't go all the way toward him, but now close to him, she replied. Hello, yes? The man looked her over for a few seconds, long enough for María Eugenia to feel the hairs on the back of her neck stand on end. Do you know where El Corte Inglés is? *Oh, he's lost.* Yeah, yeah, of course. You've gotta go back up, head up, and then make a left. If you follow Diagonal, you'll see it there on the right. She said all this while signaling with her arms and indicating where he had to go, proud of knowing her way around after so little time. And do you know where La Caixa is? the man asked again. She thought about it for a few seconds and this time, subconsciously, got closer to the car. You have to go down and head straight along this street, it's on the left, she replied, once again demonstrating the way with her arms. What about the town hall? sighed the man.

Oof, she had no idea. She rolled her eyes for a few seconds to analyze her mental map, but the town hall wasn't on it. And in that fraction of time when she looked up and to the left to think, she spotted out of the corner of her eye a weird, unusual movement. She snapped her head back to witness how the man was stroking his hand up and down, jerking himself off. She blinked with surprise and, to her rage, stammered the only thing that came to her in that moment: Oh, sorry.

As if she were the guilty party. When inside she wanted to scream at him: *Disgusting, pervert!* But no, with all the phrases that were swirling in her head, her lips remained empty. The fear paralyzed not just her body, but her voice.

Hey you! Bloody whore. Get over here, you slut. She moved away from the car, her hands shaking and sweaty. She grabbed the bike as best she could and tried to get on it, but the car was still there, alongside the pavement and, for the first time, she was aware of the terror she felt. Yes, terror. At once, she felt so vulnerable, in the middle of this place that she really didn't know beyond what Google Maps told her. She didn't have an emergency contact or anyone she could turn to. She didn't even know the number for the police in this country. *How could I not know that? What the fuck am I doing here alone when I'm always told to avoid isolated places?* The man kept shouting things at her and she ignored him. She decided the best thing was to leave right away and, even though fear was still making her clumsy, she set off down the avenue, propelled by her own weight.

She thought she was safe, the pressure in her chest was beginning to dissipate, when the car accelerated and started to gain on her. She was forced to pass by its side again and didn't know what to do. She stopped for a few seconds that seemed like minutes, waiting to see if the car would move on, but no. *I'm not moving from here, he can move.*

She grabbed her phone as if it were a gun, her only weapon, and started to film. *I've got your license plate, you sick fuck. And if anything happens to me, I'm going to report you. Okay, but can I make a report without papers? What if they ask me why I was here so late, what I was doing? What happens when they ask for my ID and I only show them the card I laminated myself? What if they send me back when they see I'm here illegally? What if they arrest me and not him?* She was super nervous; as she remembers everything that happened then, she gets the same feeling in her stomach, in her chest, that nausea emanating from every corner of her body. The man turned on the light inside the car and she saw that he had his hands up, as if apologizing. Sorry, eh? I thought you were one of them, I'm sorry, he shouts in the same tone as before.

She felt her heart in her mouth. *What does one of them mean? Who are they? Is any woman who might be out alone in the early hours one of them? And what if I were one of them, huh? What happens then? Does every woman alone in the street in the early hours have to endure these goddam creeps?* A million thoughts crossed her mind. She pedaled slowly, ignoring him; she was so afraid that she couldn't think forward to what she would do if he decided to get out of the car. Flee on her bike? Run? Scream? Or even worse, if he rammed her with his car.

After a time, she couldn't say how long, a moment that seemed to go on forever, the car accelerated and he took off, leaving her with a metallic taste in her mouth; she had bitten her tongue so hard that it was bleeding. It was her anchor to reality, a way not to let herself be consumed by panic. *Calm down, calm down. We're getting out of here now.* She couldn't give herself the luxury of letting her guard down anywhere, no matter where she found herself; first or third world, men are the same all over.

That scene plays in her mind for the time it takes her to cross the avenue on her bike, now more aware of the dangers she faces for being a woman and being alone. In the end, her mom was right with all her warnings. She looks at the flowers with nostalgia. Some girls wave as she passes, and she waves back. When she used to smoke, she sometimes shared cigarettes with them, just to talk with other women. The hookers were friendly. Nobody asked probing questions, they just shared jokes, were kind and funny. There everyone, including her, was just passing through. María Eugenia let herself be wrapped up in their laughter and their joy, which could well have been a false or drunken joy, but she didn't care in that moment. When she felt sad and she was in the area, she knew that stopping by there meant a guaranteed laugh, even more so if she gave them cigarettes.

Before Camp Nou, she had never spoken to prostitutes. She is transported back to that day, many years ago, when she was in her youngest uncle's car, where, in the company of her cousins, she became aware of the existence of prostitutes on Avenida Libertador. She was about seven or eight and her other uncle, the elder one, had taken his own life. A bullet straight to the head. After the wake, the youngest uncle took all the cousins to Wendy's; that was the last time they were all together. And even though the death of their uncle was hanging over them, she remembers it as a fun and happy moment for having spent time with her cousins, playing with the toys from the Kids Meals, and because her uncle decided to grant the wish of the eldest cousin, who at that time was around fifteen, and go show him the prostitutes. They stopped at a light and, windows down, had their first glimpse of the semi-naked women who walked in towering heels, their glittery eyeshadow and silvery smiles, their graceful movements. Their strange voices, or so it seemed to her at age seven. Women with a smile stamped onto their faces.

When she came across them farther on, after the gross jerk-off had driven away, she discovered the meaning of the phrase I thought you were one of them. Did she really seem like one of those girls? If she was wearing athletic gear, had a bike and a yellow bag on her back? When they appeared in front of her, she had to stop and have a smoke. She watched them. These women weren't as naked as the ones she remembered from Caracas. *The climate, duh.* They did wear short and skin-tight dresses, a ton of makeup, lots of perfume. One of the girls came over and asked her for a smoke. She couldn't help telling her the story of the masturbation, her hands still shaking, emphasizing her outfit and her delivery backpack.

The girl stared at her for a few seconds, she seemed to be processing all the information and finally she burst out laughing; a guttural wrap-around sound. María Eugenia, almost automatically, joined the laughter and for a moment enjoyed the blind euphoria of laughing for the sake of it.

Oh, you poor girl. Sure, all men are pigs, don't you worry about it. Look, you know that around here, if you come back, you'll never ever be alone. All you gotta do is shout and one of us'll come out from here. We're always here, alright? Yep, you don't gotta worry. We're always here, come rain, thunder, or snow.

She remembers her velvet laugh and smiles. *They're always so good and so kind.* Talking to those girls by Camp Nou caused an abrupt change in her perception of prostitutes. At first, she saw them as victims, as women with no other option who let themselves be violated for money. But it turns out she was wrong, most of the women out there are prostitutes because they want to be, nobody is forcing them and they don't see themselves as victims, nor as women who need saving.

Walking along Avenida Joan XXIII after nine at night is like walking along Libertador, and even though it's much later and much colder than over there, María Eugenia closes her eyes, cycling blind down the avenue which she knows is empty. She pretends she's on the other side of the Atlantic. She keeps pedaling and imagines that she is leaving behind the Previsora buildings, then the Vallés funeral home and La Campiña. She hears the fleeting conversations of the girls on the pavement and their frugal laughter; their accents transport her. The cool air hits her face, she feels free. María Eugenia is still amazed by the things and situations that make her feel at home. The most unlikely things, the ones she never really gave any importance to. Is that how memory works?

Does it boil down to this?

A car appears ahead and dazzles her. She returns to the present and puts aside her daydreams. *Things are going well here now. But I think so much about going back that . . . Over there I couldn't think about anything but leaving, and here I can't think about anything but going back.* Yes, the hookers are still there and farther along there's still the giant man, even though it's a year since she first discovered this route. Time seems to have stood still and simultaneously feels more violent. She can't believe everything she has done in a year, all the friendships put aside, and the new responsibilities born of necessity. Over the year, there is little she has cried about and much she has swallowed, kept quiet, put up with: now, all of a sudden, she feels like she's getting misty-eyed. *That's just great, Marugenia. Now you're gonna lose your shit over the Camp Nou hookers?*

It's almost one a.m.; she's drowsy and the silence isn't helping. She has discovered that she likes the silence in these nocturnal hours. Her thoughts flow when there's no noise, she's much more attentive to what is around her, more active. Pedaling in silence is the closest thing to meditation. She's spacey, dragging her feet on the pedals, still fantasizing about streets that are similar but not the same, when at last her phone wakes her with the *bum-ba-da-dáh-da da-da-dáh-da.*

Surprise, surprise, it's a special order: she has to go to an address that the app places in Poble Sec to pick up something she'll have to take elsewhere. She's never had something like this before, but they pay better than several orders combined. That fires her up and she quickly leaves Camp Nou behind. *Goodbye pretend Previsora and beloved hookers of the new Libertador.*

Today she is not going to let the pain in her legs beat her, or let fatigue bring her down; nor that voice note from her parents that she still hasn't listened to, probably saying how proud they are, that now she has had three hundred and sixty-five days proving to herself that she can do it, that it's difficult but not impossible. Of course, her mom will have said that she should give thanks to the universe and that she will soon be rewarded.

But with what, what are the rewards?

She pedals until she feels heat in her calves and, even then, she keeps going and keeps going until she reaches Avenida Parallel. The pain consolidates until it disappears. *Now straight on until Poble Sec.* What might she have to do at this small hour? What kind of person sends a special delivery at this time? *Don't be scared, dumbass.*

She catches a light, checks her phone and, still not replying to her parents, opens the chat with Cheo, who has just sent her a photo: him, Diego, Andrés, Nacho, Keiber, and the guys' roommate, a Catalan who has a very common name here that she can't remember right now. They're sticking their tongues out displaying tiny pieces of paper on the tips. She imagines them screaming like in Scary Movie. Get over here, the message read, with emojis of a little plant, a cyclist, a beer, and the devil. She smiles. She's about to reply when another message arrives. Invite your roomies if you want. Nanda's coming too. Flamenco dancer emoji. You're being so bad, she replies. As soon as I finish this order, I'm on my way.

Sticker of a girl in sunglasses giving two thumbs up. You said it. Emoji of several guns, bang bang bang.

She needs to go to Carrer d'Elkano. It's a small building and the walls are stained. She has to go up to the first floor. She enters and searches for the porch light with the flashlight on her phone; the bulb illuminates a narrow corridor and some rickety old stairs. Balancing her bike on her shoulder, she goes up and rings the bell. Nothing. She rings again and counts before going to ring once more. As she reaches out a finger to press one last time, the door opens. Before her is a hunk of a guy; blond, topless. As a reflex, she takes a few steps back; the man's gaze intimidates her, she feels uncomfortable before his nudity and his eyes. His cold stare. Her voice wobbles when she speaks.

Hi, good evening. I've come for a special order. What do I need to take? As soon as she's said it, she feels ridiculous; it often happens to her, especially when she's in front of male clients. Sasha turns his head and makes a quick movement, as if he were calling someone. For a moment, María Eugenia thinks he's going to say something about her usurped identity, she takes another step backward, ready to run if need be. She hears footsteps and Nataly comes out, holding a small gift bag.

Hi, how are you? Yep, this is it. She holds the bag out to María Eugenia, who grabs it without hesitation. And the direction? María Eugenia briefly thinks she's asking her, but before she can react, Sasha replies with something she doesn't understand and Nataly repeats, patient and firm: The direction, Sasha, the address, you have it? I already have the address, don't worry, María Eugenia intervenes. Look, when you do this kind of special order the customers enter the address themselves, see?

She shows her phone screen and Nataly smiles. Chama, you're from Venezuela, right? María Eugenia nods, she doesn't return the question because it's more than obvious. Oh, me too! Nataly turns back to Sasha, bouncing. From Venezuela también, understand?

Sasha nods and starts looking at her in a different way, as if trying to find some physical similarity he had missed. María Eugenia doesn't know if she can go now or if she should wait for anything else. Nataly, who also doesn't understand what she should do, thinks she is waiting for a tip and slaps her forehead. Oh, wait, wait.

She disappears inside the apartment. It's impossible for María Eugenia to sneak a casual look inside because Sasha is covering the whole doorway. Nataly returns and hands over a ten-euro note. María Eugenia is confused. Do I give this to the other person too? she asks.

No, hon', no, that's for you! Nataly giggles. Sasha laughs too, he seems to understand the confusion, in his way. Ah, okay, okay. Thank you so much. No worries, mami, thank you. Good night. Nataly closes the door. María Eugenia is happy; it's the first time she's received a tip like this, nobody had ever given her ten euros.

Once she is back in the vestibule, she puts away the gift bag with great care. It's one of those small and simple little bags, she's seen them several times in stationery stores, they're cheap. She's surprised that there's no card, no message, nothing. For a few seconds she is tempted to pry, to snoop and to see what is inside, but it's well sealed with tape and she doesn't want to ruin it. *Plus it seems like something Diego would do. Then he'd be unbearable if I told him I'd opened that stupid bag.* It's heavy for a bag so small and, even after squeezing it gently, she can't guess its contents. *A mystery.*

She checks the address and understands the reason for the ten-euro tip: she has to venture out to Pedralbes, the high part of the city, a very bougie area of Barcelona. She's had very few deliveries there. Now she has to push her legs hard; it's almost half an hour away, and, worst of all, uphill. *Oh, fuck. Well, there's nothing for it. Let's pray to the Virgin Mary that they give me another tip when I get there, that my legs don't hurt too much, and that the time goes quickly.* And with this silent prayer, she gives herself over to the meditation of pedaling.

She goes up as far as Rocafort on Carrer de Calabria, turns at Consejo de Ciento and ends up on Carrer del Comte d'Urgell, where she carries on straight for a while. She goes fast, concentrating; she runs several lights, but as there's no one around, she doesn't care. It's one of those times when she imagines she's competing in the Tour de France and she has to give her all. She's also projecting onto her retinas the photo that Cheo sent her on WhatsApp. She wants to finish work soon, she's craving the escape and synthetic joy that will make her forget reality for a few minutes. As she turns in the Plaza de Francesc Macià, she remembers that she didn't update Sara. *Will she still be awake?* She told her that she wasn't working tomorrow and that she'd wait up for her. *Fuck it, okay.* She puts her feet down to brake and sends her a message. I'm going to Cheo's. Wanna come? Everyone's there. They've got fun drugs. Crazy face emoji, alien head. *Sara is writing.* Sure. Send me the address. She sends the street name and number, keeps pedaling. There's not far to go now. Just this section of Diagonal and she's there.

On her left, she passes the L'illa shopping mall; for her it's the San Ignacio. Both buildings have an open structure and play with space. The most notable similarity, however, is when she enters through the parking lot. The few times she does it, even though she knows what's coming, she still feels that weight in her guts as she goes in and feels transported.

It's identical to the San Ignacio, there's even a musical instrument store. She imagines for a few seconds that she is on Avenida Blandín. *Mmm, if only I could get close to the Danubio for just a minute, smell the pastries . . . Enough, Marugenia, stop this nonsense.* At last she's at Maria Cristina and starts going up and up until she reaches her destination on Avenida de Pedralbes. She would love to live in this area. *I'll have to ask the Virgin for that too.* She likes it. The buildings are pretty, the streets seem cleaner and more spacious, the pavements are well cared for, the entrance halls are lit up, no dark and narrow entrances, no buildings crammed together and full of piss. *This is something else.*

Now her legs do hurt, she's starting to feel tired because she knows this is the last push. She stops at number 176, a small brick building, four floors at most. Shrubs and flowers everywhere. She's nervous as she buzzes the intercom; a trilling like a telephone call until someone answers at the other end. There's a camera in front of her and she knows she's being watched. She smiles slightly, feeling stupid. Hi, good evening! I've got your order, she shows the gift bag to the camera. Wait there, a woman's voice replies. María Eugenia does as she's told, obedient. She hums the Héctor Lavoe song she heard earlier, what was it? *Fuerte fuerte, hacha y machete, fuerte fuerte, hacha y machete.* She hears something and looks over, intrigued; the elevator doors open and a tall and slender woman appears.

At first, María Eugenia thinks she's wearing a sheet, but then she realizes it's a sheer dress that fits her perfectly. The woman smiles before opening the door. Lipstick, makeup, long nails, gold earrings. She's pretty dolled up. Subconsciously, María Eugenia starts to smooth the hairs sticking out from under her helmet; her face is greasy and her nail polish is chipped. She feels so insignificant in front of this immaculate woman who exudes financial comfort.

Thank you, darling, the woman says, accepting the gift bag. Thank you, she replies. Here, she puts a folded note in María Eugenia's hand; it looks blue, but she doesn't pay much attention to it in front of the woman. Bye. Thank you so much, good night.

She can't place the accent, the woman closes the door without looking away from her, then turns, fading away in her dress of smoke. She checks the note: twenty euros. *Yesss!* She bounces with joy, like a little girl. *Please, send me all the special orders in the world. I'll take them wherever's necessary, I don't mind.* And then, just in case, she gives a quick kiss to the Virgin hanging around her neck.

Finally free, she launches herself along the streets without braking; she's overjoyed with the thirty-euro tip that she's going to send straight to her parents' account. Cycling the whole length of Diagonal again, she hums the song, trying to remember the lyrics. *Something like . . . Palante alta la frente, de frente vamos a demostrar, que lo nuestro no fue un golpe de suerte . . . fuerte fuerte, hacha y machete.* At Plaza del Cinc d'Oros, she makes a left and slowly goes up toward Gràcia, until she reaches the guys' apartment. She presses the intercom. Open up, dummy. A buzz and the door opens with a push. She hoists her bike to fit into the elevator and once she's out she removes her backpack like someone taking off shackles. They left the door half-open and from the elevator she hears the music and the laughter. When she enters, the shouts of welcome embrace her: her new family is waiting for her to give her the sacred host. They all bear the relaxed faces and loose smiles of artificial happiness, except Sara who had been holding back, waiting for her.

What's up, Marugenia? How was the route, was it busy? Awesome, look, look, she shows off her thirty euros of tip with pride. The group all cheer. Fuuuuck, chama, that's how you do it, says Diego. Nah, do you know what this one did? asks Keiber, pointing to Cheo with his chin. What did you do? I didn't do anything! He laughs. He pushed his bike over a taxi, Nacho summarizes. How? Fuck, the asshole was in the bike lane and wouldn't move, I don't know what the hell he was doing, but he wouldn't let me by and it was my lane. And get a load of this, he shouts at the driver to move and everything, the driver tells him to eat shit and here comes Cheo, he grabs the bike and bam! Pushes it over the car, as if it were nothing. Everyone laughs. And what did the taxi driver do? What was he gonna do? Get pissed, of course. He started screaming things at me but I didn't pay any attention, just grabbed my bike, got on like nothing was happening, and left that wacko talking to himself. Marico, there were people filming you and everything, Keiber added.

Nacho puts a rum in her hand and María Eugenia takes a few sips. Santa Teresa, for you, cheers! They clink glasses. To better things and piles of cash for everyone! *Cheers, amen.*

Put some music on then.

In a matter of hours, the sun will start to rise and María Eugenia will have been living with the Mediterranean for over a year. Cheo, three. Nacho, two. Diego's not yet at a year. Keiber, almost two as well. Sara, six. Me, five.

Jordi cuts the air with his laughter, learning new expressions that he tries to repeat in his best accent, a fusion of two such similar worlds. From her corner in the living room, sitting with her back against the wall and also laughing at her friends' absurd comments, María Eugenia observes us one by one.

Yes, me too. We observe each other, glimpsing ourselves in the other's gaze. And even though we don't speak, we understand each other.

She gives in at last and goes out on the balcony to listen to the voice note from her parents, the effusive greetings from her little brother, and the cannonball drops from her throat straight to her heart, where it seems to be stuck for eternity.

Nostalgia is a bitch and at the same time the fuel that moves all these tired bodies, trying to cope with loss as best they can. Being a migrant means feeding yourself on loss, on what could have been, the infinite possible nuances of that history which will forever remain hidden but present. We don't fully understand that feeling-trace born from the savagery that lives within us and that watched us grow, the savagery that allows us to be, to act, and to take a bite out of the day-to-day, and also to get a little chewed up ourselves; but we venerate it, we respect it, because only one desire pounds above all others: to return one day.

Que es santo el amor de la tierra, que es triste la ausencia que deja el ayer, Cheo sings at the top of his lungs. How sacred is love for the homeland, how sad the absence left by yesterday. María Eugenia dries her tears and joins the chorus because, what does it matter? What's the point of crying if we're all in the same boat? Todos vuelven a la tierra en que nacieron, al embrujo incomparable de su sol! Everyone returns to the land of their birth, to the incomparable charm of its sun. Hell yeah, watch out boys, here comes Marugenia!

With unspoken complicity, María Eugenia holds out her hand and asks me to dance.

A NOTE FROM THE TRANSLATOR

From Savagery holds nothing back. From the unflinching depiction of death and decay in a broken Maracaibo that opens the book to the menstrual blood that stains María Eugenía's bike during another grueling shift as a delivery rider in Barcelona, the stories in this collection immerse us in the full humanity behind the statistics of mass migration from Venezuela. The fast-paced orality of the prose is the language of a lost generation, the twenty-somethings fueled by rage, frustration, desire, dark humor, and grit. The first time I heard Alejandra Banca read from these stories, in a crowded Madrid bookshop in 2022, I fell in love with these characters, who have an honesty and soul unlike anything I had heard before.

Nanda, Cheo, María Eugenia, Nacho, and the other worker bees we meet in *From Savagery* are among the more than seven million Venezuelans who have left their country since the mid-2010s. Approximately one quarter of the population has been driven out by the hyperinflation, scarcity, desperation, and omnipresent violence, referred to by Venezuelans simply as "the crisis." Banca does not linger on its political background—the Bolivarian Revolution, which began in 1999 with President Hugo Chávez, and has been led since his death in 2013 by his successor, Nicolás Maduro. Interested readers can find many excellent journalistic and academic texts analyzing the "twenty-first century socialism" of this government, its overreliance on oil production and economic mismanagement, Chávez's cult of personality, and the growing authoritarianism of the regime. Instead of talking about politics, the characters in *From Savagery* are busy sending money home to their families, dreaming of being reunited with loved ones, making connections, surviving, living. It would be easy to see the mass migration from Venezuela as exceptional. Banca, however, places this exodus within a context of global migration while also hinting at the deep roots of the precarity that her characters experience. In both respects, language is key.

From Savagery is a polyphonic novel. Voices weave in and out, often with no explicit indication of who is speaking. As readers, we must pay attention; we must unpick sense from context and from the way in which each character speaks. *Desde la salvajada*, Banca's original collection, contains a multitude of Spanishes: the distinct Caraqueño and Maracucho dialects of the Venezuelan protagonists; the Peninsula Spanish of bosses and clients; the immigrants from Morocco or Pakistan getting by with language inflected with their home tongues; the Puerto Rican wife who quotes salsa singer Héctor Lavoe when she is mad with her husband; the Argentinian sex workers sharing cigarettes and laughs; the sociolects of students and drug dealers. In my translation, I attempt to capture some of this with multiple dialects of English from the US and UK, shifting sometimes within the same sentence as characters come into contact and their forms of expression collide. In a similar way, tenses shift between past and present, reflecting how traumas have distorted the characters' sense of time.

The idiosyncrasies of the Venezuelan language tell the country's history. "Chama," a key form of address found throughout *From Savagery*, reflects how, for most of the twentieth century, Venezuela was a country of immigration rather than emigration. Some insist the term comes from "chum," a legacy of North American migration to Venezuela during the boom years of oil extraction beginning in the 1920s; others that it is from the Portuguese "chamar," meaning to call oneself, reflecting the history of the Portuguese, Italians, Spanish, and other Europeans who came to look for work opportunities and escape their dictatorships. In the story "Damp," Lucía is a relic from this era, having migrated from Italy as a child the best part of a century earlier. Her physical and mental deterioration is a metaphor for the country's downturn. She and Pedro, a young man who takes care of her, use the term "matando tigres," killing tigers, which is an exclusively Venezuelan phrase for taking on odd jobs. This phrase, too, has multiple proposed etymologies. The most common is that a wealthy landowner asked his workers to kill a tiger for him to decorate his hacienda in exchange for extra pay; another is that freelance jazz musicians would often

play the "Tiger Rag." Between them, these accounts encap-
sulate aspects of Venezuelan society—enduring inequality
combined with a cosmopolitan, modernizing drive—that
have shaped the country to this day. In this translation, I
have kept "chama" and the loan translation "killing tigers" to
acknowledge the histories of migration and precarity that are
embedded within the language.

During the twentieth century, Venezuela was more stable
and prosperous than many of its Latin American neighbors, so relatively few Venezuelans left. In the late 2000s, a
trend began to appear in Venezuelan literature of questioning attachment to the country, in the context of a strongly
nationalist government. The term "desarraigo," meaning a
sense of uprootedness, became more common. Critic Luz
Marina Rivas notes that the question of whether to stay or
to go became a recurring theme in narrative. A decade or so
on, the deliberation has been replaced with a harsher reality:
the characters in *From Savagery* had no choice but to leave, to
work abroad in under-the-radar jobs and send remittances
to their families.

As Venezuelans negotiate what it means to form diasporas
for the first time, language stands out as something shared,
something familiar in the face of change and uncertainty.
When Nanda visits Madrid, she keeps her ears open for
Venezuelan accents, listening for words in which she recognizes herself. In her darkest hour, hearing "chama" from a
stranger who offers help allows her to trust him. The Spanish

of Venezuela is uniquely rich and vibrant, a language bursting with imagery. While translating, I often found myself lamenting that English is far less evocative. My favorite example is "Qué ladilla!" The phrase is used to express annoyance, but its literal translation is "What genital crabs!" "What a pain in the ass!" comes close but lacks the precision of the original. Throughout *From Savagery*, I've loaned certain Venezuelan expressions to share the joy I find in them with English-speaking readers.

Language can also be contentious. Along with the multitude of Spanishes, Catalan is present throughout the book. In "Insecurity4U," older, more affluent residents of rural Catalonia speak only Catalan with the intent of excluding the migrant workers who have come to install their security cameras and whom they cannot look in the eye. Meanwhile, for the young activists in "I Already Know," Catalan is part of their group identity, while Spanish is the language of the oppressor. *From Savagery* was written as Catalan nationalism intensified and led to wide-scale protests, which our narrator Nanda witnesses, though she notes that this is not her struggle. Nanda understands only fragments of the conversations she hears. Where not essential for the plot, I have left this in Catalan—we pick up familiar words like "emocional" and "premenstrual" along with Nanda, understanding enough to respond to the situation while recognizing the unfamiliarity of her new home. María Eugenia and Nanda use Catalan in pragmatic ways. They have learned "carrer" for "street," the most common type of address they encounter, but still use "avenida" instead of "avinguda" and "plaza" instead of "plaça," as these Spanish terms will be understood.

From Savagery confronts the multiple ways in which people hurt others. These stories do not sanitize the reality of abuses and aggressions, including racist, misogynist, and ableist language. A particular challenge was "subnormal," Cheo's response to the racist driver who knocks him off his bike in "Karate Kick." "Subnormal" is defined as an extremely offensive term for a person with an intellectual disability, and is frequently translated as "retard," which was my first draft. "Retard," though, is more hurtful in English than "subnormal" is in Spanish. Banca explained that the word is not common in Venezuela but is often used in Spain as an insult without consideration. In the heat of the moment, Cheo expresses fluently the lingua franca of offense that he and his compatriots regularly receive. After much reflection, discussion, and reading about activism against ableist language— and workshopping translating offensive language as part of the master's level translation class that I teach—I settled on "moron" as a term that is similarly used by people in the UK without necessary reflection on the history of discrimination inherent in the word.

In this context, this battlefield of idiomatic savagery, Cheo, Andrés, and Jordi's apartment is special as a place of linguistic exchange, of gathering, and of comfort. Venezuelans Cheo and Andrés use the Catalan word "home," and Jordi, who is from Catalonia, uses the Venezuelan word "marico." Both are terms used to greet a friend; the latter stems from a slur that, while still used only in a homophobic sense in some parts of Latin America, has been reclaimed and resignified in Venezuela. The apartment is also where the characters laugh, dance, and sing together. Amid xenophobia, precarious labor, and homesickness, these small moments of connection bolster their resilience. At the heart of *From Savagery* is a celebration of that resilience. Like Nataly, the sex worker who just wants to pay her taxes, none of these characters want to be seen as victims. Orianna Camejo, founder of *Lecturas de arraigo*, which published the original Spanish edition, established the publishing house to "tackle [. . .] all the issues that have marked us, all the bad and all the good, [. . .] to think about ourselves in the future, to have fun in that possible future." That possible future shines through this collection of stories. The "savagery" of the title refers not so much to the conditions in Venezuela that the characters have escaped—though these are truly horrifying—but rather to a force beyond the rational, deep within them, which drives them to keep going. Banca coins the phrase "sensación-huella," which I have rendered as "feeling-trace," to express being marked by this feeling, a remnant from home, that is not easily named. And as poet Andrea Sofía Crespo Madrid writes in her introduction to *Desde la salvajada*, the collection "speaks of unbreakable lives, rebellious like the flowers in the garden of an abandoned house, which continue to bloom."

ABOUT THE AUTHOR

ALEJANDRA BANCA was born in Caracas, Venezuela, in 1994. She earned a BA from Andrés Bello Catholic University in 2016 and made her debut in 2021 with two poems in UBICUO, published by Lecturas de arraigo. Her poems were published in the third edition of *Anthropología de fuego* (2022) and she received a digital publication mention in the Venezuelan poetry contest Ecos de la Luz, both from Ediciones Palíndromus. *From Savagery* is her first work of fiction.

ABOUT THE TRANSLATOR

KATIE BROWN teaches contemporary Spanish and Latin American culture at the University of Exeter and holds a PhD in Venezuelan literature under the Bolivarian Revolution from King's College London (2016). She is co-editor of *Crude Words*, an anthology of Venezuelan texts in English, for which she also translated six stories. She is part of the women's UK, US, and Venezuelan translation collective, Colaboratorio Ávila. Her translations frequently appear in Latin American Literature Today.